A MARSDEN ROMANCE
VOLUME ONE

A MARSDEN ROMANCE VOLUME ONE

DAWN BROWER

MONARCHAL GLENN PRESS

CONTENTS

A FLAWED JEWEL

EXCERPT: ALL THE LADIES LOVE COVENTRY

DAWN BROWER

A Flawed Jewel

My stepsister, Amanda, encouraged me to write a book, and in less than a day I had a really rough draft, in less than a week a short story ready for submission. If she hadn't goaded me into it, this book wouldn't exist.

Thanks to Melanie for reading my really rough first draft—I know it was a mess of epic proportions in the beginning, to Hailey for her words of wisdom and showing me my many errors in a humorous light, and finally to Victoria for pointing out I was a little too bloodthirsty and for answering my endless questions. If not for all of your encouragement and help, I would have been lost. The three of you helped me more than words can express. Thank you for being my rock when all I want to do is hide under one. I love you girls.

Mostly I want to dedicate this book to my dad. He always believed I should write a book, but I never believed I had the patience for it. I wish he could have

been here to see me finally getting around to doing it.
I miss you daddy.

CHAPTER 1

March 3, 1861

"You need to suck in more, Miss Pieretta."

Tully, her maid prodded and pulled at the strings of Pieretta's corset to tighten it as much as possible. One of many torturous things a lady must endure to remain fashionable. It was her job to get Pieretta ready for the biggest voyage of her life. There was nothing Pieretta wanted more than to stay on the plantation where she grew up, but her presence was required at her grandpere's estate in France. She had no real desire to go anywhere. Everything she knew was in Charleston. She had no choice but to go live in a country she knew nothing about.

Tully yanked on the laces one last time squeezing Pieretta's ribs tightly inside her chest. She struggled to breathe. Pieretta squirmed in an effort to loosen the stays. "Miss Pieretta, please, we need to tighten this corset a little more, or you will never fit into that traveling dress you had the seamstress make for you. We all know you're only stalling so you don't have to leave the plantation. Your grandpere is expecting you, and you need to be on that ship."

"Oh be quiet, Tully. The laces are too tight. Fix them before I can no longer breathe." Stupid know-it-all maid thought she could order her around. It was bad enough that her entire life was about to change. Now she had to deal with Tully ordering her around. "The dress will fit and still allow air to enter my lungs. Mind your own business and do as you're told," Pieretta scolded her.

As a southern belle, she didn't have to do anything more than host parties and help her father manage the house. The most traveling she had ever done was to attend picnics and soirees at neighboring plantations. She had never traveled more than fifteen miles away from her home. The idea of sailing all the way to France—Pia hated to admit it, but it terrified her.

Pieretta had never boarded a ship, now she was expected to sale on a long voyage. She, at least, had seen one or two while they were in the Charleston harbor, but it had never crossed her mind ever to give one a closer look. It was not an experience she ever expected to have.

Her happiest moments were in Charleston, in the heart of the only home she had ever known.

Pieretta didn't want to leave everything behind. It was hard to comprehend why her grandpere insisted she come live with him in France. The fact she didn't have any living male relatives in Charleston shouldn't matter. She could look after the plantation and deal with the overseer. Her father made sure she understood every aspect of running the plantation. She had the best education possible. He believed females had a right to learn more than just how to run a household or proper etiquette.

Oh, Papa, I miss you so much...

A sting of pain hit her chest. She was reminded again of her father's death a month ago. Each day without her father was more unbearable than the one before it. Pieretta couldn't believe she had to live in a world where he no longer existed. His death had been so sudden—had suddenly just quit breathing. It had been so devastating to realize someone could die without any warning.

Pieretta was all alone in the world.

She had no brothers or sisters, and her only living relative was her grandpere. So it was with a heavy heart that she prepared to make the journey to live with him in France.

Her mother died when Pieretta was born, and her father never remarried. He loved her mother too much to ever envision a life with someone else. The only females Pieretta spent time around on a regular basis were servants. Without the benefit of a maternal influence, Pieretta had more masculine ideas about her future. It would have been all right to stay and run the plantation if she had been a man, but as a woman, she had no real say in her life until she reached her majority.

Until then, her grandpere, Comte Renard Dubois, had the right to tell her how to live her life.

Because she had never been to France, she didn't know what to expect once she arrived. Grandpere had told her stories about his estate and how large it was, but she had never had the opportunity to visit. He outlined the many gardens and the different foliage that it encased. Pieretta looked forward to walking amongst the roses and counting the various shades his gardener cultivated.

She had never seen an actual rose, but her grandpere's description made them sound like the most beautiful flower on Earth. The blossoms were rumored to be filled with an aromatic scent that tantalized the nose. Rose buds bloomed in a variety of colors from the shade of a blushing bride's cheeks to the various hues of sunshine bouncing through the windows of her sitting room. Even with the allure of seeing roses for the first time, she still had no desire to travel such a long distance.

All of her trunks were packed and already aboard the ship. The only thing required of her now was to get herself ready, get in the carriage, and travel to the docks.

Pieretta wanted to throw a fit and stomp her feet, but that would be out of character for her. While her father often indulged her, Pieretta was not prone to temper tantrums. She did occasionally let her displeasure be known, but most of the time she was able to hold back the temptation to scream. Pieretta took a deep breath and exhaled slowly, preparing herself for whatever the journey might entail.

She stood up straight as Tully finished tying the

corset's laces. She didn't want to stand still any longer than necessary and keeping still ensured the bows on her dress were tied evenly.

In her mind, fighting the inevitable would not help her situation. The servants needed to make sure she made it on the ship. Even though Pieretta didn't to move to France, she could make the best of the situation. Her life on the plantation had a repetitive quality to it—nothing ever changed.

Instead of harping on the negative, she could look at this forced trip as an adventure.

"Almost done, Miss Pieretta."

"It's taking forever," she groaned. Sometimes being female was a nuisance. Surely it didn't take this long for a man to get dressed.

"It'll be all done before you know it and then we will be boarding a ship to France."

Did Tully have to give her a reminder of it?

Tully finished lacing her stays, and the corset hugged every curve of her torso. She walked over and picked up Pieretta's traveling gown and opened it for Pieretta to step into. Once she was fully within the confines of the dress, Tully pulled it up and began the long process of latching all of the hooks up the side. She opted not to wear any petticoats or a hoop skirt, as it would be ridiculous to wear them in the small confines of the ship. Her traveling costume was made of the finest dyed black wool.

Black Wool was ever so dull and boring, but Pia didn't mind wearing it to honor her father. She'd miss him for the rest of her days. When she received the letter from her grandpere, Pieretta visited her favorite seamstress to have a few traveling costumes made for her crossing to France. She had no idea what the current fashion was and figured more gowns could be made upon her arrival at her grandpere's estate.

Besides only so much could be done to make a black gown look good...

She was trying to be practical, and Grandpere wouldn't mind. He would want his little princess to be happy. After all, one couldn't be happy if one wasn't fashionable. Grandpere believed she didn't have the brains for anything besides frivolous things such as fashion. He did not realize Pieretta had a lot of things on her mind, and fashion wasn't always at the forefront.

Soon he'd realize how mistaken he was about her character.

For instance, her love of mythology consumed

her. Some of her favorite books housed stories of the gods and how they had fallen. She read everything from Norse to Greek mythology. Her favorite had always been Thor. Pieretta often wished she could visit Asgard and have the opportunity to meet him and Loki.

"Tully, please tell me you remembered to pack my favorite books."

"Yes, ma'am" Tully nodded. "You have more books packed than you do gowns."

"Books are more important."

"hmmph" Tully snorted. "I wouldn't know as I've never had the opportunity to learn to read."

"Maybe I will teach you on our voyage. Not like we have anything better to occupy our time with."

"I don't know how much use I'd have for learning." Tully frowned. "Why don't we just wait and see how the crossing goes. You might find something to entertain yourself with."

Pieretta sighed. No one truly understood her—especially her only living relative.

Grandpere knew next to nothing about what Pieretta actually liked. He assumed she was similar to her mother, Dominique Dubois Carlyle, who only thought of frivolous things such as the latest styles and idle gossip.

Her grandpere couldn't be more wrong.

He usually visited her at least twice a year, staying for a few weeks and then returning home. Her mother was his original princess. Grandpere had doted on her his whole life. When her mother died, he had been heartbroken. When he saw his new granddaughter with her mother's royal blue eyes and pale blond hair, he had decided that he had a new princess to coddle with affection. It had helped to ease the sting of his loss, finding a near carbon copy of his beloved daughter. He'd found a way to fill the empty hole in his heart with Pieretta.

Tully finished connecting all of the hooks on Pieretta's dress. She inspected her work, trailing her fingers over the dress to smooth the lines. Stepping away, Tully motioned for Pieretta to sit down on the chair next to her vanity. "Miss Pieretta, you need to sit down so I can fix your hair."

She had no idea what Tully meant by fix her hair. She hadn't touched it. "What are you going to do to my hair, Tully?" Pieretta asked.

"Don't you worry any, Miss Pieretta. I am just going to pull it back a bit so it's out of your way. You're not going to want to deal with it on that there ship. It needs to be more manageable."

Pieretta sighed and sat in front of her vanity.

Unfortunately, she had to deal with Tully even though she was a meddlesome nuisance. Tully had helped raise her, the servant believed she had a right to dictate how Pieretta should live her life. Tully's many lectures were a normal part of her day. In Pieretta's mind, Tully was overstepping her duties and trying to take the place of the mother she never knew. The maid was traveling with her only because a young unmarried lady could not travel alone. She was going to be the only person Pieretta would bring with her into this new life.

"I suppose you're right," Pieretta agreed. "It would be rather tiresome to constantly push my hair out of the way."

"Trust me, I know what I'm talking about."

Pieretta rolled her eyes. "Oh? And exactly how many ships have you sailed on?"

"I haven't always been on this plantation," Tully informed her. "I came over here on a ship when I was a tiny thing. Of course, my hair didn't have the opportunity to get blown around, but I do remember the howling winds."

"Howling winds?" Pieretta gulped. "What do you mean?"

"There was a nasty bit of storm for half the

journey. The winds whipped right through the ship leaving an eerie whistling piercing our ears."

That didn't sound—appealing.

Tully pulled Pieretta's braid tighter and wrapped it around her head. Pieretta sighed, fighting tears as Tully continued to plait her hair. It was difficult to keep her emotions from welling up and spilling out of her. If she had one wish, it would be to find a way out of the situation her grandpere had forced her into. Her only option wasn't really an option in her mind. She could get married, but she didn't want any person to have that sort of power over her life. Relinquishing control meant fighting for the right to make any decisions for herself. Marriage was the one thing Pieretta had never wanted.

When she turned twenty-five, she would gain control of the plantation. It would be a long seven years living with her grandpere, but if anyone could do it, she could. Pieretta had to make sure her grandpere knew she was never going to get married. In Pieretta's mind, any woman had the capability to make her own decisions. It would be a cold day in hell before she allowed a man to have any kind of control over her life or her inheritance. Her father had made sure she was educated far beyond her station, and she had a working knowledge. She was intelligent and intended to use everything she learned to further her ambitions.

Tully finished fussing with her hair. Her pale blond locks were now securely wound around her head in a practical plait. Pieretta brushed a tear from the corner of her eye. Would she ever be happy again? She had serious doubts that happiness lay in her future. Pieretta stood and flattened her dress, smoothing the lines and wrinkles along the side of her skirt so it fell evenly as she moved. She glanced in the mirror. The dress wasn't designed to be flattering, but Pieretta believed she could make anything look good. She may be pale and sad, but she was still beautiful. She was curvy in all the right places with a small waist.

"All right, Tully, I guess now is as good a time as any," Pieretta said. "Go and have the carriage brought around. I'm ready for an adventure. That's how I'm choosing to see this change in my life."

Eerie winds and all...

Pieretta stood and looked around her bedroom one last time. Several years would pass before she could return and take control of the plantation. It was important that she store all of the good memories so the years in France would be easier to bear.

The fight to gain control over her life would be

tough, but the things that mattered the most were worth fighting for. Even though at times she felt like she would never be happy again, Pieretta had hoped that she would find a reason to smile. Changes were always hard to make.

She wandered over to her bedroom door and pulled it open. She began the long trek down the stairs to the main hallway. At the bottom of the steps, she looked up as Tully made her way down the long staircase. No one ever promised life would be easy, and if Pieretta knew one thing, it was that she could get through any hurdle life put in her way. This was only one bump on a very long road ahead of her, but in the end, she knew she would get what she wanted. After all, Pieretta always did.

THE DOCKS WERE NOT A PLEASANT PLACE TO walk. They were filthy and smelled of unimaginable things. The scent of rotten fish and fresh salt water permeated the air. Pieretta needed to board the ship as quickly as possible, before she stepped in something disgusting.

The waterfront was booming with activity, and the noise was deafening. It was hard to ascertain the different sounds and locate where they might be coming from. The combination of the odors stung her nose and throat. The smoky air made her eyes water. Pieretta covered her nose with her hand in an effort to block out the stench but was forced to wipe the tears from her eyes as they started to stream down her face. Tully followed behind her as fast as she could. They both wanted off the docks as fast as they could manage it.

"Miss Pieretta, we need to move faster. I don't like it on these docks. Some of those men are making me uneasy. They're looking at us like we're a special treat they want to lap up."

"Don't be ridiculous Tully, they wouldn't dare harm us. We'll be fine. Just the same, there's our ship. Let's board quickly and be done with this area."

A lump formed in her throat. She gulped it down and refrained from looking at the men Tully referred to. They made her just as uneasy, but she refused to admit it.

They moved quickly to the gangplank so they could board the clipper. The ship had three large masts each filled to the top with five sails. When they stepped on deck, the first mate and captain greeted them.

The captain folded one of his hands behind his

back with the other one tucked in front just below his chest and bowed to Pieretta. "It's a pleasure to have you aboard, Miss Carlyle. I am Captain Devere, and this is my first mate, Cam. I know Comte Dubois is anxiously awaiting your arrival in France."

"Do you know my grandpere well then?"

"As this is one of his ships, I have had many occasions to spend time with him, discussing how his shipments are to be handled. You are one of our most important cargos. He made sure to have a meeting with me before I left France and gave me the strictest instructions regarding your safety on this crossing."

Did he? She shouldn't be surprised, and yet she was.

"Grandpere can be very protective. I'm surprised he didn't make the trip himself."

"He wanted to, but an emergency arose at the last minute on one of his estates. It was something that required his personal attention. It is why he gave me instructions as to your passage and care. I hope your crossing with us is pleasant."

Pleasant? As far as she was concerned, there really wasn't anything that could make this journey tolerable let alone pleasurable. It took every ounce of her will to not come back with a rude comment. The need to get to her cabin and rest was starting to become a top priority to Pieretta. She needed to vacate the captain's company with as much haste as possible.

With as much politeness as she could muster, she cleared her throat. "I certainly wouldn't want it to be unpleasant. Who is to show us to our cabin?"

"My first mate will gladly give you a brief tour of the ship and show you to your cabin. We would prefer you remain in your quarters for most of the trip. It is the safest option. We will have a tray brought to you for all of your meals."

Was the captain mad? How could he expect me to be confined to a small room for three weeks? She would have to make her needs known from the very beginning or be stifled inside of a cabin with Tully for the lengthy passage. Her throat closed up just at the thought of it—she hated being confined.

"I couldn't possibly stay locked inside a small room the entire journey, Captain. We are going to be on the ship for at least two weeks. I would go mad for sure. I must insist on daily walks above deck."

The captain studied her for several seconds before he nodded.

"Very well, but limit them to thirty minute intervals twice a day. Do not walk on deck once night falls for any reason. If I tell you to get below deck, you are not to argue. Just go. I wouldn't insist unless it was a matter of safety."

"I can agree to that."

"Very well, Cam will see you to your cabin now."

The first mate guided Tully and Pieretta below deck and escorted them to their accommodations. There wasn't a lot of free space aboard the ship. The captain gave his quarters to the two women for the trip. Pieretta wondered where the captain would stay during the crossing to France. It would be cramped for all those involved.

Pieretta sighed as she entered the cabin. The limited space didn't leave much room for her to share with her maid. The journey across the ocean stuck in such a tightly confined room with Tully constantly telling her what to do might drive her mad. Tully scrambled in behind her, scuffling her feet as she settled into the small room. If only Grandpere hadn't demanded she come live with him. Why must females be dependent on their male relations?

"Thank you, sir. I think we will be fine for now. How long until we set sail?"

"If all goes well, we should be on our way in an hour's time. Please remain here for the rest of the evening. It will be too dark to walk on deck, and it is easy to fall overboard when you can't see in front of you."

"I will heed your advice, sir. I have no desire to swim, or sink, any time soon." Pieretta shuddered.

As the first mate left the two women, Pieretta only had one thought. *It's going to be a very long and grueling excursion across the immense ocean.*

CHAPTER 2

A week later...

"*C*aptain Thor, sir. The ship has been spotted. The one you've been waiting for," bosun Cornelus informed him.

Thor lounged in his bunk. It had been an uneventful few days aboard the Sea Rover. He had waited patiently for the vessel leaving the American shore to cross paths with him. It carried a package he was desperate to get his hands on. That particular parcel held extreme importance to him—for one reason and one reason only. He needed it in order to finally get even with his former partner Renny Dubois.

The bloody man had organized Thor's early departure from this world.

If he hadn't been quick, he would instead reside in his eternal resting place. The bullet Renny had put into his shoulder would have entered his heart if he had not seen the glint of the pistol out of the corner of his eye. Since then, he had been patiently waiting for the opportunity to enact his revenge. As far as Renny knew, Thor died on that fateful night. The comte certainly hadn't bothered to check before he exited the docks as fast as his pudgy legs could carry him.

Thor had been twenty-four when his father died. At that time he inherited his father's business holdings along with the entailed property. Dubois-Marsden Shipping Firm was one of his more profitable business ventures. Thor had met with Comte Renard Dubois to learn more about the business side of the shipping company. He'd had a lot to learn before he could make sound business decisions. Renny took him under his wing and taught him everything. He trusted him completely. He'd been like a second father to him.

So it had come as a shock when Renny attempted to murder him. The brutal betrayal stung his pride and made it next to impossible to trust.

Thor had been on the docks in Paris overseeing the shipment of their latest cargo when everything changed. He'd looked up and saw Renny walking toward him. He turned to say something, and Renny pulled out a pistol, firing it at him. Thor had turned just enough preventing the bullet from hitting anything vital. His shoulder was nicked and he'd lost a lot of blood. With each wave of pain, he grew light-headed, causing him to lose his balance. His head had bounced off of the hard surface below him and knocked him unconscious. Renny, the bloody bastard, had left him for dead.

When he finally awoke, he had been surprised to find himself aboard a ship with his shoulder already doctored. Another captain had seen the whole thing and had Thor placed on his ship. It was on that ship, the Sea Rover, where he had made a life for himself.

It changed his life and from that moment on he became a new person, one that held no qualms about what must be done. Thor became an unscrupulous pirate—no bounty to small. Until the day would come when he'd become the Sea Rover's captain and his revenge became possible.

He worked his way up the ranks and, after a few years, he made first mate. When the old captain was killed in battle, Thor was promoted to captain as the laws of the ship dictated. He had been a pirate for five years now.

Snapping out of the distant memory, he looked up at his bosun with a smile on his lips. Thor had been planning his revenge against Renny Dubois for a very long time. All of his plans were finally going to become a reality. Today was going to be a very good day.

A cocky grin filled his face. "Corny, ol' man, that is the best news I've heard all day. Make the call, all hands on deck. We're about to plunder us a ship."

Soon he'd have his hands on the means to take down the most evil man he knew. It didn't matter that Thor had to sink to his level to obtain it. In his mind the means more than justified the end.

If Pieretta Carlyle let him he'd try to make it up to her later—hell even if she wouldn't he'd find a way.

Pieretta was on the deck looking out at the ocean. She had taken well to sea travel and enjoyed having the wind blow on her face. If only she was allowed more than thirty minutes on deck each day to enjoy it, her life on board the ship would be more ideal. The waves danced and rolled across the ship's hull, crashing into it and creating white crested waves atop the cerulean horizon. She looked across the indigo waves and saw a ship in the distance. In fact it looked like it was moving toward their ship, growing closer with each gust of wind. As the other clipper's sails brought them closer to her, Pieretta squeezed the guardrail of the ship tightly. She bit her lip, the sting of her teeth drawing a minuscule droplet of blood. Surely they could see the two vessels were going to cross paths. There was a commotion to her left so she turned to see what was going on.

"Captain! Captain!" the first mate called out.

She looked over as the first mate ran toward the captain. His face was flushed bright red from running across the windy deck. Once he arrived at his destination he stopped suddenly and with a high pitched voice delivered the imperative message to Captain Devere.

"Sir, there be a pirate ship drawing close. It's flying the red flag, we're about to be attacked."

"Hurry, all hands on deck. Make sure our important passenger gets below deck," he shouted as he ran off.

"Wait. What does it mean when it's waving a red

flag?" Pieretta asked the first mate. By the way Captain Devere and his first mate acted, Pieretta knew it wasn't a good sign.

Her heart beat hard against her chest. Pirates? Surely they were mistaken.

"Don't you worry none about that, miss. Just get below deck like the captain said."

"No, I am not going below deck until you answer me."

The first mate kept shooing her, his hands waving wildly in front of her face. He made sure she turned around and started the trek back to her cabin. When she didn't move fast enough, he pushed lightly against her back in an attempt to get her to move faster. If Pieretta didn't start moving faster, it was very likely he would shove her all the way to her cabin. He clearly didn't have time to deal with the hysterics of a young girl. From the expression on his face, it was evident he was weighing his options. He kept lifting his eyebrows and looking back at the approaching ship. They continued their journey to Pieretta's cabin. The first mate needed to follow the captain's dictate to ensure her safe return to her cabin.

He turned back with a frown on his red face. "It

means they're going to give no quarter." A tinge of fear colored each word he spoke.

The words didn't mean anything to Pieretta. The term was foreign to her. "I don't understand. What does give no quarter mean?" she asked him.

"They're not going to leave any survivors. They will kill us all if we allow them to board our ship. Go below deck as you were told." He scurried away. He had followed Captain Devere's orders and delivered her to her cabin—why should he care if Pieretta stayed inside. It was up to her to make sure she remained safely inside.

Pieretta's heart beat faster as the blood drained from her face. It frightened her, knowing that if the pirates boarded the ship they'd murder everyone. Pieretta quickly went inside the cabin and slammed the door shut. It was the only place she felt truly safe, but with each breath she took, she felt less and less protected on board the craft. She had never been more helpless than in that moment, thinking she was going to die. *What should I do?*

When she calmed down enough to look at her surroundings, she was surprised to see Tully paid no attention to her. Tully was unfolding one of her dresses and laying it across a table to smooth out the wrinkles, a complete waste of time in Pieretta's opinion. It wasn't as if she was going to wear it anytime soon. They were confined to the cabin.

Pieretta hadn't even considered this possibility when crossing the ocean. How could she have? She had lived a very sheltered life. It occurred to her in that moment— she really didn't know anything. She didn't want to have regrets, and more importantly, she wanted to live. She had never been given the chance to do any of the things she wanted with her life. More importantly, she had plans—beginning with an expansion to the plantation and making the lives of the slaves better. Pieretta didn't believe in slavery, but she didn't have the authority to make any changes until she had gained her majority. There were so many books she hadn't gotten a chance to read, and so much she still wanted to learn. Damn those pirates for making her fear for her life.

"Tully, we are going to be attacked by pirates," Pieretta shouted, frustration flowing through each word she enunciated. "Put those away, we need to take cover."

"You be a silly girl, Miss Pieretta. We are not under attack by no pirates." Doubt was evident in Tully's voice. Instead of heeding Pieretta's advice, she turned her back and resumed her work.

Pieretta gasped. Why wasn't she taking her

seriously? She stormed over to her side and shook her.

"Tully, I was just on the deck. I heard the first mate and the captain. They are preparing for battle. Do not call me a silly girl!"

"Hmmph," Tully said, ignoring the warning. "Leave me be. I have work to finish." Tully turned around and resumed her task. Two seconds later she screamed when an earsplitting explosion hit the ship.

Pieretta jumped onto the bunk and covered her face in her skirts.

Tully joined Pieretta on their bunk, and they held on to each other. Tully squeezed her so tight it took everything Pieretta had to not push her away. They shook uncontrollably when another thunderous blast rattled the ship.

Pieretta closed her eyes, blocking out everything. She had never been a truly religious person, but in that moment, it wasn't hard to remember some of the prayers her pastor said during church services. The Lord's Prayer popped in her head, and she could hear the words loud and clear as if she was attending mass. With a shaky voice she began to recite them aloud, hoping if she died, the Lord would grant her some absolution.

THOR MADE HIS WAY ONTO THE DECK OF THE ship. With each movement his stride became more of a swagger. Most of the ship's crew were already tied up and secured in the empty cargo hold. His men were pretty savage when they worked, but they kept the casualties to an absolute minimum. A laugh rumbled through his chest, echoing across the deck. This vessel had been much easier to capture than Thor had anticipated.

It was a grand day to be a pirate.

The captain would be required to answer a few questions before they vacated the vessel. Thor walked over to where the captain was tied to the center mast of the ship, blood dripping from his mouth and a resentful look in his eyes.

"Well sir, I commend you on a fine battle," Thor said. "You didn't make it too easy. However, your job isn't quite done. You have something I want. Now, Devere, be a good sport and tell me where I can locate it."

The captain spit blood at him in response, hitting him square in the face. Thor wiped it from his eyes with the sleeve of his jacket. If the captain was looking to make Thor angry, he was doing a tremendous job so far. Captain Devere had better start cooperating before Thor would have to do something he disliked. He did not enjoy killing people and avoided it whenever possible, but the captain might just force his hand.

"Now, mate, that's not the way to go about this. If it's death you are looking for, I would be happy to oblige, after you tell me what I want to know. Where is Pieretta Carlyle? Tell me where she is, and I will consider letting you live."

The captain looked up at him through swollen eyes, now turning various shades of blue, black, and purple. "Why should I tell you anything? You are going to kill us anyway. I don't see the point of putting that girl through something that she doesn't deserve. I have no doubt that what you have in store for her is terrible. No one deserves to be tortured, even irritating females."

A cocky smile formed on his face. "Well that is no concern of yours."

The captain's face turned several shades of red at Thor's comment. "Go and bloody find her yourself." Each word uttered from his swollen lips was strained with barely contained rage.

"I know you work for that deplorable man Comte Dubois. I want to wring his neck more than yours. Don't be bloody stupid and save your own hide. Otherwise, I'll leave you for my men to torment. The choice is yours, mate. Now tell me where I can find her."

"You call him deplorable when you're a damned pirate. What makes you any better than him?"

Thor glanced at the captain's bloody and inflamed face, trying to decide how to best answer his question. He crossed his massive arms over his chest as he tilted his head up, looking at the billowing sails. After some careful internal deliberation, he chose the truth. "I keep my word."

The captain stared at Thor, disbelief clouding his eyes. His swollen lids folded down into tiny slits narrowing just enough to see the small specks of his black pupils shining through. "Why should I care about that?" he asked.

The man might just have a brain after all. He seemed to be considering his options.

"Well I guess that doesn't really matter, as your life is of little consequence to me. Whether or not you are still breathing depends on your willingness to help me locate Pieretta. Would you like to die now, or live to fight another day?"

Devere didn't take long to answer the question. He looked up at Thor. "She should be in my cabin with her negro maid. Good luck handling that one—she's a spitfire and stubborn as hell."

The Captain's head rolled back into unconsciousness. It bounced off the tall mast and landed hard against his left shoulder. The man would surely wake up sore if he remained in that position overly long. Thor couldn't muster enough energy to care and left him where he was.

Being a pirate was bloody business.

He stopped letting his principles get to him years ago. It was a hard life at sea every day, plundering ships for supplies. It went against his nature to kill, but if he was forced to, he never thought twice about delivering a fatal blow. Because he didn't believe in murdering someone without cause, he decided to leave the captain and his crew alive.

Thor wanted to make them suffer. He hated anyone working for Comte Dubois. Renny was rotten to the core. His precious granddaughter was the key to his undoing. Pieretta Carlyle would ensure his vengeance. Joy burst through his heart at the idea of finally making the comte pay. No words could express his delight.

He walked away from the captain's slumbering body to make his way below deck. He had a lady to locate so he could properly kidnap her. This was the fun part about being a pirate. A huge smile formed on his lips making his eyes crinkle at the corners. Miss Carlyle would be the best prize he had ever plundered from a ship.

He couldn't wait to make her acquaintance.

The rest of the ship's occupants would be left tied up securely below the ship's deck, while the captain would remain tied to the ship's mast. It would depend on their will to survive if they managed to stay alive once the pirate ship left them to their own devises. If they were creative enough, one of them would come up with a way to free themselves and gain control of the ship. It would take some time for them to accomplish that task and would give Thor plenty of time to put some distance between them.

CHAPTER 3

*S*he paced back and forth from one end of the cabin to the other. The quarters she shared with Tully were small so she didn't have much room to do it, but she couldn't stop herself. She twisted her fingers together in frustration, debating what could possibly be done. Pieretta stopped walking and wiped her hands on her skirt to remove the dampness building there. She continued her futile trek between the two bare walls of the tiny room. The cannons had stopped firing, and it was eerily quiet. Tully had passed out from fear hours ago, rendering her useless. Pieretta wondered if she should venture out to see what had happened. She feared the ship's crew was already dead. Pirates were surely all over the ship by now.

A loud racket shook the walls of her cabin. She jumped when her door crashed open. The doorframe swallowed up by a man, his body filling almost every inch of the opening.

She swallowed the lump building inside of her parched throat. She had never been intimidated by a man before, but his demeanor was imposing. His whole body was nothing but muscle. He walked into the cabin and approached Pieretta. Once he was inside, she got an even better look at him. The more she saw of him, the more she wanted to escape. The pirate was perhaps the largest man Pieretta had ever laid eyes on.

And he seemed solely focused on her...

As the pirate moved around the cabin, she saw that black clothing covered every inch of his body. His pants were tight over his thighs. The man's shirt hung loose and flowed over his chest. It was open at the navel, revealing a small trail of hair. His immense stature towered over her small frame.

He was so—huge.

The pirate had to be at least six feet tall. His dark black hair was pulled back with a leather tie. A light dusting of stubble covered his face and added to his appeal. He was terrifyingly gorgeous. The pirate was the type of man that made you want to simultaneously run from and toward. He was by far the most handsome man she had ever seen.

How scary is it the only man I had ever been attracted to was a damn pirate?

Once he stepped into the light from her small lantern, she was able to get a better look at all of his features. His cobalt eyes narrowed into tiny slits with a purpose she could only guess.

Pieretta scrambled back towards the bunk in an attempt to get away from him. In her haste, she tripped over the dress Tully had been working on earlier and fell onto the bed face first. He stalked toward her and pulled her to her feet.

Pieretta looked up at him and saw a smirk forming at the corner of his mouth. One side was upturned in a lazy half smile. Her meager attempts at getting away were thwarted by the stupid dress Tully had carelessly left laying on the floor.

Even if I managed to get away from him where would I go?

They were on a ship in the middle of the ocean. She resigned herself to being at this pirate's mercy, at least for the time being.

"Ah, I have found a fine jewel to add to my treasure." He pulled her firmly into his tight embrace.

A musky smell tinged with a hint of sandalwood and chocolate filled her senses.

Delicious...

"What?" Pieretta dumbly replied.

How am I going to survive when looking at him makes me brainless?

"What is your name, girl?"

Should I tell him my name? Why does it matter to him what it is? Pieretta didn't know much about pirates, but the little she was aware of told her they didn't care about the people they attacked. Her name shouldn't matter to him. Still locked in his arms, Pieretta was forced to tilt her head back to stare up at him. The look in his eyes told her all she needed to know. It was best to just answer his questions and pray for mercy.

With great reluctance, she told him her name. "Pia."

"Ah, Pia, you're coming with me." He yanked her toward the door.

"No, I don't think so—I think I would rather stay here," she replied.

She really didn't want to go with the pirate. If she had the choice, she would rather stay on the ship and die with the rest of its inhabitants. Pirates were not known for their mercy or for treating prisoners well. A female prisoner would suffer a fate worse than death.

Pieretta was horrified, and she did her best to fight her way out of his arms in an attempt to escape. She thrashed and pulled with all her might—only to have him laugh at her.

"The captain was right."

"About what?" She asked, stupidly. What else could she say?

"You're a feisty one. We're going to have a spot of fun." A cocky half smile filled his face. "Don't fight me. I promise you won't regret it."

Oh Lord. She started to pull again—harder this time. She had to do something—anything to escape.

Her efforts were futile as his grasp was so tight she could barely breathe. She squirmed in his arms with one last insufficient attempt to get away from him. She raised her small fists and pounded them with all of her might against his hard chest.

What is he going to do with me? I can't escape him. Where would I go?

Pieretta was at his mercy, on board a ship under his control in the middle of the ocean. She hadn't even told him her real name and had no idea why she did that. On further reflection, maybe she did know why. She had always hated her name, and Pia rolled off the tongue and sounded prettier than Pieretta. She decided right there from that moment on she would be Pia to everyone, including herself.

His amusement became evident as a rolling chuckle bubbled from between his full lips as he watched her struggle within the confines of his arms. It was the kind of laugh that rumbled through your soul. Once it started, Pia felt it all over her body, making her shiver with a need she didn't understand. She wanted to rub herself against him. Pia was suddenly aware of where she was. That little compulsion terrified her more than anything she had ever encountered. She needed to get away from him before she did something she would truly regret.

"Please don't take me with you," Pia begged again.

He stared down at her, disbelief clouding his eyes. "So you would rather die along with everyone else?" he asked her.

Pia felt the lump in her throat forming again. *He wouldn't kill me, would he?* Well if she was going to die, she would do her best to remain as brave as possible. There was no reason to give the man any enjoyment from her death. She wouldn't cry—would remain strong to the very end.

With a nod she said, "Yes, I think it would

probably be better than whatever you have in store for me."

The pirate freed her long enough to grab her wrist and drag behind him. "Well it's good for you that I don't take orders, I give them. Come along, Pia. You're much more valuable to me alive than dead." He shook his head and frowned. "Lucky for you, my plans involve you still breathing, or I might have indulged your childish whims."

Good Lord, has the pirate captain claimed me as part of his treasure? If only there was some way to flee. She tried to pull away again, but he just laughed. Her attempt at escape had barely caused him to move an inch. Pia was doomed.

"You're a real bastard, aren't you?"

"I assure you, my father married my mother, and I'm legitimate." His amusement spread across his face as his lips curled into a smug smile.

Did he have to be so frustrating? He continued to chuckle at her attempts to pull out of his grasp. Pia had to restrain herself from using her free hand to slap him, for fear of what he might do to her if she gave in to the desire. He treated her like a bug that was easily ended with one stomp of his heavy boot. Perhaps the problem was the pirate could kill her without giving a second thought to what ending her life might mean. With her arm still firmly within his grasp, he continued to drag Pia along as they made their way topside.

"You know what I meant," Pia shouted.

"I don't read minds, and I don't assume to know what you mean."

Pia snorted. "How do people bear to be around your arrogance?"

"As long as they follow my orders, I don't care what they bear."

Her mind raced...the visual images almost made her fall over. What would this man look like bare? Pia had the sudden urge to fan her face with her free hand to alleviate the hot blush forming across her cheeks.

The sun hung low on the horizon, and she realized that she had been below deck for several hours. Tully had been passed out on the bunk for at least half of the—Wait a minute, what were they going to do with Tully? She should at least make an effort to save her. Tully had been her nurse since she was born. She may be bossy, but Pia would never wish her dead.

"I can't leave my maid. It isn't proper for me to travel alone."

"I could care less about your maid. My plans do

not include carrying around any extra baggage. Your companion will remain here in your cabin."

Pia was at a loss for words. She opened and closed her mouth several times before she was able to convey her shock at his causal dismissal. "You mean you're going to leave her here to die? That's deplorable. You're a wicked man, and I hate you."

The damned pirate ignored her as they continued their journey across the deck. He made his way to what could only be part of his crew. The group consisted of some men Pia had never seen before. She was familiar with most of the crew on the ship from her daily walks on deck, and she didn't recognize one person standing before her. That could only mean one thing; these were the pirates who attacked her grandpere's ship.

The pirate captain approached an older man with snow white hair and dark brown eyes. "Bosun Cornelius, take this treasure to our ship. Put her in a secure spot so I can deal with her later. Pia and I have much to discuss."

"Aye aye, Captain," he said, as he took over the captain's grip on Pia's arm. There were several red marks forming on her already sore wrist. The bosun yanked her across the plank connecting the ships. Pia looked up at the sky and saw the red flag flying above her.

How can they live like this, taking the lives of the innocent? She could still see them plundering the ship, taking all the valuables. She wondered what they would do when they were done. The ship was badly damaged. Would they sink it?

"Where are you taking me?" Pia demanded.

The bosun acted like he didn't hear a word she said. Pia stomped her foot in frustration. She was strong and capable, and she would survive. The pirate could do his worst. She knew something he did not. She had a will stronger than most people, and she was a force to be reckoned with.

Cornelius marched her below deck, shoved her in a cabin, and then locked the door. Pia looked around the room. It appeared to be well kept. It was interesting to see the pirates were not slobs and took care of their belongings. The space was cramped, but it was not nearly as small as the cabin she had previously inhabited. The room held a large bunk and table. There was a trunk pushed up against the wall near the bed. Everything was bolted down to ensure it wouldn't move. The room was decorated in bland colors, everything a muted brown. Even the bedding was dark brown. As she finished surveying the room, she had a realization. Pia was in a room surrounded entirely by things the shades of dirt. Staring at everything in the place, it occurred to her she was probably in the pirate captain's cabin.

THOR SUPERVISED AS THE REST OF THE CREW plundered all of the bounty the ship had to offer. The cargo from Comte Dubois's ship would bring in a good price. It was just another reason Thor was happy with the results from attacking the ship. That ship had been fully stocked with Dubois goods. There were crates full of rum, brandy, and several bolts of silk. It was a double win for him. He now had the comte's precious granddaughter and his cargo.

Thor had made sure every crew member had been breathing before they sailed away. Enough food remained in their galley to ensure they didn't starve. That is, if they managed to get themselves untied. He left the maid passed out in the cabin where he'd found Pia. If she was brave enough, she would free the crew members so they could continue their voyage to France.

Anything that could be used aboard the pirate

ship had been taken. As a token of good will, Thor made sure his crew retrieved Pia's trunks. He wouldn't give any of them to her right away. He would make her earn the contents. He was going to enjoy every aspect of it too. Thor had already thought of several ways she could receive some of the things encased within her many trunks.

Thor walked on deck and sought out his bosun. He located Corny near the quarterdeck where he was issuing orders to some of the crew. "Make sure these cases of liquor are stored in the ship's cargo hold. Take the food to the galley and give it to cook. We will be eating well for the next couple of weeks." The crew members quickly marched off to move the cargo to the areas he had designated.

Corny turned at Thor's approach. "Captain, I was just making sure the bounty was secured," he said.

"Good. Corny, is everything where it needs to be?" he asked.

"Aye, Captain. We are ready to set sail as soon as you give the order."

"And my personal treasure?"

"She is in your cabin, as you ordered Captain."

"Very well, tell Jamieson to set sail. Those tasked with cargo organization can finish that as we sail.

Have all hands on deck to open the sails and hoist the anchor. I will be in my cabin. I do not want to be disturbed unless it is a dire emergency."

"Aye aye, Captain."

Thor turned and made his way to his cabin. It was time to get better acquainted with his precious jewel. She truly was beautiful. The lovely woman only had one flaw, her irritating and evil grandpere. It wouldn't be long before Thor erased that flaw from existence. The only way to ensure the man paid for his crimes was to take away the one thing he valued more than money, his granddaughter.

CHAPTER 4

*T*he cabin walls were beginning to close in on Pia, suffocating her with the knowledge that she had no clue what she ought to do. It had been several hours since the pirate's bosun had shoved her in the cabin, and she was slowly going insane. She was both uneasy and excited at the prospect of facing him again. Did he really murder everyone on board grandpere's ship? If so, why would he spare me and kill everyone else?

The pirate was a devastatingly handsome man, but his arrogance knew no bounds. Against her better judgment, she found herself attracted to him. Pia chewed on her bottom lip, concerned about what his plans were for her. She couldn't let that attraction be her undoing. She knew it was unnatural to feel the way she did, because he was clearly an evil man.

From what little she knew about him he didn't think twice about murder. Her body reacted to him of its own accord. Pia's heart beat faster and her face flushed with heat when she was near him. If she had met him in any other way, she would have seriously reconsidered her no marriage policy. He was the only man who had ever made her think it might be worthwhile to sell herself on the marriage mart.

Yeah, like a pirate would marry anyone. She snorted at the silly idea.

More likely he would plunder every inch of the woman's depths, leaving her well satisfied and alone for the rest of her life.

Well, now that's an idea.

She could not have those kinds of thoughts. She was a virgin and a lady. Women of her station did not consider gifting their virginity to pirates.

No matter how delectable they smelled or how utterly gorgeous they were.

He was immoral and diabolical, giving her the impression he was capable of almost any vice known to man. Pia couldn't help wondering why he took her aboard his ship. There was something he wasn't telling her, and her mission was to discover that reason. The first order of business would be to gain more information and ascertain why the pirate kidnapped her.

Pia roamed aimlessly around the room growing more frustrated at the lack of things to do. The room was stifling, and she was starting to feel claustrophobic from being confined for so long . She was not used to such idle musings and desperately needed something to occupy her time. Pia wished she had access to her trunks. She had lots of books, and it would be spectacular if she could get her hands on one of her treasured tomes.

It was very easy for her to get lost in books because she thirsted for knowledge. Her current book involved her favorite mythological characters: Thor, Loki, and Balder. Pia found Thor's hammer, Mjölnir, the most fascinating part of Norse mythology. It was rumored to be able to crush anything and could only be wielded by Thor himself. She could read about Thor for hours.

Pia desperately needed something to do and wished—again—she at least had some reading material to help pass the time. Even if there was some sewing, at least it would occupy her mind. Normally sewing would have caused her to want to poke her eyes out. Taking the sewing needle and blinding herself would have been preferable to sitting for hours and pulling it through some cloth. Sewing or cross-stitching was such sleep inducing work. In the meantime, she was bored out of her mind with absolutely nothing to occupy her time while she was locked inside the cabin.

She refused to give in to her frustrations or worry over something she had no control over. Surely there had to be a way to convince the pirate captain to release her unharmed. Her grandpere was wealthy— she was wealthy—between the two of them they could surely buy her way out of this predicament.

Yes, that was a plan she would broach with the pirate when he deemed her worthy of his presence, the rat bastard.

The sinfully attractive rat bastard.

She heard footsteps nearing the cabin door. Maybe that was the dreadful, gorgeous man now. Goodness gracious, she had to stop thinking of him in those terms.

How am I going to negotiate if I am constantly salivating over him?

He may be one of the best looking men she had ever encountered, but he was also the same man who ordered the attack on her grandpere's ship and killed its occupants. Well, except for her. Poor Tully, she didn't deserve to die. She irritated Pia, but she would never have wished her harmed in any way. The door creaked open, and the man himself walked in. He looked her over like she was his favorite dessert, and he couldn't wait to lick the plate, alleviating it of every inch of its sweetness.

Heat filled her chicks at his unadulterated gaze. Where was a fan when she needed one?

"Oh good, I can see you have been anxiously awaiting my attention," he drawled. Amusement laced through every syllable.

She opened and closed her mouth several times like a fish out of water trying desperately to breathe. Pia couldn't tell how many times, because she stood there dumbfounded at his audacity.

I should be terrified right? Pfft.

She had let go of that useless emotion hours ago. She didn't have time to be frightened anymore, and it wouldn't do her any good to give the pirate anything to use against her. It was high time she did something to make things go the way she needed them to. She would buy herself out of this situation with any means at her disposal. It was a good thing she was a very wealthy heiress, because it might just come in handy in this particular situation.

"I assure you, Captain Pirate, I have not been

anxiously awaiting anything. What I have been is bored silly. If you were trying to kill me with ennui, then by all means stay the course. If not, well I will surely expire before long. Maybe that is your intention? It's less messy, and it's a great means of torture. It is a miracle I haven't already gone insane from sheer boredom over the past several hours."

A rich throaty laugh echoed through the room.

The man dared to laugh at her. It was like he couldn't help himself, and it just burst out of him every time she tried to speak to him. It was the kind of laugh that made you weary and excited at the same time.

When she first heard it, it made her shiver from the inside out.

She was starting to realize it might always have that affect on her. It tickled down her spine and made her tremble.

His laugh was dangerous.

Oh Lord. A devilish smirk curved his lips. She was a goner for sure. Damn man, why must you have such an appealing face. She was so lost in her own thoughts she almost didn't hear him when he finally spoke.

"Thor," he replied.

"Excuse me?"

"I am Captain Thor, not Captain Pirate."

It was Pia's turn to laugh. Only moments ago, she had pondered her favorite book on Norse mythology, and here the blasted pirate was named after her favorite hammer wielding god.

"I suppose you carry a hammer only you can lift right?"

"Oh, I don't have a hammer per se..."

She sucked in a breath as he delivered the innuendo. Pia choked, finding it difficult to express the words flowing through her mind. Surely he didn't mean what his words implied...

Thor's face lit up with his roguish smile, and he crossed the short distance between them and whispered in her ear. His hot breath caressed her neck as his words softly flowed through her eardrums. "I can assure you it will be my pleasure to share it with you."

Pia moved away quickly before she could take him up on his offer. Her heart beat faster. Its rhythm pounded through her ears and steadily gained pace with each breath she forced between her open lips. The more space she put between them the better off she would be. It was unfortunate the cabin was so tiny because it left her very few options. Pia needed to gain some distance between herself and the pirate. She took a deep breath and steadily exhaled with slow measures to gain some control over her body's reaction.

It was an attempt to remind herself she was supposed to be livid with him, not attracted to him.

Once her breathing was under control, she looked up into his blue eyes. "I am not interested in your over-inflated ego and images of grandeur."

Thor's lips upturned into a devilish half smile. There was once again a drop of mirth in each word he enunciated. "Oh, my ego is definitely not over inflated—or anything else. Trust me. It is well earned. However there is a part of me that is...inflated." He took a step toward her and asked, "Would you like me to show you?"

Thor's said the most outrageous things—Pia didn't know how to respond. Every sound and gesture he made was a form of seduction she was sorely unprepared for. Pia needed to steer the conversation on to another topic, one designed to ensure her virtue stayed intact. This one was taking her places she did not want to go—at least she didn't think she did.

Who was she kidding? A large part of her wanted to look him in the eyes and tell him exactly what she wanted him to show her. Her curiosity was going to get her into trouble.

What Pia needed to do was turn the conversation back on him. If she could make sure he didn't get any closer, she could remain relatively safe. "Pirate Thor?" she asked derision in her voice. "You imagine you are equal to a god?"

"I can't help what my parents named me, now can I?"

Disbelief coated her voice. "Your parents actually named you Thor?"

"Thor Williams, at your service," he said, making a production of bowing, much like a gentlemen would before a lady.

He seriously went by that moniker? His parents named him after a Norse god? No wonder the man had an overinflated ego. If he lived up to her fantasies about the god of thunder, then this Thor would certainly be her undoing.

Pia cleared her throat. "Sooo—I am Pia Carlyle. I don't know why you decided my life was worth keeping. Not that I'm not glad that you did, but I've had a lot of time in this room all by myself to consider my options. I thought maybe we could strike a bargain."

The man had a perpetual smile on his face, as if

everything she said was the most comical thing in the world. The real problem was his smile was so attractive she was having a hard time concentrating on her main purpose. If he kept doing that, she was going to climb all over him and beg him to show her his mythical hammer.

"Exactly what I came to discuss with you, Pia."

"Good. I am glad to see we are of the same mind."

He nodded. "I concur."

"I don't know if you are aware that my family has money. They will pay any ransom you demand."

"Oh, I am more than aware of who your family is, love," he replied.

"Good. So you will send notice of the ransom for my release?"

"I will do no such thing." He shook his head.

Pia's mouth hung open in frozen disbelief.

She recovered quickly while he continued to grin at her shocked disposition. In that moment, she realized this might not be something she could gain control over, but she still needed more information before she could assess what needed to be done.

"Why not?" she asked.

"I have other plans for you, dear. None of them involve extracting money from your grandpere."

Well that was a development she had not been expecting. She assumed because he was a pirate he could be easily bought off with her inheritance. Her limited knowledge of pirates suggested they were mercenaries. From what Thor had said though this very well could be a personal endeavor of his, and her grandpere was deeply involved. "You know my grandpere?"

"I know him better than you do. In fact, he and I have a debt that will not be easily settled with the exchange of money. You are going to help me to do that, and in the process, we will get to know each other very well." He wiggled his eyebrow suggestively. "We'll be as close as two people can possibly be when this is all said and done."

With each sentence Thor uttered, Pia felt the color drain from her face. "What do you have planned for me?"

"You will find out soon enough. For now, we are going to get some rest, you and I. We have a long journey ahead of us. No need to rush into it right now. Our more pleasurable pursuits will happen in due time."

He dragged her toward his bunk. It was fairly large for a ship, but not nearly big enough for two people. Especially if he was one of those two people. It would definitely be a cramped sleeping space.

"Surely you don't expect me to sleep there with you."

"Oh, I assure you, not only do I expect it, but you will do it."

"It isn't big enough for both of us."

Thor smirked, and a small chuckle echoed throughout the cabin. He shoved her over to the side that hugged the ship. Pia curled up against the wall in an attempt to make herself as small as possible. She watched as Thor sat and removed his boots, setting them next to the bed. After the task was complete, he rolled over and lay next to Pia on the bunk. He pulled his arms over his head and tucked both of his hands beneath his dark locks. Pia tried to find a comfortable spot on the small bunk, but his body engulfed more than half of it.

"We fit just fine. You fretted unnecessarily, love. Don't worry, you will soon be very used to having my arms wrapped around you, in sleep and in other things. For now just lie down and get some rest."

"I'd rather not."

"Well that is too damn bad, lie down and go to sleep. You have no idea when you will have such a luxury again. I have many plans for you, and sleeping isn't exactly on my agenda."

Pia did what he asked, at least as much as she was able. What else could she do? He was right in some ways. Pia would need some sleep if she was going to be able to properly deal with her dastardly pirate. She needed to survive, and Pirate Thor wasn't going to take advantage of her, much. She was still fully clothed at least. From what little he shared with her, she knew nothing was going to happen on this night, getting a little sleep would only benefit her.

Pia lay her head down on the bed next to Thor. Once she was curled up next to him, he rolled over and wrapped his entire body around her. She could feel his hammer nestled against her rear. If she gave him the slightest encouragement, she was sure he would show her what he could do with it. With what little preservation Pia still had within her, she ignored what that meant. She did not want to find out what losing her virginity felt like any time soon.

ONCE PIA WAS ASLEEP, THOR LEFT THE CABIN and locked it. He couldn't stay in the bed with her any longer. She was too much of a temptation. He had plans, and using her body wasn't on the list.

Yet.

She called herself Pia. He liked it much better than Pieretta. It rolled off of his tongue like a lover's caress, and they would be lovers. Every blush staining her cheeks told him how attracted she was to him. Her breathing became labored when he pulled her near, and he could feel her pulse racing beneath his fingers when he held her wrist in his hand. It was only a matter of time before she was completely his.

Thor hadn't known exactly what she looked like when he'd started this crusade. He had only been given a general description so he would know who to look for on board the ship.

She was stunning. He wanted undo her braid and run his fingers through her pale blonde hair. He needed to spread it out across his bunk. Then he wanted to strip her luscious body of her drab mourning garb and lick her all over. He would start at her ankles, and work his way up to her pretty bosom. Her breasts were plump and just large enough to fill the palms of his hands. He loved how her waist curved into a nicely rounded derriere.

Thor had a fierce need to pull her on top of him and slide inside of her tight channel. Having her wantonly ride his shaft and find pleasure remained on top of his most desired fantasies. He wanted to get her naked so he could taste every inch of her and hear her scream with satisfaction. She was everything he had ever considered to be perfect, and he could not have dreamed up a more ideal woman to find pleasure with.

He had to snap out of this line of thought. It was too early for this part of the plan, but it would happen and soon. He needed her to be a willing participant in her own downfall. He had never forced anyone in his life, and he was not about to start with his jewel. She was far beyond anything he could have expected, and he found he wanted more from her than he had originally planned. He was beginning to think he just might want to keep her forever, something he had never considered with anyone else.

He made his way topside. He needed to talk to his first mate and bosun. They needed to set a new course. They were going to make a stop in southern France instead of Calais. When he had looked through the captain's logs, he had discovered the comte had traveled to his southern estate, and that was where they would see each other again for the last time.

He needed as much time with the feisty Pia as he could manage, before they had their final meeting with her grandpere. He needed her to fall in love with him. He would use every tool in his arsenal to make that happen.

What Pia didn't know was that their lives had been forever entwined before they ever laid eyes on each other. If not for her grandpere, they would never have met. The actions of the comte ensured they would forever be linked.

Thor had to admit he was actually looking forward to getting to know her better.

He intended to have his cake, and he would savor every sweet bite.

CHAPTER 5

*L*iving the life of a lady had many perks and advantages. Pia had no qualms about using every one of those resources to ensure she came out on top. As an only child, Pia's father indulged all of her requests. Mr. Carlyle only had one rule he stood firm with concerning her. She could basically do anything she wanted, but if it was something he deemed dangerous, it was forbidden. Fortunately for Pia, his list of perilous things was not very long, so she pretty much ran wild on the plantation. As long as Pia was safe, her father did not object to any activity she wanted to experience.

Pia did have the benefit of a more formal education. The instructors her father hired taught her Latin, history, and math. When she wanted to learn about mythology, science, and, Greek, her father hired the best tutors he could find. She probably, in some ways, had a better education than some of the gentlemen in Charleston.

No one had a thirst for knowledge quite like Pia did. Getting lost inside the pages of a book was her favorite past time. The stories weaved lead her on adventures she couldn't have imagined herself. There were adventures to be found all from the safety of her library. As she studied with her tutors, she encountered Norse mythology and learned of the various gods. Thor had been her favorite, so it shouldn't surprise her that she was attracted to a man with the same moniker.

Her father even hired a fencing instructor when she expressed a desire to learn. He made sure the foils were dull and harmless before the lessons could commence. Pia was an apt student and excelled at everything she attempted. There was no one else more aware what her many flaws were than Pia, but she equally knew every one of her assets.

She had been locked inside his cabin for twelve days. Twelve days of doing nothing. She wanted to make sure the pirate felt at least a small amount of her frustration. Thor needed to feel it, but she had no way of accomplishing this daunting task. Pia had plenty of time and not a thing to do, except get lost inside her own mind. She could be patient, but after so long with only the pirate's occasional company, she started to slowly lose her mind. The ennui of her existence was torture only a strong person could survive. Pia questioned if she was capable of the kind of strength required to endure beyond this moment in her life.

It was beyond her comprehension why she couldn't bend Thor to her will. The pirate delivered innuendos and implied a lot, but he never acted on any of it. The more she knew about him, the less she understood what his intentions could possibly be. He made no secret that he hated her grandpere, but he failed to express how that information actually applied to her. The banter between her and Pirate Thor continued every time they were in each other's presence.

Thor remained stubborn in his desire to make her sleep next to him each night, and he absolutely refused to let her out of his cabin for any reason. Each night when he deemed it was time to rest, he made her lay down on the bunk. Once she was settled in, he would lay next to her so she could sleep inside the warmth of his embrace. It was beginning to feel safe locked in his arms as he hugged her close, her head resting above his heart. The one thing Pia knew for sure was she should not relax in his company, because it was the most dangerous place she could be.

Each night Pia experienced the same thing, and she grew more and more confused. What exactly does he have in store for me? She needed to find a way to make him talk. Well, she needed answers. He had no problem talking, but it was usually filled with innuendo. With each word he uttered, she became more confused. She wanted to hold on to her anger, but she also craved the companionship of another human being. All Thor offered her were baseless conversations leading nowhere. Pia was tired of only having him for company.

Pia was no stranger to the insinuations he alluded to every time he deigned to speak to her. She may be a woman, but she went unnoticed much growing up and had overheard men discussing their sexual exploits. Most of her knowledge was gained from books, and very few offered good illustrations of what they were talking about.

Pia had only been kissed once, when she was sixteen years old. There was a man on a neighboring plantation who thought she would be a suitable wife and had begun to court her. During a picnic at his home, he had lead her behind a tree and kissed her. It wasn't very notable, and Pia felt next to nothing, except wet and messy. What was enjoyable about a man leaving saliva all over your face? The sensation was disgusting, and his groping at her hadn't helped much. The man may have enjoyed it, but she never let him touch her again. She had doubts she would ever want to be kissed again, because the experience had been so distasteful.

She knew what desire was as she had inadvertently witnessed some clandestine meetings. Pia had just never really felt it before, and that was one of the reasons she didn't think she would ever get married. She just wasn't interested in what a man had to offer her.

That was until she came across a certain pirate. *Why do I have to feel something for a dangerous pirate?*

Losing herself in her own thought, she imagined the many things she would do to him if given the chance. They alternated between kissing him and strangling him, depending on the direction her thoughts wandered. The more she was reduced to keeping her own company, all Pia wanted to do was scream at or kill a certain pirate.

It was while she was doing her daily pacing the

pirate did the unexpected and returned to the cabin in the middle of the day. He generally left her alone until it was time to settle in for the night. Apparently being the captain of a ship kept him busy, leaving little time to entertain her.

Pia hated to admit it, but she was excited. As her only source of company, she anticipated his arrival every night. At least with him around she had someone else's voice to listen to. His presence helped keep her sanity in place. If she were left alone any more than she was, she'd have gone stark raving mad by now. Pia had reached a pinnacle in her situation, suddenly willing to give anything a try in order to have a variation in their daily routine. He wouldn't tell her how he knew her grandpere, and she was hoping to goad him into doing so.

"Ah. I see you are as busy as usual, Pia."

She glared at him, but said nothing. Pia traipsed over to the bunk and sat on the edge.

"Are you attempting to give me the silent treatment? How novel of you."

Thor sauntered over to his desk and pulled out the chair. The stool was the only piece of furniture not bolted down in the cabin. Pia watched as he sat on it and pulled himself closer to the desk. Once seated, he pulled out a key and unlocked the cabinet attached to the side of the writing table. Thor slid open the cabinet and pulled out a piece of paper, followed by a quill, and then ink. It was sad that watching him sit at his desk was entertainment to her. He made a production of setting everything on the table in preparation to write.

Pia studied the back of his head. His sun-kissed black hair was pulled back in a leather tie. It was the only way she had ever seen him wear it. Her view was blocked from seeing what he was actually doing, but she was happy just watching his shoulders move as he scribbled something across the blank pages.

When he had entered the cabin, she had been determined to ignore him, but her eyes kept being drawn back. It was too easy to watch him with an unguarded gaze. Pia felt herself wishing they could have met differently. She wanted to give in to the urge to stroke her hands over his shoulders, and it wasn't long before she started to wonder what he would do if she licked his neck.

Pia let out a whoosh of air from her lungs, and a loud sigh emerged from between her lips. She couldn't help it. The cabin was beyond tedious. If she didn't stop these fantasies about the pirate, she was going to inadvertently act out one of them. By the time the actions took place, it would be too late to change her course.

Thor was too busy to pay her any attention. Pia wanted to know more about the pirate but was unsure how to go about getting her questions answered. *I simply have to find a way to get him to open up to me.* No matter how many questions she asked, he never gave her any personal information about himself. Any efforts on her part to gain insight into his persona were met with little success.

Pia had little recourse but to spend time with Thor. He became the only thing occupying her thoughts. Her days started with him next to her and ended the same way. The in-between hours were spent thinking of ways to extricate herself from the situation she was in. She saw no clear way out.

Pia lay down on the bunk and tapped her fingers together while daydreams of a dashing pirate floated through her imagination. In her mind, he was really a gentleman caller approved of by her father. The dashing man courted her and asked her to be his wife. Of course she said no. Couldn't they just have an affair instead? He was shocked, but agreed to her suggestion, leading him down a pathway to sin. He was willing to do anything for her as long as she was his. Pia was such an impious girl, if only she knew what to picture that wickedness to actually be. She could guess, but she was sheltered so she didn't know.

Pia had a one track mind and these days it involved her and the pirate in various compromising situations. She stopped being terrified of him. Pia was so used to his company even the fact he towered over her became completely natural to her. She didn't understand how she could have come to be so accepting of him in such a short time.

Lost in the world of her imagination, Pia didn't realize Thor had stopped writing and was watching her. He had placed his stuff back in the cabinet, and she hadn't heard a thing. Pia often got lost in her mind and drowned out the rest of the world. The only noise that existed was the music of her own daydreams.

"Is this what you do all day?"

The pictures running through her mind made it almost impossible to hear what he had said. Unfortunately for Pia, his voice was a huge part of her daydreams so it bled through, bringing her back to reality. Choosing to ignore his question, she kept the images dancing in her mind. He was ruining my fantasy.

Irritation corded into each word as Thor spoke. "I asked you a question."

She hummed her favorite song as she imagined dancing at a ball in his arms. *Why can't he say things I want to hear?* Things like: of course I will let you go, no I didn't kill everyone on board your grandpere's ship, or how about a kiss, Pia.

Wait, she didn't want him to really do that last part, did she?

"I think that this is quite enough, Pia. I am not going to tolerate your silent treatment for much longer."

What did he expect me to say?

Pia stuck her tongue out at him in defiance.

He laughed at her as he pulled her up and off the bunk. The sound echoed across the cabin walls, amusement filling the room with each chuckle that escaped his lips.

"I think you need a lesson on some things you can do with that tongue. If you stick it out at me again, you can expect this..."

The only thought Pia had as he pulled her toward him was: be careful what you wish for.

He plundered her mouth in ways she could never have imagined. Fantasy? What fantasy? Reality was much more exciting and fulfilling. If she was capable of thought, she would have started planning on ways they could do this again.

When his tongue intertwined with hers, they danced to a tune only they could create. Any thoughts of remembering how to breathe failed to find their way into her befuddled brain. Her hands wrapped around him, and she pulled him closer. Pia felt a strong need growing inside of her. She felt Thor's hands as they roamed across the back of her head, locating the braid secured at the nape of her neck. Once he had it securely in his palms, he pulled her tresses, tipping her chin up. With her head tilted back, he placed soft kisses along her décolletage. He kissed her neckline and stopped at the base of her ears. He trailed his lips across her cheek, placing little kisses along the way, and then plundered her mouth all over again. Their tongues entwined for what seemed like hours but were no more than mere minutes. Surely there wasn't anything better than this?

He whispered in her ear. "You taste so much better than I could have imagined."

Oh he did too—so so delectable.

She enjoyed kissing him just as much, but it had to stop before she did something irreversible. She began to pull her face away from his, but he still had his arms wrapped securely around her. Pia wasn't going anywhere just yet. Thor settled her firmly against the wall of the cabin and lifted her up so her bosom was level with his mouth. His tongue found the crevice between her breasts and licked upward. He brought his mouth to hers for one last mind blowing kiss as he eased her down the wall and swung her toward the bunk.

He stepped away from Pia, putting some much needed distance between them. Pia lost her balance and fell backward onto the bed. She sat there in silence and stared at him. Words escaped her, as she had no way of describing all of the emotions flowing through her body and soul. Her mouth was swollen from his attentions, and she felt a tingling in her lower regions. Her breasts were tight and heavy, and she knew what true desire was for the first time in her life. None of the books she had read had described it with any kind of accuracy. So this is why it was forbidden.

A wide grin spread across Thor's face as he gazed at her. She felt heat stinging her cheeks, and her heart raced wildly beneath her breasts. The mirth shining in his eyes told her all she needed to know about how she appeared to him. She had been well and truly pleasured by everything he had done with his mouth and hands. What that man did with his tongue should not be permissible.

"Do you still insist on giving me the silent treatment?"

Oh yes, absolutely if you kiss me as punishment. More please, oh I am quite certain, I want you to punish me more.

Pia was equally certain she had a lot of horrible ideas lately. She was a bad girl. She needed to talk to him before he did more than kiss her breath away. He finally was doing instead of implying. Maybe, just maybe, she could get some actual information out of him. So she decided to take a nonchalant approach to the whole situation.

She shrugged. "What is there possibly to talk about?"

"Perhaps you would like to know what I have planned for you."

"Oh, you think I have finally earned the right to know that?"

He shook his head. "No Pia, dear, you won't know exactly what my plans are for you until the very last second."

There was no other person alive who could frustrate her more than her pirate. Yes, he really was her pirate in her mind. He still needed to talk about things that mattered to her, or she wouldn't be held accountable for her actions. With as much indignation as she could muster, Pia looked up at him. "Then why are we discussing this?"

"Because your life is going to change forever in a short time."

What an asinine statement. Pia let out an unladylike snort. Hadn't it already changed forever?

"And that is different than the past week how? Why don't we talk about you instead? Like what a murdering fiend you are for what you did too everyone on that ship."

Thor folded his arms across his chest and leaned back against his writing table. "Because my plans for you will be irreversible once everything is in place."

Damn, that didn't sound good. Pia frowned. She had to try to get him to talk more. Her life depended on what he was going to do. So she needed to do something to get him to tell her what his plans actually were.

"Seems like that is also already true, what could be so different today? One thing is certain, you are very good at evading questions. Why don't you tell me why you needed to kill everyone aboard my grandpere's ship?"

"I never told you I killed everyone on that ship. You just assumed I did."

"An assumption that you never corrected. You wanted me to believe the worst in you."

Thor shrugged. "It suited my purposes at the time."

"So are you going to tell me anything else, since you are in such a sharing mood today?" Pia inquired.

"I grow weary of your persistent questioning. I have answered all you need to know for now."

"You answered nothing, you only implied you didn't kill anyone, much the same way that you insinuated you murdered a whole ship of people."

"Believe what you want Pia. The truth will be evident when it matters. I don't need to confirm or deny anything."

"Okay, I'm tired of your non-answers. Why did you come in here to bother me?"

"We will be making port in a couple of days. You will be able to come on deck. Once you are topside you will agree to everything I ask you to do. No matter what it is you will do it. If you don't, I will personally make sure that your only living family member dies."

"Are you saying you would murder my grandpere?"

Thor leaned down and looked her directly in her eyes his intentions crystal clear as he enunciated each syllable. "In a heartbeat."

Pia didn't want to think he would kill her grandpere. It just didn't make sense to her why he would do something so evil to someone she loved. "I don't believe you. Why not threaten my life?"

"Because it's clear you have no regard for your own life. I figured, if I threatened someone you love, then you would be more willing to follow my lead and do as I say. It also helps that I have a deep hatred for your grandpere. His death is nothing at all to me."

He had her there. She would die before she let him control her. Her grandpere though? Pia had to protect him.

"You are despicable."

"You enjoy it though, love. I could have done whatever I wanted to you earlier, and you would have followed me to hell and back. You were so hot, you seared my skin. Maybe talking with you isn't the best use of my time? In the future, I'll just show you what I want instead."

Without thinking, Pia slapped Thor across his left cheek.

Thor's amusement still hung in the air. His

laugher echoed through the cabin as he sauntered out of the room.

Pia had a lot to think about. Would the pirate actually kill her grandpere? She believed he would. He made sure she knew he harbored no tender feelings for her grandpere. Oh yes, Pirate Thor would follow through with his threat to kill the comte. He left her little choice. If she wanted to ensure her only living family member remained alive, she would have to do everything he asked of her, even if she hated every minute of it. The only option Pia had was to pray she could actually follow through with whatever plans he had in store.

He had almost gone too far with Pia. If he had stayed there even a moment longer, he would have ravished her completely. He needed her, and as he got to know her, his plans changed course, moving in a completely different direction.

She was supposed to fall in love with him. He had blundered a bit there. He would have to make her forget he had threatened her grandpere's life somehow. Not that Comte Dubois didn't deserve to die. He was an evil man. If not for him, Thor would never have become a pirate. But that also meant he would never have met Pia. Thor's conundrum was his constant craving for Pia. It hadn't been in his plans to want her as much as he did.

He had intended to offer her some of the things from her trunks. It was clear to him she was restless. Thor would offer her a boon the next time he talked to her. Peace was important to have between them. It did not bode well with his plans to always be so overbearing and obnoxious with her. Although, she did appear to enjoy being kissed.

He walked up to the deck to check their progress. They should be in Bordeaux in less than two days. His plans would be in full motion once they were in port with the anchor dropped. When it was all done, he would be able to have what he wanted most. Revenge. Thor would also have something he was starting to desire almost more than that. Almost.

When he got topside, he located his first mate to make sure they were on schedule. Jamieson was at the bow of the ship with his sextant measuring the angles on the horizon.

"Are we on our scheduled course, Jamieson?"

"We are, Captain."

"Excellent work. Let me know if we run into any

problems. I don't want to have anything spoil the plans I've made."

"Aye aye, Captain."

Thor walked away making his way to the galley. With his cabin occupied by a tempting beauty, he couldn't spend his leisure time there. He would make the cook get out his bottle of scotch and pour him a glass.

He was desperately in need of something to assist him while slumbering alongside Pia in their shared bunk. It would prove difficult to find any rest lying next to her later that night in his current state. Thor hoped the alcohol would help him pass out and prevent him from groping her...much.

CHAPTER 6

*T*hor started to speculate about life and the choices he made. A person's existence could become their own version of hell on Earth. Sadly he knew more about that than anyone else did. The choices he made often demanded every ounce of his blood, sweat, and tears. The very essence of his soul had been devoured whole, chewed, and spit out with nothing good remaining to maintain its life force. His soul remained on the brink of being lost, never to be retrieved again. At the same time life is inherently full of surprises at every turn, both good and bad depending on which path is chosen. The course he selected determined how much of his soul was beyond redemption or if it had one last chance to achieve salvation.

Watching the sun rise above the ocean announcing a new day, Thor thought of all of the reasons he set himself on this particular path. Revenge was the course of action he had taken, and he couldn't extricate himself from it even if he wanted to.

Pia was a revelation he had not anticipated. When he had heard she was traveling to live with Comte Dubois, all he could see was a way to enact his vengeance. The reality of it all was more of a shock than having his partner put a bullet through his shoulder. He was beginning to need her. He knew he had to alter his course before he crossed a line.

The port of Bordeaux beckoned him. Some plans already set in motion were irrevocable. Once the anchor dropped, he would need to make some quick alterations to his plans. In the missive he had written in front of Pia, those changes would be hastened. He just needed to send one of his crew to deliver the message of their arrival, and once it was done, everything should go smoothly.

His heart would never recover if he lost it all because he couldn't correct some of the mistakes he had already made. As it was, there was still a lot that was unforgivable. Sadly events to come might hamper any effort he made. Pia was still an essential part of his plan, but the difference was how she would be used in his revenge.

He still needed to make sure the comte paid for his treachery. The modification was in how much of it would destroy the humanity that remained of his soul. What he was doing to gain retribution wouldn't blacken him to the core. It was something he could, and would, happily live with. Some things were worth whatever price needed to be paid. This was one time there would be no regrets. There were times when he thought he would never be able to make Renny Dubois pay for his betrayal, and it was finally within his grasp. He just had to reach out and take it. He was so lost in thought he hadn't heard his bosun approach until he started to speak.

"Captain we are almost to the harbor of Bordeaux. I have Timmy getting ready to take a dinghy to shore. Is your message ready?"

Thor pulled out the missive. He had carefully written all of his instructions on the day he'd gotten his first taste of Pia. She had been so occupied with her own thoughts she hadn't even been curious about what he had been writing. At first that had disappointed him until he turned around and saw the expression on her face.

There had been such a look of longing in her eyes as she chewed her bottom lip. He lost control when her tongue slowly rolled over her lips leaving them a shiny invitation to be kissed. He couldn't restrain himself after that. He had to taste her. It was nice to see a lighter side of her personality emerge. If she had never stuck her tongue out at him, he may never have given in to his desire to kiss her.

He rolled the missive between his fingers remembering how much that day had transformed his outlook. His needs had altered so much because of that one moment of weakness. He wouldn't go back and change any part of that day, even knowing how much it would change him or what it forced him to admit about himself. After spending the past two weeks with Pia, he knew she was meant to be his. That day had sealed it for him. Thor turned to his bosun and handed him the message.

"Tell Timmy to wait for the reverend and bring all our guests back with him. The crew and I will await their arrival. Also, make sure he is aware I would like them here as quickly as possible. I want to have enough time to make sure Pia is back below deck before the sun sets tonight. It will be too dangerous to allow her to remain on deck after the ceremony."

"I will make sure that Timmy follows your directions, sir. After all it is a good night for a celebration."

Thor laughed. "It is indeed, Corny. It is indeed."

"The cook also wanted me to let you know that tonight's meal would be remembered for a long time to come. We got quite a haul from the galley of the ship we plundered, including a nice case of brandy and scotch. He wants to know if you'd like us to break it open for the celebration tonight."

"I think that's a fine plan, Corny. Also, any unnecessary crew can have shore leave for the night. Tell them they can go after tonight's celebration and remind them they need to be back on the ship before sunset tomorrow night. We will set sail after everyone's returned."

"Aye aye, Captain. I will take care of everything."

Thor found himself smiling in anticipation. Soon he would have everything he desired, including the alluring Pia. Her charms were something he ached to sample. After the blazing kisses they had shared, he knew her desire was equal to his. Pia was full of a fire that would consume with the right amount of fuel feeding her flames. It would be his honor and pleasure to share that bliss with her. After the ceremony just before dusk, she would be his in every way. Once the formalities were out of the way, they could explore what made each other burn.

I‌F P‌IA D‌IDN'T S‌TOP W‌ALKING B‌ACK A‌ND F‌ORTH, she was bound to wear a hole in the cabin floor, clear through to the cargo hold. If that damn pirate showed his face today, she was going to pummel it with her fists. He needed to let her out of this cabin. He could at least have given her something to read. Then again, he did have that locked cabinet.

Staring at the cabinet as if seeing it for the first time, she analyzed it for weaknesses. Maybe it is possible to unlock it. With little to amuse herself, she was desperate enough to try anything. She scoured the room, looking for a tool that could help her pry it open. She turned the bunk inside out, throwing things on the floor. The blankets and pillows hit the ground with a soft thud. There was nothing there. She pulled the mattress up and pushed it against the wall. She looked beneath it. When she did not find anything of use, she let it flop back down haphazardly on top of its wooden frame. She turned and spotted the pirate's trunk. Rushing over to it, she tried to lift the top with her bare hands. The bloody thing was locked too, and she kicked it in frustration.

Nothing. There was nothing in the room. This was the worst torture ever imagined. She moved over to the cabinet to see if she could pry it open with her hands.

Pia kept trying to tear it open unaware that Thor had entered. He watched her for several seconds before he spoke. "Perhaps I could help you with that?"

Pia jumped back, startled by his voice next to her.

"Must you be so damned quiet?"

A chuckle rumbled out of his chest, developing into a full blown laugh. It was like a bolt of lightning striking the ground and spreading a light through a dark room.

"It was not my intention. I can see you have idle hands. Perhaps, I can give you something to keep them busy."

"Really? What? Do you have any books? I would love to have something to read. It would go a long way in curing the chronic boredom I've developed while being held captive."

"Sadly, pirates have little use for books. We don't have time for any leisurely pursuits. I might have a map or two you could entertain yourself with, but that wasn't exactly what I had in mind."

"I am almost afraid to ask. What exactly do you have in mind?"

"Well we could always continue where we left off the other day. That wall there was quiet handy in keeping you in place and what you were doing with your hands—purely inspirational."

Pia glared at him. Is he serious? Please let him be serious. She wanted to kiss him again and feel his hands roaming over her body. She wanted him to suck her nipples and squeeze her breasts. Wait, where did that idea come from? It was a fine idea indeed, and it needed to happen. I really, really need it to happen. She was about to make her demands when she remembered she was supposed to discourage such actions. She had to be sensible, and the pirate had already proven his kisses made her brainless.

"That is not what I had in mind and you know it."

"Pia, love, you are the most amusing woman I have ever encountered. I can see the conflicting emotions all over your face. No worries, my dear, I do have something else in mind. I thought perhaps you would enjoy a bath and a change of clothes."

She raised an eyebrow. "Is this some kind of trick? What's the catch?"

"No trick or catch. I want you to be comfortable and feel your best today. We are having a celebration tonight, and you will be able to come on deck."

"Really? I can leave the cabin now? I'd been starting to think you were lying about allowing me out of this blasted room."

"Yes, for an hour or so. Your attendance at the celebration is much desired."

"Then yes, absolutely, I would love a bath. But, I don't have any underclothes or another dress that I can put on when I'm done."

"Don't worry. I'll make sure you have something besides that drab dress you choose to wear."

"Are you serious? It isn't like you have given me a change of attire since I have been on your ship."

"I didn't have a reason to before. I was commenting more on your choice of attire, period. It's dreadful, and you need to wear something with more color. Black, my dear, does nothing for you."

"I'm in mourning, my father died. That's what you wear to honor the dead."

"I know. All the same, you will no longer wear black. I don't like it."

Pia pursed her lips together, letting her

displeasure be known. She looked at Thor. "All right, Captain. As I have no choice but to follow your dictates, I guess I will have to agree if I want a bath and a change of clothes."

He smiled at her, and she felt her heart flutter faster. Damn him and his alluring smile. It should be illegal, not that it would stop him. He was a pirate after all. They never followed any laws, unless they were of their own making. If there was one thing Pia was more than aware of, it was that this particular pirate made his own rules. This ship was a nation of its own making. Any regulations were enforced by the one and only sovereign pirate, Thor.

"As always, Pia, you make things more interesting. I will send my cabin boy up with your hot water. Do not give him any trouble. If you try to leave the cabin before you are supposed to, you will regret it. Take this small peace offering and enjoy your bath."

Pia sighed. "I can't very well argue with your logic."

"Of course you can't, it won't take you long to realize that I am generally right in most situations. One more thing before I go, please clean up the mess you made before Gus comes with your bath. I know that you didn't have anything to do, but tearing the cabin apart isn't an acceptable form of entertainment. It wouldn't do very well for us to sleep on wet things tonight."

He turned and walked out the door, making sure it was secured behind him. Once it was closed, Pia stuck her tongue out at him. She didn't dare do it to his face any more. Even if she wanted him to kiss her again, she couldn't allow it to happen. They almost went too far the last time.

After reflecting on her situation, she didn't think it was wise to get too attached to the pirate. He was undoubtedly handsome and his kiss was an experience she would always treasure, but her heart would break if she allowed him to have it. She did not believe it was possible for her to have an affair without letting herself feel something for the other person. She had already begun to care about the pirate, and all they had done was kiss.

Pia sighed and looked at the room. She had made quite a mess of the small cabin. On this one occasion she conceded that Thor had a point. The room's current chaotic state needed to be set to rights. She had no idea how long it would be before her bath was brought to the cabin so she immediately began to clean up the room. It didn't take her long to put everything back where it belonged and decided she needed a break from the exertion.

Pia was lying on the bunk when the door opened. She turned to see a boy of no more than twelve come in carrying a wooden tub. He placed it near the bunk and walked out of the room. He wasn't much of a conversationalist.

Pia got up to inspect the tub. It wasn't very large. Looking at it, she wondered how anyone larger than her could possibly fit inside of it. She wondered where the captain got the tub, and if he had intended for her to bathe all along. Where did the rest of them bathe? Did they even bother?

It wasn't long before the boy returned. This time he was carrying two large buckets of steaming water. He quickly poured them into the tub. When he was done, he looked over at her and set the buckets down.

"Miss, I will be back with more hot water. Once the tub is half full, then a couple of pails with cooler water will be available so you can make it to your liking. I'm to bring you some soap and drying cloths as well. After I bring you everything, you are free to take your bath. I just wanted to let you know so that you can bathe in peace."

"Thank you, what's your name?"

"Gus, ma'am."

"Thank you, Gus. Are you bringing me a change of clothes too?"

"I don't rightly know, ma'am. I suspect the captain has everything you need ready, and you will get it when he decides you need it."

"Hmm. Of course he does. Thank you again, Gus."

Odious man.

When Gus left, Pia silently fumed. Give it to her when he wants her to have it, will he. It was time to share her frustrations with him. Thor had no idea how much he drove her insane. The pirate would soon learn exactly what Pia's capabilities were. This was definitely going to be an amusing day.

Gus continued to fill her bath. He completed his task efficiently, working as fast as his small frame could manage. Once he was gone, she didn't waste any time because the water would cool and make her bath a miserable experience. She adjusted the water to her desired temperature. While she was finishing that task, Gus came in one last time with a couple stacks of dry cloths and a bar of soap.

"Here be your soap, ma'am. I will be by later to collect the water and tub. I will knock first so as to make sure you're decent."

Pia looked over as Gus left the room. The door

shut with a quiet click. She heard the key turn, locking her inside once again. She began to undress, and it wasn't until he left that she realized she had a dilemma. *How the heck am I going to get my corset off?*

Thor had decided he needed to give Pia something to occupy her time with. When he had walked in earlier and found the cabin a mess with her attempting to yank open his cabinet, he knew she was at her wit's end. So he dug through one of her trunks, locating some books for her. He had heard her expound at length about how much she loved every one of her damned books. Apparently, she really loved mythology. So it was with some amusement he picked up a book titled: Thor, God of Thunder. He couldn't wait to see the look on her face when he handed it to her. Yes, he was attempting to do her a favor, but that didn't mean he couldn't find humor in giving her that book just to get a reaction out of her.

When Thor walked into the cabin, he found Pia struggling to untie her corset. Thor leaned on the frame of the doorway and watched her with amusement. He let out a laugh that echoed throughout the cabin like a roll of thunder, much like the god he was named after. The boisterous sound succeeded in gaining her attention.

Pia glanced back at him briefly only to turn back around, still struggling to loosen her stays. "I'm glad I can amuse you. What are you doing here anyway? I thought I had privacy to bathe?" She waved her hands motioning him to come to her. "Never mind, make yourself useful and untie this blasted thing. I don't have a maid, as you left her on the other ship, so you can act in her place."

Her face was turned away as she stood quietly with her back to him. Thor took his packages and set them on the table. He walked over and pulled at the laces of her corset, loosening them. He leaned over her shoulder, his breath hot on her neck and whispered in her ear. "Oh, I assure you I have no problem acting as your maid. I have wanted to undress you for days."

"How crude, just unlace this thing. Then you can leave. Did you bring me a change of clothes?

Forget the corset. I am not wearing it again. I don't have a maid to help with the blasted thing. It's far too much to deal with on my own."

Thor laughed as he listened to her ramble on without giving him a chance to respond. Pia talked so fast it was impossible to get a word in. Once she stopped to take a breath, Thor took the opportunity to speak.

"It was good of you to remember to straighten up the mess you made earlier. I did remember how agitated you were and thought perhaps you would like one of the books from your trunks. Yes, I did remember your clothes. They were especially made for you. I hope the dress pleases you."

"Wait, you have my trunks? Why didn't you tell me this sooner? There are things in there I could use. Why wouldn't you let me have my things?" she demanded. Her agitation showed as Pia swung her hands around in circular motion, emphasizing her disapproval through the movement.

"I didn't see any reason before now."

"I don't know why I'm surprised. Nothing you do shocks me anymore, just leave the stuff on the table and leave so I can bathe in peace."

"I have no intention of leaving."

"I beg your pardon?"

Thor raised an eyebrow, mocking her. It was clear he had her backed into a corner. She could not find a way to extricate herself from. He didn't budge on anything once he set his mind to it. Thor knew Pia would acquiesce to his demands.

"Well, love, it is as simple as this. I am going to go take a little nap over there on the bunk. I'm weary and want to rest before tonight's celebration. I won't bother you while you bathe. Go ahead and do as you planned."

Pia stared at him with her mouth gaping. Shock riddled her face, turning it a bright shade of red. It would be interesting to see what she would do. He was actually looking forward to it. He loved teasing her.

Thor watched as she reached down to check the temperature of the bath water. The water had a little steam billowing over the tub as she ran her fingers over it. Seeming to be satisfied with the temperature, she grabbed the soap and a dry cloth and set them near the tub. Her pantaloons and chemise hit the floor, leaving her completely naked before him. Her pert backside was in full view as she climbed into the tub keeping her back to him the entire time. It took everything he had not to walk over, pull her back out of the tub, and explore every inch of her body. Instead, he laid there in silence and watched as she scrubbed her body clean. Pia poured a bucket of water over her head to rinse herself off. When the water flowed over her head dousing every inch of her, Thor's eyes remained on her back as tiny droplets of water slowly trailed down the curve of her spine.

She was completely thorough in her bathing, washing every inch of herself. Thor was entranced as she slowly brought a washcloth across her neck and it disappeared from his view, down toward her bosom. He had never been so jealous of a piece of cloth in his life. He wanted to touch everything it brushed against. The longer he lay there watching her, the harder he got beneath his trousers. Siren's were fabled to tempt sailors to their doom. Pia could very well be one put on Earth to bring about his demise. The beautiful temptress scrubbing her skin pink in front of him was surely created to torture him with pleasure.

It took every ounce of his will not to strip his clothes off and pull her out of that blasted tub. His need for her grew with every breath he took. Thor assured himself he would have her soon. He could be patient and wait for the appropriate time. Thor gritted his teeth in frustration as he rubbed a hand over his aching member.

Yes, he was going to be inside her and soon. The little minx was begging him by bathing before him. No lady would have done so unless she secretly desired a man's attentions. In the evening, if all went as planned, Pia would have his complete attention. He just had to bide his time and survive this torturous experience. In the meantime, he intended to enjoy the show she provided for him.

"Pia, love, must you make so much noise splashing the water? I am trying to relax over here."

"Yes. If you have a problem with it, you can leave."

"I don't know. If you are going to be so loud, maybe I should just enjoy the scenery."

He was trying to goad her. It wasn't working. Pia just kept scrubbing her skin and removing the dirt. She was in the bath for thirty minutes before it became clear she was done. There was nothing left on her alabaster skin to scrub clean. She cleansed her body so much that every inch had turned a delightful pink. Her skin glowed from all of her ministrations. If Thor were to hazard a guess, everything Pia did was for his benefit. He was certain she was trying her best to torture him, and he couldn't let her know it was working.

Pia slowly turned her head, impishness shining in her eyes as she looked over at Thor. "Was the scenery to your liking?"

"Immensely."

Her head turned slightly so he could see the outline of her profile. Pia's voice was husky as she replied. "Hmm. Well, I wonder if there is a way to improve on that."

"I'm sure you can think of something."

"Oh, I am intelligent enough. I'm sure I could be creative as well."

It was Thor's turn to smile. He had no doubt she could be creative. He couldn't wait to find out how resourceful she could be. "I have no doubt that you could do anything."

She gave him something to look at—and he lost his cocksure smile too.

WITH THAT, PIA STOOD AND TURNED TO FACE him. The droplets of water trailed between the valley of her breasts, creating a path toward her belly button. The small rivulet flowed even farther south. Thor's eyes tracked every inch of the course it made.

Thor got up and walked over to the table where the dry cloths were placed. He grabbed one and tossed it at her. If he didn't get away from her, he was going to lick every particle of water off of her body like a man desperate for a drink. Just looking at her made him salivate.

"Please be a dear, dry yourself off, and get dressed. The celebration is scheduled to start in an hour. I'll be back then to collect you."

He managed to remain cool and aloof as he walked toward the cabin door. Once outside, he quickly secured the lock. Thor rested his head on the door and took a deep breath. That was too close. He had almost given in and ruined all of his plans.

While she stood there dripping water all over the cabin floor, Thor had been struck dumb. The sneaky, sensual wench had effectively turned the tables on him. Thor had never been a betting man and wouldn't gamble his plans away at this juncture of the operation, at least at this stage when their relationship hadn't gone beyond a few kisses. He couldn't take any chances that his carefully laid plans might fall to pieces if he gave in to Pia's charms too early. She was every fantasy brought to life. The beautiful, wet witch had done something he'd never expected. If he wasn't already in deep, that little scene would've told him one thing. He'd willingly jump into shark infested waters to claim her as his own. He'd finally found a woman who was his equal in every way.

CHAPTER 8

*P*ia still held the drying cloth Thor had tossed at her. Her hand rose to grab it out of the air as he exited the room. Pia automatically began to dry herself with the towel. Could that have been any more embarrassing? He appeared to be upset with her. Why? She thought she had read the signs correctly. Thor wanted her. His body gave that away whenever he pressed himself against her.

She felt his hard shaft pressing against her derriere as they slept each night. Its length growing as he spooned against her, holding her in his tight embrace. While in her presence, it appeared as if the pirate was hard all the time. Why did he act like I just insulted him? She may be naïve, but she knew what a man's body did when he desired a woman. Pia didn't understand why Thor had damn near run out of the room. His desire was evident by the look in his eyes. So why did he feel the need to put distance between them?

She looked through the items he had brought for her. There was a clean chemise, pantaloons, a brush, and some blue hair ribbons. But the jewel in the treasure trove was the royal blue dress that matched her eyes. The bodice was lower than she would have liked, but it looked like it would hug her every curve. It was made of the softest silk and trimmed with the finest lace. He didn't bring her any matching slippers, so she would have to make do with her sensible travel shoes. Why did he bring me something so fine and beautiful to wear?

She quickly put on her new chemise and pantaloons. Once she was partially dressed, she traipsed over and sat on the chair by the table. She grabbed the brush and untangled the knots already forming in her long blonde mane. Pia hummed a happy tune as her nimble fingers created a simple braid and laced one of the blue ribbons through it. After the braid was completed, she took another ribbon and tied it off at the end to make sure it stayed in place. After her hair was arranged to her liking, she pulled on her stockings.

Pia picked up her dress and stepped into it, pulling it up. Luckily the gown laced in the front, making it easier for her to put on without the assistance of a maid. All of her other ensembles hooked in the back. With her gown securely fastened, Pia walked over and grabbed her shoes off the floor. She sat on the edge of the bed so it would be easier to slip them onto her feet. Once she had them in place, Pia laced them firmly. She stood and smoothed the dress with her hands so it fell in even waves down to the floor.

The door opened, and Pia looked up as Thor entered the room. He had always been attractive, but in that instant, she was amazed at how good he really looked. To say he was handsome did not do him justice. He was breathtaking.

He had clearly taken the time to bathe. As usual, his beautiful onyx hair was pulled back in a leather tie. He was dressed in his finest pirate attire. He wore black leather pants that hugged his thighs, making it possible to see every inch of his body. His pearly white shirt billowed over his shoulders and was tucked into his trousers. His tan skin gleamed against the stark white of his tunic. Thor's eyes held a mischievous twinkle that made Pia a little nervous about this supposed celebration.

Thor took his time looking over Pia as he circled around her with an appreciative scrutiny. Once he had made a full circle, he stopped in front of her. "Ah good, you are ready."

"Well you did tell me I would be able to leave the cabin today. I wasn't going to delay that for any reason."

A small chuckle escaped him and reverberated through the room. A roguish smile slowly formed on his lips. "Very true, love. Come along, I have a lot of surprises for you."

"Can I have a hint?"

"Only a small one. It is something you could never guess."

Pia stuck her tongue out at him. "You call that a hint?"

"Careful, Pia, you remember what happened the last time you stuck your tongue out at me."

Pia looked at Thor with an impish grin. "Oh, I remember that quite well. I just figured you must have gotten your needs taken care of elsewhere. You didn't seem interested in touching me earlier."

Thor raised an eyebrow at her, amusement shining in his eyes as he looked down at her.

"Nothing could be further from the truth. I like to savor my treats, and make no mistake about it, you would be a treat. There wasn't enough time to enjoy you earlier."

It was Pia's turn to raise her eyebrow. As far as she was concerned, he already had his chance and blew it. She didn't believe in unwarranted second chances. So she told him the truth as she saw it. "Well, it was a onetime offer. One that has already expired, so it won't be an issue since you're not going to touch me again."

"Be careful about issuing me commands. You will soon realize that I'm the only one in charge."

"Right." Pia rolled her eyes. "Because you are the mighty Pirate Thor."

"Absolutely, it's best you don't forget that. Come. Our guests await us."

THOR ESCORTED PIA TO THE QUARTERDECK. IT was kind of nice to stroll along with her. She looked ravishing in the blue dress, but he couldn't wait to get her out of it. They had been spending all of their time in his cabin. This was a different way to see her and enjoy her company. This celebration had been planned for weeks. As soon as the intel had come to him she would be crossing the ocean to live with her grandpere in France, he knew what he had to do. Comte Dubois was the one responsible for the life he now led. He would never have been a pirate if the man hadn't tried to execute him. This was his chance to pay the comte back in kind. He would have his precious granddaughter for his own, and the comte wouldn't be able to do anything to stop him. His plan was brilliant.

"Do you remember the conversation we had a few days ago?"

"You will have to clarify which conversation. We have had many."

Thor looked at her with delight shining in his eyes. Conversing with Pia was a game he would never tire of. His voice held a tinge of devilment. "Don't play coy Pia, you know what I'm talking about. I am referring to when we discussed the day you would be allowed to come on deck. Please don't disappoint me. I'm sure you'll enjoy some company other than mine, even if it's brief."

"Ah, the one where you said I had to follow all of your orders, or you would kill my grandpere."

"Yes, that one. If you do not do everything I ask of you, I will kill your grandpere."

With a petulant smile, Pia looked up at him. "I understand. You do not have to remind me of that."

"Excellent. I'm glad you're on board with the plan, because I have an extra special surprise for you. Well a couple of surprises, I hope they please you. Don't leave my side for any reason. I promise, you will regret it if you do."

Thor wished reminding her he would kill her grandpere wasn't a necessary evil, but he needed her to comply with everything he had planned. It was unfortunate they had to meet this way. She really was perfect for him. In a very short time, she had become the most important person in his life. He sincerely wished they could have met at a different time.

Life had sent him on a path, and he hadn't been given a choice. He had learned to embrace it as the tool that would eventually give him the revenge he sought.

His Pia was beautiful, but more importantly, she was also feisty and smart. He had a feeling she would always be able to surprise him. It was his deepest wish to have her with him all the time so she could continue to astonish him for the rest of their lives. So it was with a heavy heart he continued on his chosen path, hoping that one day she would be able to forgive him for what he felt must be done.

"I already told you I would do what you ask. You don't need to remind me again," Pia said as she stopped. "Is that my grandpere?"

Thor had been walking her toward where Comte Dubois was standing, guarded by several of his crew. He had been brought to the ship by one of the pirate crew. Comte Dubois was a man of average height, an olive complexion, and dark ebony hair dusted with grey. He was stout and had a small pouch of a belly, showing how comfortable he was getting as he aged. Everything was coming together nicely. Thor couldn't wait to see the reaction on the comte's face when he married his granddaughter.

"How did my grandpere get here, Thor?" Pia demanded.

"Thor? Pieretta you are mistaken. This man's name is not Thor." Comte Dubois told his granddaughter.

Pia stood looking at Thor in shocked silence. She tilted her head at him, confusion clouding her face. Thor knew she wanted to know what was going on, and the answers she needed from him would become apparent momentarily. His gaze was firmly on Comte Dubois as he responded to his statement.

"Your grandpere would know exactly who I am, Pia. He did try to murder me after all."

"I did not try to murder you. I was trying to save you. Standing directly behind you was a pirate, and he was aiming his pistol straight at you. When I fired mine, I was aiming at him."

"Really, Renny, you expect me to believe you shot me while trying to save me? Then why did you leave me there to die?"

"I did no such thing. I went to get help. By the time I came back, you were gone."

Thor raised an eyebrow in disbelief. "So you took it as a sign I had died? You rushed to have me declared dead so you could gain control over our business. I'm actually amazed they took your word for it. There was very little evidence of my supposed demise."

Thor kept a close eye on Pia throughout his exchange with Comte Dubois. He saw the confusion spread over her features. She looked back and forth between the two of them, her face growing paler with each statement.

Looking directly into Thor's eyes, Pia asked. "Who are you really? Grandpere says your name is not Thor. I want your real name."

Thor shrugged his shoulders, dismissing what

the comte had told her. The comte didn't really know him or the name his loved ones had known him by. He looked down at her. "Thor is my name."

"That's a lie. His name is William Thorston Marsden, Fifth Viscount Torrington," Comte Dubois shouted.

"He is correct. I go by a shortened version of my second name. Thor is short for Thorston. I was named after my father, and my mother wanted me to have my own identity. To my family and close friends I was always Thor. You wouldn't have known that, Renny. You always referred to me by my title. I was always Torrington to you. Did that make it easier to murder me? Was it more impersonal that way?"

"I told you I didn't try to kill you, Torrington," Comte Dubois insisted.

Thor had listened to enough of the comte's lies. It was time to end the charade and finish everything once and for all. He wanted the comte off of his ship and out of his life for good. He looked at the man with contempt, distaste filling his mouth from spending time in his malicious company. If his presence wasn't so important to fulfilling his vengeance, the comte would not be aboard, talking to them. He waved his hand at him dismissively. "No matter, I don't care. That is not why you're here."

"What do you want with me then?"

Thor looked at him. "I couldn't very well marry Pia without her only family being present to witness the union now could I?"

Thor heard Pia gasp. He knew it was a shock to her. He didn't think she would have agreed if he had outright asked her. They certainly didn't have a traditional relationship by any means.

When he had kidnapped her, his original plan had been to seduce her and return her to Renny as soiled goods. The more time he spent with her, the more apparent it became he couldn't do that to her. He knew he could never do that. This was the only choice he had if he was going to keep her safe with him. He needed to make her his wife. It was not in his makeup to just willingly hand her over to her grandpere and hope for the best. No, this is what must be done.

Comte Dubois started to spit and sputter at Thor's announcement. His voice filled with uncontrollable rage as he screamed. "You are not marrying my granddaughter, Torrington."

A wicked smile crossed Thor's lips. "I absolutely am. Pia consented to be with me for the rest of her life. I wanted to make sure she didn't have any regrets. It is part of the reason I made sure you were present. Ah, here is the priest now, it's time to begin."

THE CEREMONY WENT BY IN A BLUR. SHE DIDN'T even remember saying I do. She couldn't believe Thor wanted to marry her. She was still confused by it all. He wouldn't let her go near her grandpere. He said her grandpere was too dangerous, and he wouldn't allow her to ever be around someone so evil. Here she was, married to a pirate viscount of all things, and she would never be allowed to see her family again.

This was why she never wanted to get married. Men had all of the control. Thor had threatened her grandpere's life. If she didn't marry him, he would have killed her grandpere. With the comte standing on the deck, the threat had seemed very real to her. He begged her to not marry Thor. Pia could tell he didn't understand why she was going through with it when he shook his head in confusion. Grandpere didn't know she was only marrying Thor to protect him. She couldn't be held responsible for his death.

Please let my grandpere be okay.

Her feelings for her pirate were complicated.

They had spent only a short time together on board his ship, but Pia believed she had begun to understand him. In some ways, she felt she knew him more than she knew herself.

This whole situation felt wrong in so many ways. Marrying Thor turned her life even farther upside down. It sank deeper and deeper into a never-ending fiasco, one she could never escape. Why did he want to marry me? He attacked a ship and kidnapped me to make me his wife? Pia shook her head in confusion. Why would that matter?

Once it was all over, Thor had escorted Pia back to their cabin. Before he closed the door, he had informed her he would be back in an hour or so. He had some things to take care of on deck. Thor had looked at her directly in the eyes and said he was looking forward to spending the night with his new wife. When he left, she thought she'd be lucky if he actually gave her that much time.

She had done everything Thor had asked of her. One thing was for sure, Pia had a lot of questions, and Thor was going to answer them all. She had never wanted a husband. Thor had effectively tied her hands, making it the only decision she could make.

Pia had longed to be an independent woman.

Thor took that away from her by forcing her to marry him. She wasn't exactly delighted to be his blushing bride. It didn't really matter because regardless of how she felt about the situation, Thor was her husband now. She wasn't going to back down. He would do what she wanted for once.

CHAPTER 9

*T*hor knew he had to face his bride sooner rather than later. Unfortunately, it was several hours before he was able to get away from the crew to seek her out. After he ensured Comte Dubois and the priest were back on shore, he could deal with the ramifications of the day's events. Some of his crew had been worried the comte might try and come back on board to harm him. So he had to assure them it was okay to go ahead with the shore leave he granted them. He wanted them to have some time to themselves before they set sail again.

Thor made his way to the cabin to deal with his new wife. He was prepared for a temper tantrum. In fact, he was looking forward to it. He liked when she got mad and feisty. It made things a lot more interesting.

He wasn't prepared to explain everything to her just yet. He wanted to show her everything he wanted from her first. He yearned to express all the bottled up desire and longing he had been holding back. Thor wasn't always good with words and often found actions were a much better way of getting his point across. They would have to talk eventually, but he was hoping to put it off for as long as possible. For now, Thor wanted her to feel everything he was feeling. He needed to experience what it was like to be inside of her. He patiently waited until he could love her the only way he knew how.

Pia was his wife, and he finally had the right to explore every inch of her luscious body. She had given him a very brazen invitation after her bath earlier that evening. It hadn't been the proper time to accept it, but he was more than ready now that they were legally wed.

He walked into the cabin and was surprised to find Pia asleep on the bunk. She had taken off her dress and draped it over the chair by the table. Thor stopped to stare at Pia for a while, admiring her beauty. Her chest rose and fell with an even pace.

She was utterly and completely beautiful. To him she was perfect, but more importantly...she was his.

Thor removed his boots, and the rest of his clothes followed shortly after. He crawled onto the bunk with his wife. Her instinct made her curl next to him. She was used to sleeping with him and didn't rouse when he pulled her closer. He slowly caressed her, hoping she would awaken. He needed her conscious for every part of the loving he was going to give her.

PIA WAS HAVING THE BEST DREAM. IT FELT SO real. She was almost afraid to open her eyes and discover it wasn't. She didn't want it to stop. Phantom hands wandered down her body. She felt light kisses across her cheek and trail down her neck. The warmth spread all over her body, increasing with each new sensation. Her body had never felt so amazing from such simple contact with another person. Wait, there really is someone's lips floating over my body, drowning it with kisses.

Her eyes flew open, and she found Thor staring into them.

"Good of you to wake up, love."

"What are you doing, Thor?"

"I'm loving my wife."

If Pia had been capable of snorting at that moment, she would have. He claimed her grandpere was the master of lies, and here falsehoods spilled from his lips. Both Thor and her grandpere expected her to believe them, but she didn't really know either one of them. She wanted a real conversation with her grandpere, but Thor would never allow that to happen. It was up to her to find a way.

In the meantime, she had to deal with Thor's amorous intentions. He said he was going to love her. She didn't believe he actually loved her in any way, shape, or form. But he did desire her, and as her husband, he would want to express it. Fortunately for him, she equally desired him, and she might as well get something out of this sham of a marriage. Her gaze drifted up to meet his. "You do not love me, Thor. I am just a pawn in your revenge against my grandpere."

"Nevertheless, we are going to find pleasure in each other."

Before Pia could get another word out, Thor kissed her. He peeled off her drawers and chemise. When she was completely nude, he caressed her body, placing soft kisses along her breasts. Pia moaned when he brought one of her rosy nipples into his mouth, savoring its taste. The man sure knew how to kiss, and Pia wanted him to put his lips all over her body. Wherever his mouth touched, her body blazed with need and pleasure.

Thor drifted down and kissed the inside of her thighs. He spread her legs wide as his face drifted to her very core. He used his hands to open her wider, and one of his fingers gently stroked her. She moaned when his tongue darted out and found her sensitive spot. He licked and sucked until Pia thrashed wildly on the bed. She felt the culmination of something grow inside of her. As his mouth caressed her, his fingers stroked her, pumping in and out, until she screamed out in ecstasy.

The pleasure was so intense she didn't know how much more she could possibly take. He kept moving his fingers in and out of her, while his thumb caressed the sensitive nub. Every sensation made her burn, and her flesh heated, turning a rosy pink as moans of pure bliss escaped her mouth. She bucked against him, needing something more, but she didn't understand what her body craved. All she knew was something was missing.

Once again she saw stars as the world exploded around her. It was the most amazing feeling she had ever felt. It wasn't possible to feel this good. *What has Thor done to me?*

Before she finished the thought, Thor shifted her. He spread her legs wider and entered her slowly. He inched his way inside of her until he was fully seated within her quivering body. The pain caused her to bite her tongue and whimper. It hurt to take him inside of her. Everything had felt so good, and then he went and ruined it by pushing himself inside of her narrow passage.

"Shhh, it only hurts the first time, love. I promise the next time will be all pleasure."

He moved in and out of her, his pace steadily increasing. At first, she wanted to shove him off, but the more he moved, the better it felt. Pia's desire grew with each thrust. She wanted him deeper, harder, faster. She wrapped her legs around his waist, finding her own rhythm to match his movements. The sensations building up in her grew and Pia craved more. She couldn't get enough of him.

"Yes, like that, squeeze me, Pia. Good God, you feel so good. I can't hold out much longer. Come with me."

He kissed her again as he thrust deeper and faster. The movements brought Pia over the edge, and it was even better than the explosion she'd experienced earlier. This was a completion. It was just—right.

She screamed Thor's name as she came. He whispered her name as if it was a benediction. He soon followed and released himself inside her. He rolled to his side pulling her along with him. He curled his body around hers and held her as he fell asleep. Pia couldn't believe he was able to sleep after something so monumental, but she soon drifted off herself.

*P*ia woke up in slow degrees, and Thor was still passed out next to her. She extricated herself from his embrace, getting out of the bunk as quietly as possible. She located her pantaloons and chemise lying on the floor where he had discarded them. Pia grabbed her dress and stepped into it, fastening the buttons as quickly and quietly as she could.

Now they were married, she hoped Thor would be more lenient in his desire to keep her confined in their cabin. Surely now he would start leaving the door unlocked. Pia was desperate to get off of the ship and go see her grandpere. She picked up her shoes and carried them out the door Thor had left unlocked. Thank the Lord. I can try to get away.

He must have felt secure in his ownership of her, because he hadn't bothered to ensure she couldn't escape. Finally, the pirate was getting sloppy. He would soon discover she was capable of taking care of herself. He may have just given her the greatest pleasure she had ever known, but he also had used her in the worst possible way. She didn't want to consider what other complications might arise from what they had just done. Pia was well aware they could have created a baby, but she didn't have time to think about it. She needed to get away, and this may be her only opportunity.

When she was far enough away from the cabin that she felt safe, she put her shoes on. It was difficult, but she managed to be as silent as possible as she crept on deck. Pia walked on her toes across the creaking timbers, cringing every time a small squeak emitted from underneath her feet.

She looked up realizing they were still anchored in the harbor at Bordeaux. The docks were in the distance, but it shouldn't take her long to get to shore. She scanned the sides of the ship and spotted two of the crew climbing up a ladder. They vacated a dinghy to board the ship, and the bosun greeted them as they walked onto the deck.

Pia's heart beat heavily in her chest as she hid

from their view. She was terrified they would discover her hiding place. Standing as still as possible, she controlled her breathing so she wouldn't make any unnecessary noise. Pia took the time to still all of her movements, relaxing enough to listen to their exchange.

"Is everything taken care of?" the bosun asked.

"Yes, sir. We dropped the priest back at his parish and dumped the comte at his estate."

Estate? Grandpere had an estate in Bordeaux? Pia had thought he lived in Calais.

"Very good. You may retire for the night and give a full report to the captain in the morning. He is not to be disturbed tonight. The captain changed his mind, and we will set sail at dawn, please be prepared to lift anchor."

There were no crew members anywhere else on deck. The ship was almost like a ghost ship. That couldn't be how it was normally. Where did all of the crew go? Who was taking care of the ship? Pia had to try to get to the dinghy and row to shore. Then she could find her grandpere. Once she saw him, she would have the chance to explain everything. He would understand she really didn't have a choice.

As soon as the bosun was far enough away, Pia scrambled to the ladder and climbed down into the dinghy. She wasn't concerned for her own well-being, but she was desperate to see how her grandpere had fared. She may be the pirate's wife, but she could still make decisions for herself.

Her arms grew sore with each push of the oars through the water. Her strength was limited because of her small stature, but she managed to row herself to the nearest dock. Once the boat was next to the dock, Pia scrambled to the top and walked as fast as she could. Her breaths fell in pants from her mouth in the cold night air. She rubbed her hands together trying to warm them as she strolled across the docks.

The first thing she needed to do was find out where her grandpere's estate was. Pia didn't get very far before she was grabbed. She didn't even have time to scream before the unknown assailant dragged her away.

THOR WOKE UP AND STRETCHED. HE HAD NEVER felt so relaxed in his entire life. He wanted to experience those sensations all over again. Thor was blissfully happy at the results of loving his new bride. He rolled over to pull Pia to his side.

He sat up with a start. His cheeks heated with

anger. She wasn't in his bed. Where did the little minx go? She couldn't have gone far. Thor rolled off the bed and pulled on his clothing. He stormed up to the quarterdeck. Thor stomped his way to the cabin shared by his bosun and first mate and knocked on the door.

Thor waited for someone to come to the door. It opened to reveal his bosun, staring at him. "Corny, have you seen my wife?"

"No, Captain, I assumed she was with you."

"Well clearly she is not. Search the ship. Locate her at once." Thor watched as Corny woke the first mate.

The bosun and first mate rang the bell for all hands on deck. The crew searched everywhere, but Pia was nowhere to be found. It was only after several minutes of searching they realized the dinghy was gone. Pia had jumped ship.

Thor roared at them to get another dinghy ready. He was going to search for his wife and wring her little neck once he found her. She was his. How dare she leave him. He was blistering mad, his face heating with every word he shouted. Never before had he experienced a mixture of anger and fear. Thor required Pia be safely returned, but mostly he just needed her.

❄

PIA WAS SHOVED INTO A CARRIAGE AND QUICKLY settled onto a seat. She didn't know who had grabbed her, but it couldn't be good. She slapped him. She was getting tired of people kidnapping her. Damn them all for thinking she was something they could throw around. What's wrong with people these days?

The man who had grabbed her rubbed his face to alleviate the sting. "Now, was that really necessary?"

Captain Devere sat across from her in the carriage. So, Thor hadn't killed him. She really did assume a lot about the man that was probably not true.

"Yes, you had no right to grab me and shove me in this carriage. I was frightened. It wasn't like I knew who was yanking me into this conveyance. It's a natural reaction for someone being kidnapped."

"I can assure you, I only have your best interests at heart," Captain Devere said.

Pia looked up at him. "Why did you take me?"

"I was asked to retrieve you by Comte Dubois. You made it a much easier task by rowing to shore. I must thank you for that. It made my job less dangerous."

"You are taking me to grandpere?"

"Yes, my dear, you may rest easy. You will be safe in his care in less than twenty minutes."

"When did you get here?" Pia asked. "I thought the pirate murdered everyone on board the ship. Is Tully alive? Thor had implied that he didn't kill anyone. Well he kind of told me that he hadn't killed everyone—but how was I to know if he was telling the truth or not. I'm relieved to see you are alive and well Captain."

"Yes, your maid is fine. She is at your grandpere's estate. He had her settled into the servants' quarters, and she will be there to assist you tomorrow."

Pia nodded her head. "Good. I know you mean well, Captain, but I don't know you. I want to look in on her myself as soon as possible."

Pia settled down on the seat, resting her head on the side of the carriage. One thing was certain. Her grandpere was alive. He wouldn't have been able to send someone to retrieve her if Thor had murdered him.

She needed to speak to her grandpere. There were a lot of questions she wanted to ask him. Pia hoped he was prepared to answer all of them, because she wanted the truth. Once she heard both sides of this sordid mess, she could decide the best course of action. She knew Thor would eventually come after her. Thor was tenacious and would not give up easily. Pia only hoped she had enough time to hear her grandpere's side before Thor caught up with her. She was grateful Thor hadn't murdered the ship's crew or Tully. It made it easier to accept her growing feelings for the wicked pirate.

CHAPTER 11

*T*hor needed to beat on something in the worst way, so he swung around and punched the nearest wall as hard as he could. The pain he felt pulsing through his fist helped him focus on the real issue. His needed to retrieve his wife and forget about his increasing fury. His rage was so great that if any of his crew members had gotten near him they would have encountered serious bodily harm. Before he had boarded the dinghy, he had bellowed at his crew to get the ship prepared to leave port. When he returned with Pia, he fully intended to set sail immediately.

They had been too slow getting the dinghy ready, and as a result, he had missed Pia by mere minutes. Thor arrived at the dock just in time to see

Pia being shoved into a nearby carriage. Captain Devere quickly jumped into the conveyance after her.

Thor found a hack as soon as he was able and demanded the driver go to the comte's nearby estate. It was the only place Devere could possibly be taking his wife.

The journey to Comte Dubois's estate would be brief, but it gave him time to reflect quietly on the situation. He should have realized Renny would try to take his granddaughter back. Thor had gotten sloppy, thinking he had won. Damn the comte for being such an evil bastard. So it looked like he would have to kill the comte after all. Thor was not leaving his wife in that man's care. Pia had become his everything in a very short time. He would not leave her in the vindictive hands of the comte. Thor wouldn't put it past him to harm his own granddaughter if it suited his purposes.

Thor sat back, leaning his head against the side of the carriage combing his fingers through his disheveled hair. He wouldn't be able to live with himself if something bad happened to Pia. Thor tilted his head toward the sky praying he would get to the estate in time to get Pia out unharmed.

PIA ANXIOUSLY CLUTCHED HER HANDS IN HER lap as their conveyance navigated the narrow road. The carriage rattled, shaking the seats as it traveled down the lane to her grandpere's estate. Captain Devere had assured her it shouldn't take more than twenty minutes for them to journey there. She sincerely hoped he was correct because the carriage was becoming increasingly more uncomfortable with each bump it rolled over.

Pia was growing weary of all the drama surrounding her life over the past couple of weeks. She should have been able to mourn her father in peace. Instead, she had been forced to leave her home and then kidnapped.

As they traveled, Devere told her what happened on the ship after Thor had taken her. Tully had been the only one Thor's crew hadn't tied up. When she wandered on deck and found the captain tied to the mast, she quickly freed him. The captain then went down and released his crew out from the cargo hold. They raised the sails and sailed toward France with due haste. There had been minimal damage done to the ship when Thor had attacked it. The damage inflicted had been meant to intimidate more than harm anyone aboard the ship.

Once they had arrived in port, they traveled to the comte's estate. He had been too late to meet him before Thor's men had taken the comte aboard the Sea Rover. Once the comte was dropped off at his estate, he dispatched Captain Devere to retrieve her from Thor.

When they arrived at her grandpere's estate, the captain escorted her into the house. It was a beautiful manor at the end of a long driveway lined with large trees. As impressive as it was in the dark, it had to be breathtaking during the day.

Devere lead Pia into her grandpere's drawing room where she found him lounging in a chair nursing a glass of brandy. He jumped up as she marched into the room and hugged her tightly in his arms. Pia felt safe snuggled deep in her grandpere's burly arms. She heard Captain Devere shut the door as he left the room.

Comte Dubois took a step back and looked at Pia. "Thank the Lord they were able to save you from that demon's clutches."

"Grandpere, did you really try to kill him?"

"Don't be ridiculous, Pieretta. I never tried to kill

him. He was like the son I never had, and his father was one of my dear friends."

"Then why does he think you tried to murder him?"

"It is a misunderstanding, I assure you. I loved the boy. I would not have killed him. It is sad what he has turned into. I cannot abide the life he has chosen to live. I was trying to save him, as I tried to explain on the ship. Perhaps, if I had gotten to him sooner— he is just not the same man I knew. He is dangerous, and you should not have married him. I'm sorry, my dear, but that was very reckless of you. We will have it annulled as soon as possible."

"That would be difficult to get, considering the marriage was consummated," Thor said with a drawl as he sauntered into the room.

Pia gasped. How did he get to Grandpere's estate so fast? She was sure he had been fast asleep when she left the ship. She assumed she would have more time to get answers. Why couldn't he have been a little slower in coming after me?

Comte Dubois took one look at Thor and then shouted for Captain Devere to come back into the drawing room.

"If you are looking for the captain, he is

indisposed at the moment," Thor said as he made his way over to Pia.

"Damn you, Torrington. You cannot have my granddaughter."

Thor ignored the comte and continued walking toward Pia.

"Why are you here, Thor?" Pia asked him.

"I thought that was clear, love. I missed my wife. I came to find her, because clearly she's lost. Wives are supposed to remain naked in bed next to their husbands awaiting another round of loving. We clearly have some miscommunication going on between us. You know where you belong, Pia. Get ready to leave now."

Pia looked at him with barely restrained belligerence. "No."

The shock and anger on Thor's face was palpable. His steely blue gaze was glued to her face as the lines of his mouth became tight from clenching his jaw. The muscles in his cheeks twitched, his face flushed with anger. He glared at Pia. "I must have heard you wrong, dear. You are my wife, and you will leave with me now. Did you forget our agreement?"

"No. I remember it quite clearly, and I want to make a new agreement."

"I must admit you have piqued my interest. What changes did you want to make, love?"

"I will not remain with a man that clearly does not love me and has no respect for my wishes. I want to be able to visit my family. My grandpere is all I have left."

Thor scoffed at her statement, his eyebrow raised with derision. His gaze locked with hers. "Your grandpere is a murderous villain, Pia. I will not tolerate you being in his presence. We will work through the rest of our issues once we take leave of this wretched place."

"Well that's too damn bad, because I will spend time with him."

"Enough," the comte shouted.

Pia and Thor turned to look at Comte Dubois. He was holding a pistol, and it was aimed at the both of them. Her grandpere had been lying to her. He had always meant for Thor to die. Her husband had been right for the pistol was clearly aimed at him.

"If the marriage can't be annulled, clearly Pieretta, dear, you need to be made a widow."

"But Grandpere you said you didn't try to kill him!"

"I lied. It's what I do. I couldn't afford for him to see that I was pocketing some of the funds from the company. I wasn't solvent and needed them to get by. The dowry I gave your mother was all I had left. It took me years to build my fortune back. I will not let this pirate take away everything I have built."

"You built it using my money, Renny. You had no right to help yourself to my funds. My life has been turned upside down by your greed, and I'll make sure you pay for that," Thor said.

Thor pushed Pia aside, diving for the gun. He struggled with Renny to gain control over the pistol, each trying to get a firm grasp on it. The two of them fell to the floor, rolling around. They wrestled for control of the pistol, trying to get it away from one another. As they struggled to gain control, the gun went off.

The sound of the gun echoed throughout the room. Everything started to move in slow motion. Pia's scream rattled the windows. Nothing was clear, and no one was moving quickly enough for her to know if either one of them had been hurt. With her heart pumping wildly in her chest, she ran over and fell beside the two motionless bodies. What should I do? Please let them be okay. Grandpere was a bad man, but she still didn't want him to die. Thor meant more to her than she wanted to admit.

A small movement caught her attention out of

the corner of her eye, and she turned her head to see if it was real or not. Thor slowly turned over, and Pia immediately noticed a spot of blood near the top of his white shirt.

"Thor?" Pia asked hesitantly. Was he okay? In that moment, Pia realized how much he had come to mean to her. Without realizing it, the damned pirate had found a way into her heart.

"I'm okay, Pia. Your grandpere is bleeding all over me though. Send someone for a physician."

Pia ran out the door calling for a servant to come quickly. The butler arrived in response to her deafening screams for help. Pia grabbed his jacket, telling him to send for a physician. He pulled himself out of her grasp and retreated to find help.

Pia's attention immediately returned to her grandpere. She felt faint. The comte's face was as white as a ghost, and Pia scrambled over to his side. She had to do something to help him. She looked across the room. Thor stood in the corner watching her.

"Don't just stand there, go get me something to hold on his wound. He's bleeding all over the carpet. Help me please, Thor. I know he is your enemy, but he will always be my grandpere."

Thor nodded at her and pulled a handkerchief from his pocket, handing it to her.

"It won't help, Pia, but it is yours to use as you wish."

"Thank you, Thor, I appreciate your help. I have to do everything possible to help him."

Pia knelt next to her grandpere, placing the handkerchief on the wound. His color wasn't improving. She turned his face in her hands and leaned over to see if he was still breathing. His breaths were shallow. Pia feared he wouldn't survive long enough for a physician to help, and tears welled in her eyes and rolled down her cheeks. She silently begged the Lord to save him.

As she wordlessly prayed, Tully ran into the room.

"Miss Pieretta, I heard you scream. Oh dear," Tully said, as her face grew pale at the sight of the comte bleeding all over her charge. "Is he dead?"

"Not yet, you fool. Don't just stand there, go in the hall and wait for the physician. Bring him in here immediately upon his arrival." Pia scolded her.

Tully ran out of the room. At least that was one less thing she had to worry about, she knew for sure Tully was well.

Pia watched as her grandpere opened his eyes.

The pain glazed his expression. His voice broke with each word he tried speak, begging for her to understand.

"I'm sorry, Pia. Wanted what was best for you. I love you..." Those were the comte's final words as his last breath drifted away. Pia screamed in agony.

CHAPTER 12

*L*ife was full of decisions, and Pia had to make plenty in her lifetime. She knew there were certain things thrust upon a person in their lifetime which they had no control over. Love and death were prominent reminders of this. Pia's experience with love had been very limited. She knew one thing for certain: love could bring her joy or unimaginable sorrow, even if that love happened to be reciprocated. Death on the other hand had its own judgment and resolution. Her grandfather had paid for his actions with his life.

Pia prepared to bury her grandpere and say her final goodbye. Several important thoughts floated through her mind as the final preparations were made. Was Grandpere really gone forever? What was going to happen with Thor, now that he finally had his revenge? *How can I forgive him?* Does he even care about me?

With the help of Grandpere's solicitor, she was able to get through all of the funeral arrangements. Pia buried her grandpere at his estate in Bordeaux. It was a small service. The only people in attendance were a few of her grandpere's servants, Tully, Pia, and of course, her husband. Thor stayed by her side through it all, offering what little comfort she would allow.

All she saw when she looked at him was his chest covered in her grandpere's blood. She didn't know if she could stay with him. She still didn't believe he loved her. It was clear her feelings for him had changed during the time she had been his prisoner. She never believed she would ever fall in love.

When he kidnapped her, she had been so very afraid of what he would do to her, but, in the end, she had begun to trust him. At the very least she had come to believe he wouldn't truly harm her. It helped to see the evidence that he wasn't as dastardly as she'd believed. Tully alive and pestering her on a daily basis was enough of a reminder.

Pia was acquainted with all of Thor's faults and well aware he was capable of almost anything. After all, he did orchestrate her abduction. Pia knew she was a fool for letting herself fall in love with him. No matter how much she tried, she couldn't stop her foolish heart's devotion to him. How is it possible to fall in love so fast? She wanted him to return her love, and she desired him with an intense passion. But nothing would torture her more than staying in a loveless marriage. If he wasn't capable of caring for her, let alone loving her, she wouldn't stay with him. She needed more. If she couldn't have it, she would seek out someone to file for a divorce herself.

Still lost in her own thoughts, she didn't hear Thor walk into her grandpere's study. Pia had enclosed herself in the room, sitting on a comfortable divan to wallow in her misery. When she looked up and saw him standing so close, her heart skipped a beat.

He looked down at her with sympathy in the depths of his blue eyes. "Pia, the ship is ready to set sail whenever you're ready." His voice was interwoven with understanding.

With a petulant look firmly fixed on her face, she looked up at him. "I am not sailing away with you, Thor."

"Like hell you're not. You're my wife, and you belong with me."

"Do you honestly think I want to live like a pirate? What kind of life is that? What if we have children? Will they join the crew and plunder ships for bounty alongside you?"

"No. We will go back to England. I have responsibilities there that have neglected for far too long. I am a viscount, and I have an estate to reclaim. Your grandfather had me declared dead, so I will have to fight to regain my title. I don't want to be a pirate, Pia. Please come with me so we can build a life together."

Pia nodded. She could see he needed to do that. He did not need her with him to accomplish it. There was no give and take. He took it all and gave nothing in return. He said nothing about loving and needing her. Once again, he selfishly planned on using her to gain something he felt was his due. The sad thing was he didn't even need her to reclaim his title. He could go back and live his life without ever seeing her again if he wished.

"You do not need me, Thor. You don't require me for anything. You should go back and claim your title. While you are there, file for divorce. I don't care on what grounds. We are better off without each other."

"No," Thor said with belligerence in his voice. "I

will never be better off without you. How could I be? Please, Pia, don't fight me on this. You are my wife, and I want you to board the Sea Rover with me today."

"I'm not going to fight with you, Thor. I am not going with you, and I will not remain with a man who doesn't love and respect me."

"Who the hell told you I don't love or respect you?"

"Well you haven't exactly told me that you do. You fail to take my desires into consideration. You dictate to me and never ask if I am okay with your orders. I am not going to live with someone who is going to take me for granted. No, I would rather die. Because you no longer have anything to hold over me, that is the only option left."

Pia turned her back to him, deciding the conversation was over. She leaned her head against the back of the couch and closed her eyes. She assumed he had left because he ceased speaking. Pia's eyelids fluttered open, and she saw Thor's blue eyes staring directly into hers.

Thor cleared his throat and spoke, his voice shaking, overflowing with emotion. "Pia, I have loved you from the moment I saw you. I never intended to actually marry you. My original plan involved pretending to do it and then using you, but meeting you changed everything. No one ever plans to find love, and I certainly never planned on finding it with you. The thought of you leaving scares me more than anything. I cannot imagine a life without your fire to warm me each night. From the instant I met you, I planned on keeping you. I know I've blundered with everything I've done. Not respecting your wishes was only to protect you. Your grandpere was an evil man, and you didn't see it. With every part of my soul, I swear I never meant to make you feel less than you are. I could never hurt you."

Pia stared at him. She waited, wondering if she should believe him. There was nothing she wanted more than to believe what he was telling her.

His voice had faltered and became husky with emotion. Thor's expression showed remorse. His gaze implored hers as if pleading with her.

"If you don't love me, I will understand," he said. "Being without you could never make me happy, but I will let you go if that's what you truly want. I would rather take my dagger and push it through my own heart then ever knowingly hurt you again."

Pia stared at him in shock. She never expected that he would actually return her feelings. She looked down at her arm and pinched herself to make sure it wasn't a dream. Ouch, nope this is real. Thor always had a way of stealing her breath, surprising her at every turn. Her lips curled up into a sumptuous smile as happiness overtook her soul. Her heart pounded with excitement when she finally accepted his words.

It was imperative she heard him say it one more time to make sure she'd heard him right. "You really love me?"

"Yes, I love you. Do you love me, even a little? Can you stay with me? Please come back to England with me. I need my viscountess to help me reestablish my holdings, and I need her to hold each night. I want her to be the mother of my children. Without you, my life wouldn't be worth living. Please, Pia, come home with me."

"Yes. Yes, Thor, I love you too. I will come home with you. There isn't any place on this Earth I would rather be." She stood and rushed over to him, throwing herself into his arms.

Thor gathered her tightly against his chest wrapping his arms around her as he hugged her close. Pia tilted her face up and met his eyes as his lips pressed down on hers. Thor plundered her in all the ways she loved most, and Pia enjoyed every minute of the passion they shared.

EPILOGUE

*I*n the past, Thor had many demons hiding inside of his soul, and they soured certain aspects of his life. He had something miraculous happen to him that allowed him to exorcise those dark areas. An angel of mercy had taken pity on his possessed black core and helped to bring him back to the light. In those moments, his life changed as his heart started to feel again and the darkness bled from its depths.

When Thor found Pia, his soul was cleansed. She was the angel who showed him how love could change his life. His existence was forever altered when he fell in love with the spirited beauty. If someone had asked him before he met Pia if he believed in love, he would have laughed at their audacity. Love? No that was for fools. *Well color me a fool because I am blissfully in love with my wife, and I wouldn't change it for anyone.*

If he had never kidnapped her to get revenge on her grandpere, his soul would still be a dark carcass of unhappiness. Thor needed her light to balance the dark shadows that overtook his spirit. They were opposites, put on Earth to balance each other out. To have her love him as much as he loved her was a blessing he didn't feel he deserved. He would never make the mistake of hurting her again. He had made a promise he would never break. Pia was everything to him.

Sitting in his study on his main English estate, Thor was lost in thought, reminiscing about the day he met the love of his life. She wasn't perfect. Everyone had flaws. He loved every one of her imperfections, because to him, she was beyond perfection. She was more priceless than the most expensive jewel. Her flaws were what made her unique. Pia was irreplaceable. She was his flawed jewel.

Thor rested his chin in his hands as a contented half smile tugged at his lips. He had a good life with Pia and their two children. It wasn't long after they returned to England, they got the happy news that Pia was expecting their first child.

As with everything in their lives, it shouldn't have been a surprise that even their children refused to do things the easy way. Almost exactly nine months after their wedding, Pia gave birth to twins, a girl and a boy. Lilliana Rose was born five minutes before her brother, Liam Robert. Lily had dark hair and cobalt blue eyes similar to her father, where Liam favored his mother with pale blond hair and light blue eyes.

Nothing could make him happier than to spend the rest of his life watching his children grow. Thor wanted all of the experiences fatherhood had to offer. As long as he had Pia and the twins by his side, his happiness was assured.

Thor turned as a little girl with black curls toddled into the room. A short time later, she was followed by a petite blonde woman carrying a small boy in her arms.

Pia looked over at Thor, her face flushed red from chasing their bundles of joy. "It's your turn. They want daddy to tell them their favorite story. You know the one."

Thor knew exactly which story they wanted to hear. It was the best fairy tale in all creation. It was the story of a flawed jewel and her dastardly pirate. They wanted to hear about adventure, love, and how their parents found each other.

Thor sat on the sofa and beckoned them close. "I'm happy to tell it. Please, come sit down by daddy, Lily, Liam."

The three-year-old twins crawled up onto his lap and waited for him to begin. Pia took a seat on the corner of the sofa her gaze softening as he looked into his eyes.

He settled them against him and began his story.

"Once upon a time, a pirate set out on the high seas..."

**Read on for an excerpt from A Treasured Lily: A Marsden Romance Book **

A CRYSTAL ANGEL

DAWN BROWER

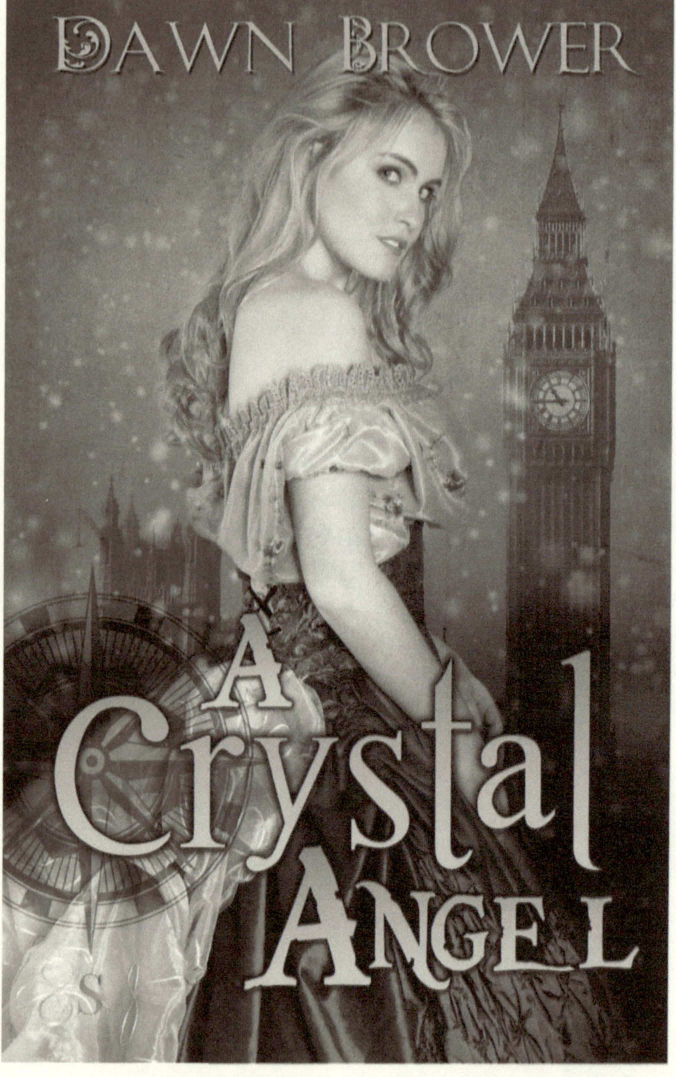
DAWN BROWER
A
Crystal
ANGEL

This book is for everyone who wants more of Pia and Thor. I hope you enjoy it as much as I did writing it. I want to acknowledge all the people who helped make me look good: Christina, Debbie, Amanda, and especially my editor, Jennifer. I can't say thanks enough.

CHAPTER 1

December 1875

*A*n emerald green vase flew across the room, hit the wall, and shattered into thousands of tiny shards. Quick reflexes allowed Thor, Viscount Torrington, to shift his head just in time to avoid it nearly connecting with his skull instead of the wall behind him.

"Pia, you really need to calm—"

This time a bronzed horse, crafted in mid-gallop, flew at him as he dodged to the right of his desk. He needed to subdue his wife before she permanently injured him. At the very least he wanted to stop her from breaking any other pieces of furniture or knickknacks lying about his study in her fit of rage.

He didn't know what had brought on this impromptu temper tantrum, but he'd already had enough of it. The previous night's overindulgence hadn't left him feeling well. His stomach churned and his head ached something fierce. He'd been sitting at his desk the better part of the afternoon staring at the same business reports, unable to decipher the meaning of them.

"How dare you tell me to calm down. I know what you did, you bloody idiot." Pia stormed towards him, waving a rolled parchment within her tight grasp. She twirled it around in circles with each step closer to him, her face growing a deeper shade of red. "You have a lot of explaining to do. What made you think this bit of nonsense would ever be a good idea?"

Thor pinched the bridge of his nose as pain shot daggers through his skull. He'd been out playing cards with the Earl of Devon the night before, attempting to persuade him into doing a bit of business with him. The events of the night before were a bit sketchy in his throbbing head.

"I don't have a clue what you're talking about."

"Well, if you hadn't decided to get sloshed with the Earl of Devon last night maybe you'd recall agreeing to betroth your son to his only daughter."

"What? Of course I wouldn't."

Her eyebrows rose in derision, her pale blonde curls framing her red face. "Oh really? That's why the Earl sent over this document outlining it in fine details. He even signed it. His note says it has all of the items you discussed last night and he looks forward to doing business with you in the future. Just sign it and send it to his solicitors."

Some of it started to come back. Devon had mentioned something about tying their families together. His daughter, Gemma, was a couple of years younger than the twins, Lily and Liam. Though they never really had any opportunity to interact with each other, Thor wondered why Devon would think Liam and Gemma would make a good match.

"Let me see it."

Pia threw the paper on his desk and folded her arms across her chest. Her blue eyes glared at him as he opened up the document and read it. Thor scanned the contents and clenched his fists. Damn it, she was right. He was a bloody fool.

"You're right. It's a betrothal. In my defense, I don't recall agreeing to this."

"Well, you can just send Lord Devon an apology. We do not choose who our children decide to marry."

How to explain it wasn't going to be as easy as

she thought. He didn't want to betroth Liam to the earl's daughter, but it might already be too late.

"Now Pia..."

"Don't even start, Thor. You messed up and you're going to fix it. Unless you want this to be the birthday and Christmas present you give your son this year. The twins are going to be turning fourteen this Christmas. Liam just got home from Eton. Are you prepared to spoil the holiday with your foolishness?"

"I don't know if it's that easy." Apprehension filled him as he stared at his wife.

"Of course it is. Go over and tell him you're a drunken idiot and you made a mistake. Trust me, if you don't make this go away, I promise you'll regret it."

Thor ran his fingers through his hair and sighed in frustration. He didn't like it when Pia was angry with him. He had to repair this damage before his wife did some irreparable harm to an important appendage of his. No doubt it would be the most heinous of deeds.

"I assure you, I already do."

"Good. Don't bother touching me until you make sure the Earl of Devon understands you are not signing a betrothal contract. I don't want anything to do with a man who plans on forcing his son to marry someone he doesn't love. I love you, Thor, but I have to do what I think is best for our children."

"Pia—wait! Stop"

Pia spun on her heels, ignoring him, as she stormed out of the room. A few strands of her pale blonde hair had come loose and floated around her neck as she breezed out. Her feet stomped hard on the ground, echoing through his study in rhythm with the pounding in his head.

"Bloody hell, what a mess."

Thor stood up and walked out of his study. It looked like he would need to pay a call on the Earl of Devon. He had to clear up this mess if he ever wanted to bed his wife again.

LILLIANA BREEZED INTO THE ROOM, SMUGNESS oozing out of her. She couldn't wait to tease her brother with a bit of the information she just stumbled into.

"You are not going to believe what I just heard our parents arguing about."

Liam looked up from the chessboard, pale blond

hair framing his face. "I don't really care. I'm trying to concentrate."

"On what?" Lily asked.

"Beating His Grace here in a game of chess."

"Don't let him fool you. He doesn't stand a chance. He has yet to beat me." Noah St. John, the Duke of Huntly and Liam's best friend, laughed as he watched him study the board.

"You should care, it was all about you after all."

Liam stopped staring at the chessboard and looked up at Lily. "I didn't do anything at school, I swear."

"Got a bit of a guilty conscience, do you?" Lily couldn't help asking him as a feeling of mischief rooted through her.

Noah's brown eyes widened with horror. "You don't think they heard about the incident, do you?"

"Of course not. No one knows it was us. They wouldn't have had time to send any notice to my parents." Liam paused and tilted his head in consideration. "Of course, anything is possible. At least you don't have parents they would send any notice to. Your guardian can barely be bothered to check up on you."

"I wouldn't call it luck."

Noah's face lost all color at the mention of his

parents, his mouth forming a straight, grim line. They died the year before in a horrific carriage accident, leaving him alone in the world. He had no family to speak of and a solicitor for a guardian. Once he reached majority he would take over control of his lands and title, but for the moment he needed someone to do it for him. It was the reason he came home with Liam from Eton on every break since his parents died.

"You shouldn't pick on your friend, Liam."

Lily didn't have any friends of her own and sometimes found herself a bit jealous of Liam's relationship with Noah. She didn't have the luxury of going away to school, and many of the girls her age didn't like her. She longed for the day she would have a friend who understood her. Of course, she was also realistic and didn't expect it to happen.

"I have to ask"—Lily's curious nature took over —"what did you two do?"

"Nothing," both boys chimed in at once.

"I don't believe you."

"We can't tell you."

Noah nodded his head in agreement. "It would break the oath we took."

Lily stared at the boys, studying each of their faces. Both of them had carefully schooled features, not an ounce of emotion showing, equally determined not to reveal their secret. She decided it didn't matter what they did. Well to be more apt, it didn't matter in that moment. She'd still get the details out of them, but her other news would send Liam into fits.

"All right. I suppose I can let it go for now."

"Good, 'cause we didn't plan on telling you." Liam turned back to concentrate on the chessboard.

"Why'd you give in so easy?" Noah asked.

"Don't see the point. Besides I think we need to discuss what I overheard."

"If it isn't about school, I don't care."

"You should, Liam. I told you it would impact your life."

"Well, what is it then?"

"Father agreed on a betrothal contract."

"Failing to understand how this might concern me." Liam waved his hand dismissively and turned back to his game. "Who is he going to marry you off to?"

"Not me you, fool. The Earl of Devon sent one over for him to sign. He's going to marry you off to his daughter, Lady Gemma Kemsley."

Liam's face turned stark white and he swayed in his chair. He turned to look at Lily as the shock settled in. His blue eyes glazed over as the astonishment of her words became clear. "Pardon me, what did you say?"

"You're betrothed, as in when you both come of age, you're getting married. Congratulations, brother of mine."

"No. Why would he do that?"

"I don't know. Have to say I'm glad it's you and not me. If I marry I plan on doing it for love. I'm not making my marriage some kind of business contract."

Noah stood up and placed his hand on Liam's shoulder. "I'm sorry. What can I do?"

"Turn back time and make my father see how unwise this is."

"I would if I could. Maybe if you go talk to him..."

"Won't make a difference," Lily interrupted him. "If mother can't change his mind, no one can."

"I'm doomed." Liam crumpled in his chair, his head slumping over into his arms, resting on the table.

Lily rolled her eyes. "Oh, don't be so melodramatic. Maybe this Gemma girl is lovely."

"I don't care if she's the most beautiful docile chit in all of England. I'm going to hate her just on principle."

Lily shook her head. "How mean and rude of

you. At least give her a chance. If you're going to marry her, you do realize you have to spend the rest of your life with her? It wouldn't be good to get off to such a horrible start."

"What do you care? You aren't the one he's making marry someone you've never met." Liam turned to glare at his sister.

Lily stared at the mulish expression on her brother's face and a wave of sympathy rolled through her. He was her only real friend and she wanted to help him if she could. She might have teased him, but she didn't want him to have an unhappy life. There had to be some way to undo what their father had done.

"Well, maybe we'll just have to come up with a plan to persuade him against it."

"You just said it was a futile endeavor!" Liam exclaimed.

"Don't give your sister a hard time for wanting to help you." Noah turned toward Lily and gave her his full attention. "What do you have in mind?"

"We could run away."

"What good would that do?" Liam scoffed at her idea.

"It would make him realize how dead set you are against it. If we leave, it would show him we would rather live alone than deal with such disrespect for our wishes."

"Where would we go?" Liam asked.

"We could go to Huntly. The servants would welcome someone to take care of."

Liam looked at Noah and appeared to think about his suggestion. He shrugged as a look of defeat crossed his features. "I suppose it's as good a plan as any. Maybe this can all be resolved before Christmas. If not, I don't want to be here anyway."

"Go pack a small bag that you can carry. We can walk over to my townhouse and hitch a carriage to take us all the way to Huntly."

"Why don't we just stay there?" Lily asked.

Liam shook his head and replied, "It'd be the first place they looked. It's too close. We need to get their attention. Going to Huntly will slow them down a bit. I think we should leave a note saying we took one of the Marsden ships to America."

"Good idea. Liam, you write the note and I'll go pack a quick bag for the both of us. Noah, you get whatever you need from your room and let's meet out front in thirty minutes."

Both boys nodded at Lily and they took off to complete their tasks. Lily went upstairs and packed a small reticule for her and one for Liam. She grabbed each bag and poked her head out her bedroom door. No one was around, so she quietly sneaked out to the front of the house to await the two boys. Soon they would be at Huntly and hopefully their father, Viscount Torrington, would realize the error of his ways.

CHAPTER 2

$\mathcal{P}$ia walked into the sitting room and found an abandoned chessboard. Earlier when she checked on them, Liam and Noah had been deeply engrossed in the match. Now the room stood empty and the game unfinished.

"I wonder where the boys are?"

"Excuse me, ma'am."

Pia turned to see Tully directly behind her. "What is it?"

"I wondered if you realized the children all went out earlier."

"No, I didn't. Do you know where they were going?"

"No ma'am, but they each had a reticule."

What were her wayward children up to now?

"Why didn't you stop them?"

"I tried, ma'am. I saw them from the upper window. By the time I got it open they were long gone."

Tully could be so vexing. She didn't know why she put up with her childhood maid. She looked back at the chess set and saw a scrap of parchment sitting on one of the chairs. She picked it up and read Liam's note.

"Those bloody fools. They get this nonsense from their father. I'm going to wring their necks when I get hold of them."

Of course, she didn't mean to actually do any real harm to the twins, but the fright of their running away ran rapid through her head. She hoped nothing serious happened to them while they were out alone in the cold.

"What did the children do now?" Thor's voice bellowed from the open doorway.

"They ran away. It's your fault too."

"How's it my fault?"

"Your stupid contract with the Earl of Devon caused this." Pia flung the note at him. It fluttered in the air and floated to the ground at Thor's feet. He picked it up and scanned the contents.

"Bloody hell."

"Exactly. Now go get those children before someone kills them."

Thor pinched the bridge of his nose and shook his head. "Pia, I'm getting tired of your constant harping. You need to take a step back and think about what you're saying."

"Don't patronize me. I have every right to be worried about our children's welfare."

"I'm not disputing that, but you need to calm down—and before you start off into another temper tantrum, you'll see I'm right. If we're going to find our children we need to have clear heads. Acting out in anger isn't going to achieve anything good."

Pia glared at him and attempted to rein in her anger, as she could see his point. No matter how annoyed she was with Thor, attacking him wouldn't get any desirable results. She needed to focus on what was important—finding the twins and Noah.

"All right, I can see your point, but I'm still mad at you."

His lips tilted into a cocky grin and he winked at her. "Duly noted. Now let's go find the children. It says they are boarding a ship to America."

"Probably Lily's idea. She always asks to go back to Charleston."

"We don't have any ships going to America until

after the New Year. I should be able to catch them at the docks," Thor explained.

Pia decided she didn't trust Thor to handle the children. They probably thought they could outmaneuver them and escape. It might be Christmas, and their birthdays, but they were still going to be punished for their behavior. They were not even fourteen yet and shouldn't be out on their own.

"Fine, I'll go with you."

"It's unnecessary, Pia. I can take care of this."

"Forgive me if I don't have faith in your abilities. You've ruined Christmas with your blundering already."

Thor sighed. "Are you going to continue to harp on me about this for the rest of the holiday?"

"Yes. You haven't made up for your mistake yet, but I'm willing to let it go for the moment. Did you talk to Devon?"

"I did. He said he wished I'd reconsider, but understood why I wouldn't sign the contract. He urged me to keep it in case I changed my mind."

"I hope you explained it wasn't likely."

"I did, but I kept the contract to make him happy. I still want to do business with him sometime in the future. I put it in one of the locked drawers."

"Fine. As long as you don't plan on signing it, I'm all right with that. Let's go get the twins and Noah."

Pia walked out of the sitting room and grabbed her pelisse. She donned it and turned toward her husband. "Well, what are you waiting for?"

Thor just shook his head and led her out the front door. The carriage still sat out front from when Thor had gone to see the Earl. The footman and driver looked surprised to see them out so soon.

"We need to go to the waterfront. Make it fast," Thor explained to the driver as he turned to help Pia inside. She shoved his hand away, lifted her skirts and stepped into the carriage unassisted. Thor pursed his lips in frustration and followed her.

The carriage ride was swift and bumpy as they traveled to the dockyard. Pia glared at Thor the entire journey, obviously still blaming him for the fiasco they were now dealing with. Once they arrived at the docks, Thor jumped out and helped Pia out of the carriage, and they began to search for signs of the three children.

"I don't think they are here."

"We need to go farther down the wharf to make sure," Thor replied. "The docks are extensive and they could be hiding behind something."

They continued down the pier, Pia trailing after

Thor, holding her skirts so they didn't skim the dirty waterfront. Night had fallen, and the only light they had to guide their path was the moonlight streaming down from above, making it difficult for them to see anything clearly. They searched the entire area surrounding them without any luck locating the children.

"I don't see them," Thor exclaimed.

"Do you see them anywhere?" Pia asked at the same time Thor spoke.

"No, I don't see them. I'm beginning to think they're not here," Thor repeated his earlier conjecture.

Pia sighed as irritation set in; Thor could be so difficult.

"So, you're ready to give up on finding them. Leave them out here alone and cold."

"Of course not. I just think this was a diversion of theirs. They probably went someplace else. Liam knows more about Marsden Shipping than you realize."

"Have you started dragging him to business meetings already? I told you not to overwhelm him with all the inner workings of your many projects. He's too young to worry about these things."

Thor stopped in his tracks and pinned Pia with a

furious glare. She sucked in a breath as rage flared across his features. She'd gone too far and now he'd finally snapped under her constant rants. "Enough, Pia, I'm not going to listen to you shriek the rest of the night. As far as Liam goes, I don't want him unprepared. It's why I was taken advantage of."

Pia knew Thor hated any reminders of her grandpère; the Comte had tried to murder him to gain control of their shared company. He failed, but it hadn't ended there. Thor kidnapped Pia to get revenge on him. It didn't turn out as planned; it had gone a whole lot better. If he hadn't wanted revenge, they would never have found each other. They both agreed everything ended the way it was supposed to. Of course, agreeing they belonged together didn't mean they always agreed on how to handle their children.

Pia forced herself to calm down and reply to him in an even, neutral voice. "Liam isn't you. He doesn't have a business partner; he only has you. Give him time to grow up." This wasn't a new argument. Pia often berated her husband for trying to get Liam working at Marsden Shipping; hollering at him wouldn't make a lick of difference.

Thor scowled at her and explained, "I haven't been. It doesn't mean the lad isn't curious. He finds himself in my study all on his own. I'm not going to turn him away just because you think he's too young to learn it."

"Hmmph. Fine. I still think he's too young, but if he comes in on his own, I see your point."

She didn't see any reason to argue any further about it. Thor believed he needed to start learning and soon. It was his belief if he didn't start soon he would be at a loss when it was time for him to take over. Pia just wanted him to enjoy his childhood for as long as possible before taking on so much responsibility. When he gained his majority he could take his rightful place at Marsden Shipping and learn all he needed to know. Pia didn't think he would ever have a disadvantage, especially with Thor at his side each step of the way.

"Do you think someone may have kidnapped them?"

"What? No, of course not. No one would dare."

"You seem awfully certain of that," Pia whispered.

"They know what I used to be and an ex-pirate isn't someone to mess with. No one would hurt our children for fear of what I might do to him. No, the kids just ran away to prove a point."

"Which is your fault."

"Don't start again, Pia. I'm not going to make Liam marry someone. When he gets married, it will be his choice."

"Still, we wouldn't be out in this frigid weather if you hadn't gotten inebriated with your crony the earl last night."

Pia couldn't stop herself from berating him, her worry for the children clouding her judgment. She wanted to find them as soon as possible and Thor made a good target for her anxiety. His face was etched with worry barely visible in the moonlight. She bit her lip and tried to prevent another irate outburst from spilling out of her mouth.

"Pia, do you really want to sit out here and argue or do you want to look someplace else?"

She inhaled and exhaled, her breath visible in the darkness. "Where do you suggest we look?"

"Noah's townhouse. They're not stupid and would know they needed someplace warm to stay. Since Noah is our guest, naturally they would go to his home."

"Do you really think they went there?"

She studied him, her pale blonde hair escaping the tight chignon and framing her face. He reached over and cupped her face in the palm of his hand. She stared up into his eyes finding her own love reflected back at her. No matter what, she knew she could depend on him. Yes, he had made a mistake, but he was willing to rectify it. He had done as she asked and retracted the betrothal contract with the Earl of Devon. He would have done it regardless because it was the right thing to do. Pia realized how awful she had been acting toward him and wished she hadn't acted like a shrew. No one else, besides her, loved the twins more. She knew if he thought the children had gone to Noah's townhouse, then they had. She needed to trust him as her instincts screamed at her to do.

"Yes, I do."

"All right. I will trust your judgment. Let's go look."

Thor led her to the carriage and helped her back inside. Once she was snuggled under one of the carriage blankets, Thor told the driver to take them to the Duke of Huntly's townhouse. The carriage rattled along the uneven road and the clip-clop of horses' hooves lulled them with their even rhythm. After what seemed like hours, the carriage came to a stop. Thor looked out the carriage window. Pia could see an ornate townhouse from the open slot in the carriage. Thor opened the door and hopped out, turning to assist Pia.

"I thought we would never get here," she exclaimed.

They raced up to the front door and knocked. After an eternity, or what seemed like one, the door finally cracked open. A wrinkled man in his bedclothes answered the door. His eyes narrowed at them, and with a gruff voice he asked, "What can I do for you?"

"Pardon the late hour, but has the young Duke of Huntly been by with our children, Lily and Liam?" Thor asked.

"His Grace was here briefly about two hours past. He ordered a carriage round to take him to the country estate. I didn't see any other children with him."

"Are you sure?" Pia bit her lip and wrung her hands together as worry nestled deep inside.

"I'm fairly certain I didn't see anyone else. His Grace came inside all alone. He awaited the carriage and after it arrived I only saw him enter it. I can't say if he picked anyone else up along the way."

"Well, there's nothing else we can do. Thank you for your time." Thor nodded at the older man and walked away from the door.

"What do you mean there isn't anything else we can do? We have to keep looking for our children."

"Of course we do, but they're not here."

"Clearly, but where are they?"

"That's easy enough; they are at the country estate of the Duke of Huntly."

"But the old man said he didn't see them." Pia's face scrunched up in puzzlement.

Thor leaned down and placed a quick kiss on her lips. "We have very intelligent children, Pia. They waited down the road and hopped in when no one else was paying attention. They tried to make it look like young Noah went home alone."

Pia bit her lip as she considered his words. She nodded her head, agreeing with his assessment. "So we're going to Huntly Manor?"

"Yes, we are. Get ready for a bit of a journey, love."

They both huddled into the carriage and sat back for the long ride to the country. The kids had a two-hour head start on them and would hopefully be safe inside by the time they arrived. There would be hell to pay once they caught up with their wayward children.

CHAPTER 3

The carriage traveled down a long, winding driveway flanked by large, barren trees, the branches towering above them. Moonlight illuminated the dark winter sky down the path toward Huntly Manor. Liam stretched his arms over his head to alleviate the kinks in his stiff muscles. Lily's head bobbed on the side of the carriage, her dark curls escaping from her long braid. Noah gazed out the window of the carriage, a solemn look on his face.

"So we finally made it?" Liam asked.

"Yes."

"Should we wake Lily?"

"Probably a good idea; we'll be at the front door soon enough."

"I know why we did this, but my parents are going to go crazy once they figure out we left."

"That's the point, isn't it?"

Liam looked over at his sleeping sister and back at his friend. He didn't like what his father had done, but what about their own actions? Were they any better? Did they have the right to worry their parents with their rash actions? Now, after hours of travel, he'd had time to think about the situation. They might have acted carelessly and should have talked to their mother first. She wouldn't have allowed him to be forced into a betrothal contract. His mother was dead-set against forcing either one of them into an unwanted marriage.

"It was. I'm not so sure about this anymore."

"There's no going back now. We're at my ancestral home now. All we can do is sit back and wait. They'll be here soon enough and it will be settled."

Liam nodded. "I suppose you're right."

"Are we at Huntly Manor?" Lily lifted her head, her blue eyes still droopy from sleep.

The carriage came to a full stop. Liam looked out the window at a large towering manor. There were at least forty tapered steps leading to the front door. Large sections of it resembled a medieval castle.

"Why didn't you tell me you lived in a castle?" Lily exclaimed, excitement filling her voice.

"Yeah, all you need is a moat and drawbridge and you'll be living in ancient times," Liam joked.

With a dry, humorless tone, Noah explained, "They were removed a century ago when the stairs were crafted. They've done a bit of remodeling, my ancestors, to make it into more of manor instead of a castle. A lot of the main structure still stands, but it is as modernized as they could make it."

"You don't like it here, do you?" Lily asked in a quiet tone.

"Not so much. It's never been much of a happy place. My parents hated each other. The best times I've had have been at your home. Sometimes I don't think you two know how good you have it."

"I'm sorry, Noah. You don't talk about your parents much. Why didn't you ever tell me?" Liam asked.

"I don't like talking about it and I've already said too much. Let's go inside and wait for your parents to come get us. I hope they still allow me to spend Christmas with you."

"Of course they will. They adore you and they'll know it's not your fault. We can be a bit—difficult— to say no to." An impish smile formed on Lily's face.

They all hopped down from the carriage and walked inside Huntly manor. They were greeted by a surprised housekeeper. "Your Grace." She curtsied. "We weren't expecting you."

"My apologies, Molly, this was a bit last-minute. Can you get some rooms ready?"

"Certainly. How many will you be needing?"

"Besides mine? I suggest getting four ready. We'll probably be getting some extra guests soon."

"Right away, Your Grace." Molly nodded her head. "Will you be requiring anything else? Perhaps some refreshments?"

"No, we're rather tired; just prepare the rooms."

"Very well, Your Grace. I will gather a few maids and have them organize the chambers for you and your guests."

Molly left to get the rooms ready. Noah led Lily and Liam into the library. The butler had lit a fire to keep them warm as they waited. They sat back and relaxed on the chaises until they could retire to nice warm beds.

"How long until you think they'll arrive?" Lily asked.

"Knowing Father, they are probably not too far behind us. With any luck we'll be asleep in a nice warm bed and they'll leave us there until morning."

"Do you think they will?"

"Not bloody likely."

Liam studied his sister and best friend. What were they thinking, running off in the middle of the night? They'd be lucky if their parents didn't murder them. He sighed and leaned his head on the chaise. Nothing to do about it now; they just had to sit back and wait for disaster to strike.

Pia's head rested on Thor's shoulder. She finally gave into her exhaustion and allowed herself to get some rest. Thoughts kept whirling through his head, not allowing him the same luxury. He couldn't help praying he was right and that the twins had coerced the young Duke of Huntly into going to his country estate. The carriage rattled along the roadway, the dark sky lightening as the sun rose in the distance. They had wasted a lot of time traipsing around London trying to locate them. At the rate things were going they wouldn't make it to Huntly Manor until dawn broke.

Pia lifted her head from his shoulder and yawned. "How much longer until we arrive?"

"I'm guessing an hour at least. The sun's beginning to rise."

"Did you get any sleep?"

"No, I have too much on my mind."

Pia's eyes pinned him. She stared at him for several seconds, biting her lip as if deep in thought. Thor didn't know what was rolling through her mind. A part of him was terrified of the answer; she hadn't been happy with his actions of late. He'd really messed up, his dealings with the Earl of Devon playing havoc on his family. At least he knew he'd taken care of it and could reassure Liam he was not betrothed to marry Lady Gemma Kemsley.

"As you should; they wouldn't have run away if not for your actions," Pia retorted.

"I've had enough of this." Thor smacked the side of the carriage with his fist, a sharp sting spreading through his fingers. "Can you just let it go?"

"I'd rather not." Pia glared. "It's all that is keeping me focused right now."

Thor nodded. "I make an easy target, love, but you know me. Just try and see it from my point of view."

"You're right. I know you better than anyone." Pia folded her hands in her lap. "They're going to be fine.

I can't keep blaming you. The twins are headstrong and it's hard to predict what they may or may not do."

"I set us on this course and I do know what my actions caused. I'm responsible for their rash actions."

Pia placed her hand on his shoulder and stared into his eyes. "You're right; you did, but you didn't tell those two to run away. They did that all on their own. If they had bothered to think, they'd realize you wouldn't have gone through with that betrothal contract."

"I know, but I can't help feeling the guilt. It should never have existed. Drinking in excess is no excuse. We both feel the same way. We want our children to be happy and dictating who they choose to marry isn't going to give them any kind of joy."

"I love you, Thor."

"I love you, too."

Thor pulled Pia into his arms and placed his lips on hers. She opened her mouth, allowing him full access. His tongue rolled over hers with gentle swirls. His hand cupped her cheek as he deepened the kiss. Thor pulled back and stared into her blue eyes. He reached down and scooped her fully into his lap and began trailing kisses down her throat and across her shoulders. A soft moan escaped Pia's mouth. Thor could feel himself begin to harden as desire flooded him. He would never get enough of his wife. He always wanted her, and he needed to be inside of her. She reached down and undid his breeches as he lifted her skirts and settled them around his lap. Pia lowered herself on his length, engulfing him in her warm passage. Once he was deep inside her, she began to ride him, up and down in slow, agonizing strokes. Thor rested his hands on her hips, guiding her to go faster, until he could feel her channel start to ripple with the onslaught of her orgasm. He could feel his own orgasm begin to crest as her inner muscles gripped him. Soon it exploded through him, draining him of energy. He groaned as pleasure washed over him in waves. Pia's head fell forward, resting on his shoulder. He wrapped his arms around her and held on tightly, his member still buried inside of her.

"We haven't made love in a carriage in a very long time."

"We probably shouldn't be doing it now."

"Why not?" she asked. "I wanted you, and you clearly wanted me. I don't see anything wrong with what we just did."

"Our children are missing—"

"But not for long. We're almost to Huntly. We'll

deal with our naughty children when we reach them."

A small weight lifted off his shoulders with his wife's reassuring embrace. They would find them and in the meantime they could enjoy each other for the remainder of the long journey to Huntly Manor.

"You're awfully sure about this, love." A warm, yet cocky smile formed on his face.

"Because nothing can go wrong now." She lifted her head and lightly touched her lips to his. "You're ready for another round, aren't you?"

"Well, we do have a little time..."

They began all over again, and Thor allowed himself to just enjoy loving his wife. Their children would feel their wrath when they caught up to them, but the worry dissipated with the assurance they were fine at the young Duke's estate.

CHAPTER 4

The sun began to stream through the windows of the bedroom Liam had been assigned at Huntly Manor, bright enough to wake him from a sound sleep. He sat up and rubbed the sleepy fog from his eyes. His gaze fell on the window.

"Should've remembered to close the curtains," he said to himself.

The bedroom door creaked open and Noah stepped inside. Tired from their journey, Liam noticed they both decided to sleep in their clothes, leaving them a rumpled mess. "I thought I might find you awake. I was so tired last night I forgot to close the curtains. As we were all exhausted, I thought perhaps you had forgotten to as well. I see your room is equally as bright as mine."

"Yeah, it sure is. Any chance we can get breakfast this early?"

Noah nodded his head. "Indeed, they are already preparing it. Should we retrieve Lily?"

"Yeah, we have a bit to discuss, though you should be prepared. Lily can sleep through anything and will be quite irritated at being awoken so early."

"I can handle it; I've grown accustomed to Lily's moods from visiting your house the past year."

Liam nodded and got up to follow Noah to Lily's room. They opened the door to find her sound asleep on the bed, the room completely dark. Lily had remembered to close her curtains. She liked her sleep and apparently had enough forethought to remember the possibility of early sunshine streaming through the window. Liam walked across the room and spread the curtains wide to allow the bright light to cascade into the room. It fell in quick succession across Lily's face, illuminating her dark curls, and her wrinkled blue dress. In sleep, she appeared angelic, but Liam knew how devilish his sister could be. The brilliant glow of sunshine was not doing much to awaken her, so he walked over to her bed and began to push on her shoulder. Lily jolted upright, her eyes flying open as they landed on Liam.

"Why are you waking me up? Are Mother and

Father here?"

Liam shook his head. "No. We are going down for breakfast and we need you to join us."

"How early is it? I feel like I haven't slept at all."

"It's still quite early, you probably only slept four hours or so." Noah's quiet voice entered the room from his place just inside the doorframe of Lily's room.

"Do we really need to get up this early?" Lily asked.

"Yes, I'm sure we will have visitors soon." Liam held his hand out to his sister to assist her from the bed. "Come on, let's go eat."

They followed Noah down to the small dining room and sat at the table. The servants began to serve them a light breakfast of poached eggs, bacon, and freshly baked bread. Liam picked up a slice of bread and spread creamy butter across it and set it on the plate of food the servant set in front of him. He no sooner picked up his fork to take a bite when the sound of voices interrupted him.

"Ah, there you three are. See, Thor, I told you they would be fine. I hope you had a nice adventure; it is going to be your last for several years to come."

His father glared at his mother and just shook his head back and forth in a slow motion. Liam watched his parents enter the room and take a seat at the dining table. Once they were both sitting, they turned their attention back to the three of them.

"So it looks like we have some things to discuss," his father said, folding his hands across his chest.

"Yes, sir." Liam nodded his head. "Indeed we do."

"You know you could have saved us all some time and just come to talk to me." Thor glowered at Liam.

"I didn't think of it at the time. I—we just reacted."

"Yes, have you had time to think about your actions and what they mean?" Pia asked them.

Liam could feel a well of emotions begin to roll through him. He still didn't want to marry some girl he'd never met. He could feel anger build up inside of him again. How could his father have done that to him? His arms folded across his chest defensively, he expressed his discontent. "You know why we left. I don't want to marry the Earl of Devon's daughter. I don't even know her. I'd like the chance to marry someone I love, if I marry at all."

"Liam, dear, you do know I wouldn't have allowed that to happen," his mother reassured him. "You shouldn't have run off."

Liam wouldn't regret his choices. He couldn't change them even if he wanted to. "I know that now, but I can't undo it." Anger and fury flowed through him as he stared his father in the eyes.

"There will be repercussions. We can't have you running off because you're scared. We need you to understand you can talk to us about anything, no matter how difficult the subject." Thor hammered home his point by pinning all three of them down with his gaze. "If you had bothered to ask, you would know I didn't sign the contract with the Earl of Devon. You are not going to be forced to marry anyone. It will always be your choice. I made a mistake and I apologize for it."

Liam lowered his head as the weight of his actions fell over him. He worried his parents and stressed over something that wouldn't have been an issue. He acted rashly. "I'm sorry, I promise I won't run away again. I will face whatever is bothering me. It is cowardly to think running will solve my problems."

The servants came in and set plates of breakfast in front of his parents, along with some silverware. His mother picked up her fork and began to cut her egg. His father continued to look across the table at them all.

"Liam isn't the only one at fault here." Lily began to play with her napkin, twisting it into a ball between her fingers. "I'm sorry too. Liam is right we shouldn't have run away."

Liam looked at his friend. He didn't say a word during the entire exchange. Noah didn't show an ounce of emotion. He continued to stare at Liam's father. When it mattered most to Noah, his emotions ran more deeply and he showed none. Liam learned his friend's biggest fear was losing those individuals he'd come to love most. They now included his entire family, and he didn't want to be cast off.

"Sir, I apologize for our actions. What do you plan to do?" Noah asked.

"I plan on eating some breakfast and then dragging you three back to London. Tomorrow is Christmas and we still have not decorated the tree. The servants should have it set up in the sitting room by now so we can direct our attention to it when we get home."

Surprise filled Noah's face. "You're going to allow me to come back with you?"

"Of course. Why would I punish you solely for all of your actions? However, there will be punishments meted out once I decide on the proper ones."

"Now, all of you eat. We have a long day ahead," Liam's mother ordered them.

Not long after they were done with breakfast, they grabbed their reticules, and all of them sat in a carriage for the long journey home. Fresh horses harnessed to the carriage had been swapped with those in Huntly's stable. They were exhausted, but anxious to return to London.

IT WAS EARLY AFTERNOON WHEN THEY ARRIVED at Marsden House, and the kids went to their chambers to rest before dinner. The Christmas festivities would start after they had eaten the evening meal. Thor followed Pia up to her chamber and closed the door behind them. He wanted to spend some extra quality time with her alone. Their argument was well over with and set aside on their journey to retrieve the children. He pulled off his jacket, folded it, and placed it on a chair near the door.

A gamine smile on her face, Pia tilted her head and stared at him. "Do you need something?"

"Yes."

She raised an eyebrow and crossed her arms beneath her generous bosom. "What can I do for you?"

Thor began to undo his cravat, pulled it off his neck, and tossed it aside. "I need you, love." He pulled his shirt off next and tossed it in the opposite direction of the cravat. His breeches undone and hanging low on his hips, he stalked Pia.

Pia took a step back. "You're not tired?"

"I'm never too tired to make love to my beautiful wife."

Thor continued to move forward as Pia stepped back. She hit the bed and fell backward onto it. He kneeled beside her, towering over her small frame. Reaching up, she ran her hands over his bare, muscled torso and squeezed one of his erect nipples. Thor reacted by lifting her skirts and skimming his hands across her thighs.

"You have too many clothes on." Lifting Pia up, he pushed her bodice down, revealing her lush breasts resting on top of her corset. Thor licked her pink nipple and nipped at it, repeating the action with the other one. He hoisted her up off the bed and turned her around. His hands roamed across her back as he undid the laces of her dress and corset, pushing her chemise over her shoulders. Thor spun her back around and pushed all of her clothing down in one full sweep. He trailed his eyes over her naked flesh. Pia shivered and Thor could see her body begin to flush with desire. Thor picked her back up and placed her beside him on the bed. He continued to lick, nip, and kiss her whole body.

"Enough. I need you inside me," Pia demanded.

Thor stood and pushed his breeches off. He spread Pia's legs, pulled her forward, and pushed his thick member deep into her. Pia moaned as her channel rippled around his length. Pia squeezed him with her inner muscles. Thor bit his lip as the pleasure raked over his sensitive flesh. He had to rein in his control and ease into loving her. If she kept stroking him with the muscles in her tight channel he would ravage her. He set a slow pace, stroking himself in and out of her. Pia raked her nails across his chest and moaned. Thor began to push himself in and out of her with deep rapid strokes. Pia's breathing became shallow and rapid; Thor could feel her orgasm begin as she squeezed against him. She screamed when she went over the edge. Thor moaned and threw his head back as his seed emptied inside of her. Afterwards he pulled himself out of her warmth and stood up. Thor lifted her up into his arms so he could pull down the bed sheets, and placed her on the bed. He crawled in beside her and spread the sheets over top of them. Thor pulled Pia into his arms; she curled into him and rested her head on his shoulder.

"I think I can sleep now," he whispered in her ear.

"I should hope so." Pia's laugh was light and throaty.

"Remind me when we wake up I have a special present for you."

"What if I want it now?"

"I'm too exhausted, love. You undo me. It can wait."

A pout formed on her face at his words. "You can be awful sometimes."

"Me? Never, wicked, on the other hand..." Thor began to trail his fingers over her erect nipples.

"I thought you were too tired?" Pia gasped as his fingers trailed down her hips and began to play with the tiny sensitive nub near her entrance. She moaned while his fingers stroked over her heated flesh. He could feel her begin to squirm beneath him.

"I believe I said I'm never too tired to make love to my wife."

Thor kissed her, pushing his tongue inside her mouth, effectively distracting her from the conversation about her present. He began to stroke her center with his fingers, rubbing over the sensitive tip, causing Pia to gasp. Deciding to distract her further, he roamed down to kiss her center. He spread her thighs and replaced his fingers with his tongue. Pia wrapped her legs over his shoulders, bringing herself closer to his wicked tongue. He began to push his fingers inside of her, caressing her channel as his tongue massaged the sensitive area of her sex. Thor licked and sucked her until he could feel her explode around his fingers. He pushed her legs off his shoulders and spread them wide. Then he crawled on top of her, pushing himself deep inside her. He began to pound into her with furious thrusts, desperate for his own release. He hadn't lied to her; he would never have enough of her, and he was always ready to make love with her. He needed her like he needed air to breathe. If not for her, he would still be a pirate roaming the seas for treasure. Pia, his sexy, flawed, perfect jewel, the angel he never thought to find in life. His orgasm hit him as he reveled in her beauty. A few minutes later he rolled off her and wrapped her tightly in his embrace once again.

"Sleep, love, we have a busy evening planned."

Pia's eyes drifted closed. Thor watched her for several seconds before he began to feel his own eyes drift closed.

*T*hor led Pia into the sitting room, where he found all three children sitting on the settee, patiently waiting for them to arrive.

"Oh good, you're finally here," Lily exclaimed.

Liam watched them with apprehensive eyes. Thor could tell his child didn't know what to expect from them. He still needed to punish them for their behavior, but hadn't thought of what would be the proper chastisement for their actions. The children needed to stew for a little while as he mulled over his options; once he decided on a proper punishment he would let them know.

"Are you in a hurry for your punishment?" Thor asked her.

"Um, no, I thought we were going to decorate the

tree..." Fear filled Lily's eyes as she stared at him. Good, she needed to know he hadn't forgotten their rash behavior.

"Did you decide what you're going to do with us?" Liam asked.

Thor looked over at his son. Resignation filled his eyes. He was ready and willing to accept whatever punishment Thor planned on assigning them.

"I will get to it in a minute."

"We have a few other things to discuss with you first," Pia explained.

Thor and Pia walked fully into the room and sat on a settee opposite the children. All three of them stared back at them, their eyes wide and curious.

"As you can see the tree is set up and ready to decorate." Pia gestured towards the tree the servants had cut down and placed inside the sitting room. "We will get to it in a moment. First we want to discuss your birthday."

Liam's eyebrows rose as he looked over at Lily. "What about it?"

"We were planning a special surprise for you, but in light of your actions we have decided against it," Thor explained.

A glum expression formed on both of the twins'

faces. Thor didn't want to disappoint them, but believed they hadn't earned the planned surprise.

"We were going to get you a carriage of your own to share. A little phaeton I was planning on teaching you both to drive; however, in light of your penchant for running away I've decided against it."

"But Father..." Lily began to say before Liam interrupted her.

"No, Lily. Father's right. I don't think we've earned the responsibility. Maybe in a couple of years, but we're too young."

Lily nodded her head at Liam and turned her attention back to Thor and Pia. "I understand. Liam's right, besides I'd probably only get in more trouble with my own carriage."

"So we will have to give you a less expensive birthday present."

Lily looked at them both expectantly. "We're still getting presents?"

"Yes and no," Pia explained.

"You still have your Christmas gifts," Thor offered.

Pia nodded. "Indeed. Our gift for your birthday is to allow you to even have a Christmas."

Both Liam and Lily groaned.

"We could cancel all of the festivities," Thor reminded them.

"No, please don't," Lily begged.

During the entire exchange Thor noticed how Noah watched and waited. He didn't know what to make of the young duke. His reserved demeanor made him feel sad. He had lost so much at a young age.

"What about you, Noah?"

"I don't understand, sir?"

"Do you still want to have the Christmas festivities?"

"I'm just glad you're allowing me to be a part of your family." Noah's voice was quiet and heavy with emotion.

"Son, you know you're welcome here anytime," Thor reminded him.

Pia held her hand over her heart, tears forming in the corners of her eyes. "Noah, don't ever feel like you're not welcome here."

Noah's head bobbed back and forth between the two of them. After several seconds he gave them a formal nod. "I won't."

Time ticked by while they talked and Thor considered how to discipline them. After they were well into the discussion, Thor decided the exact punishment to give them for their misbehaviors. He didn't want something too harsh; yet at the same time nothing equally too lenient.

"Now for your punishment," Thor began. "Each of you is going to help the maids clean for the next week. Expect to get up at dawn to assist them."

Another groan filled the room. "Unless you want more work..."

"No, Father, we'll help the maids," Liam offered before Thor could assign more tasks.

"Good, I will inform them of your duties and you're to listen to them. If even one maid comes to me with a bad report I'll make things infinitely worse. Do you all understand?"

Three heads nodded at him in agreement.

"All right. Lily and Liam, show Noah where the decorations are and we can begin trimming the tree," Pia ordered.

All three of the children hopped up and headed toward the box of decorations. With glee they began to hang up the various ornaments they collected over the past several years. Thor watched them as they hung each one up with care. Happiness radiating across their faces, they opened up each ornament and remembered when they picked it out.

"Don't you have a special gift for me?" Pia asked.

"Ah yes, I forgot."

"You did tell me to remind you."

"Indeed I did and then I got distracted."

A blush filled Pia's cheeks. "I remember how you became distracted."

His lips tilted into a smile filled with sin. "We'll have to become distracted in a similar fashion later."

"Yes, but now give me my present."

Thor looked over at his children and their friend. The tree was almost completely flowing with sparkling decorations as they continued to hang them on the green branches. Thor walked over and picked up a package near the box of decorations. It was adorned with the glittery dust of broken glass, ground down into fine grains and adhered to the sides of the box. It gave the impression of a thousand diamonds sparkling on the hard surface. A bright blue bow, matching the color of Pia's eyes, was wrapped around it. He picked it up, crossed back to his wife's side, and handed it to her.

She clapped her hands as joy spread across her face. "What is it?"

"Open it up and see."

Pia undid the ribbon with care and pulled it aside, letting it drift to the floor. She lifted the lid and gasped. Inside, against red plush velvet lay a crystal angel. A shiny gold halo floating above her head, gossamer wings spread high on her back, and her skirts hollow and fine, she shimmered much like the diamond sparkle on the package.

"Oh, Thor, she's beautiful."

"It's a special tree topper I had made for you. She's delicate, so we need to be careful when we place her on the tree. If she falls she could break rather easily."

"Will she stay in place?" Pia asked.

"Yes, there are a couple of hooks under her skirt to tie her down. When the children are done I'll help you place it on the highest branch. She's our own guardian angel to watch over us each Christmas."

"How lovely, thank you. I shall treasure her always."

Thor reached down and placed a soft kiss on Pia's lips. The children finished decorating the tree and turned their attention back on them.

"What's that?" Lily asked.

"A gift from your father," Pia explained as she turned toward Lily and Liam. "Are you ready to put it on the tree?"

"Yes," they both exclaimed.

Pia looked at Thor. "You're going to have to place

it on the tree, as you're the only one tall enough to reach the top."

Thor nodded and followed her over to the tall, fragrant pine. They placed the crystal angel on top and anchored her to the branches surrounding it. She gleamed down on them from her vantage point. Thor turned to look at his family and happiness welled up inside of him. His life couldn't have been more perfect if he tried. He looked back up at the crystal angel and smiled. Now they had a guardian angel to watch over them, a protective shield against any danger. He pulled Pia into his arms and stroked her hair with his hand. She was his living, breathing angel, and the twins their beautiful blessing.

**Read on for an excerpt from A Treasured Lily: A Marsden Romance Book **

CHAPTER 6

"I just don't think it's a good idea."

"Nonsense." Lilliana Marsden looked up at her best friend, Lady Gemma Kemsley, and frowned. "It's a brilliant idea. My father is being unreasonable about allowing me to travel to America. The plantation in South Carolina is my inheritance. It's about time I claimed it."

"It's not going to work for you to just show up and claim it though. I don't get why you are in such a hurry. You know full well you won't inherit it until you marry." Gemma reached up and smoothed over her sanguine curls, tucking a loose strand behind her ear.

"Well, that's not entirely true." Lilliana's lips twitched into a cheeky smile; it helped to have a little insight into how her parents worked. Gemma didn't know how much she'd gotten away with over the years. Eavesdropping had become a habit of hers. A person could find out the most interesting things quite by accident. When she overheard her parent's most recent conversation she couldn't help the glee that filled her soul. Reining in her excitement had taken an enormous amount of restraint. She needed to leave England and start the life she envisioned for herself. One she had complete control over. Her parent's still hoped she would settle down and get married, but they didn't know her true reasons. "I stumbled across a bit of information that may help me to achieve my goal."

"I don't understand. Did you find a way to inherit it early?"

Lilliana got up, walked to the window of the sitting room, and pulled open the curtains. She stared out at the garden and pondered how to explain what she overheard, and exactly how it fit into her idea to get everything she wanted. Various shades of roses, red, orange, and white, scattered across the garden in a pattern that reminded Lilliana of a kaleidoscope. The garden remained one of the places that she turned to when she needed to reflect on what floated through her mind. It calmed her and made it possible for her to think rationally about any issue that arose in her life. Something about being surrounded by the plant life helped her to think and form her plans with a clear head. Lilliana needed to get Gemma to aid her in her quest to leave England. They worked their magic on her as she calmly let the curtain go and turned back towards her best friend.

"I don't *ever* plan on getting married. I told you that the day we met. My parents still insisted on a season or two. They believe everyone is capable of finding love. They don't understand they are a rarity."

A sting of pain stabbed through her heart, Lilliana rubbed her chest in an attempt to erase the phantom ache. After her disastrous first season, she knew quite well how unusual it was for a love match to exist within the ton. Her choices were lecherous old men and scheming vermin only after her money. There was one man though who made her want to believe he really loved her. She found out the hard way he only wanted to use her. She was thankful he didn't achieve his goal and Lilliana came out relatively unscathed, but the damage to her belief in love sat firmly in place.

"Most matches are made for business or political

reasons. It's all about money and there is no way I'm handing over mine to a male to control."

Gemma tilted her head and crinkled her nose in confusion. Lilliana knew she didn't get it. Her friend wanted to get married and have children. The two years difference in their ages showed when they discussed the possibility of matrimony. In time, Lilliana believed Gemma would look back on this conversation with clarity. In the midst of starting her first season and barely seventeen years old, Gemma still approached life with rose-colored glasses on. For a brief moment in time Lilliana had worn that same veil of hope; her parent's love inspired her enough to want to find it herself.

Reality came crashing in like a bolt of lightning and shattered every ounce of optimism she held within her. Lilliana realized finding love at the various parties hosted within London society equaled finding a mythical creature. The chances of finding a unicorn would be an easier feat. So she gave up on love and formed a new plan for her life.

"I still think you are being preposterous. Why are you so against marriage?" Gemma folded her arms across her chest and stared at Lilliana. Her eyes pinning her in place as she spoke. "That's what a lady is expected to do after all. I just don't understand how you plan on claiming your inheritance without the benefit of a husband to help you get it."

Lilliana could feel her lips twitch into a smile. Her mother often commented on how Lilliana received all her father's traits, even his less than desirable ones. William Thorston Marsden, fifth Viscount Torrington, had a way of getting what he wanted out of people. She admired that characteristic in her father and sought to emulate it. Still, she wished she had been lucky enough to get her mother's pale blonde hair instead of her father's dark curls. In Lilliana's mind, her twin brother, Liam, was blessed because he inherited her mother's coloring.

"I suppose I should explain it so you won't be left in the dark. I'll need your assistance after all."

Gemma got up from her seat and crossed to the window where Lilliana still stood. "You're my best friend. I'll help if I can, but I'm going to be honest and say I don't like this. I don't want to lose you. Please reconsider."

"I will miss you, but I need to find my own way. Please understand this is the best thing for me."

Gemma sighed and then pulled Lilliana into her arms for a hug. Lilliana wrapped her arms around her best friend. She had been curious about Gemma once she realized who she was. Lady Gemma Kemsley had been the girl her father wanted her brother to marry when they were younger. She sought out an introduction to get her measure and hadn't been disappointed in the young woman. They had only been friends for a few months, but in all her nineteen years she had never been close to another female her age. It didn't matter that a couple years separated their age; they were a different kind of soul mate. They appreciated each other on a level that no one else ever could or would.

"I'll try to understand. I really will, but I'm never going to like it. You are my only friend. I will always wish for you to be near me..." Gemma pulled away from Lilliana and clasped their hands together. "Tell me what I can do to help."

Lilliana knew she could count on Gemma. Elation filled her as she could envision how it would all work out. Now all she needed to do was give her all the details so she could do her part in the plan.

"I overheard my parents talking. I had no intention of listening until I heard my name spoken. I found out some interesting things that I never knew. Not the least being that Mama never intended to get married and Father had blackmailed her into agreeing to be his wife."

Gemma gasped. "What?"

"Makes you stop and question the validity of their love and all that doesn't it?"

Gemma's mouth hung open with shock radiating from her eyes. After a small pause while the information sank in she asked, "Why would he do such a thing?"

"Once upon a time Papa sailed his ship, the *Sea Rover*, as its pirate captain. Apparently he had a little feud with Mama's grandpere and she became the leverage he needed to enact his revenge. They came out of it okay, clearly as they are still together." Lilliana flipped her hand dismissively as she spoke. "The point is that Mama said that by the time I'm twenty if I still don't wish to wed, she planned on giving me the deed to the plantation in South Carolina."

Lilliana tried over and over to explain to her parents how much marriage was distasteful to her, without going into too much detail. If her father knew exactly how her heart had been bruised, he would have murderous intentions. The real issue was she didn't want anyone to know how naïve she had been. Now, she knew she could get what she wanted and nothing made her happier. Anxiety filled with equal swirls of excitement tumbled through her belly.

"That's still too long for me to wait. I won't be twenty until December and that is nine months away. What I want to do is sail there now and use my family position to gain control. My plans are not going to change just because nine months pass by."

"What good will that do? Without the deed securely in your control will they allow you to oversee the plantation? Isn't someone already there taking care of the property?" Gemma asked.

"There is an overseer yes. I'm hoping to convince him that the letter giving him orders to give me control got lost on the mail packet before my arrival. Come let's sit down in comfort as we work out the details." Lilliana grabbed Gemma's hand and led her to the settee. After they were seated she poured them both tea and handed a cup to her friend. Lilliana took a sip of tea before continuing their conversation. "I've thought a lot about what needs to be done. Even if the overseer doesn't believe I have control of the plantation no one has the authority to throw me off the property because it is owned by my family. If I have to wait, I'd rather do it in South Carolina."

Gemma nodded. "Okay, I suppose that makes sense. What do you need me to do?"

"Well the tricky part is leaving without letting my parents know. First, I need to find a ship sailing to America. Once I book passage I'm going to need a way to get my trunks on board without raising suspicion. I'm not worried about funds. I've been saving all my pin money for months now." Lilliana gave Gemma a smile. Surely she would see how she thought of every possible issue in her plan.

"So how do you plan on getting your trunks on board the ship?"

"That is where you come in. Once I know what ship I'm on, I'd like you to invite me to come stay with you in the country for a week." Lilliana set her teacup down and gave Gemma her full attention. She really needed Gemma to help her. If she didn't, her whole plan would fall apart. Her eyes pleaded with Gemma as she spoke, "My family won't question it because they know that our schedule is relaxed at the moment. It will give me a reason to pack a trunk or two and have them loaded onto a carriage. The carriage with your family crest on it that is."

"Oh, I understand. You will have the carriage drop you off at the docks and our servants will unload your trunks to be delivered to the ship. They won't have a reason to let your family know that you're boarding the ship. The servants will assume they already know." Gemma nodded her head in understanding.

"I knew you'd get it." Excitement filled Lilliana's voice. "It's all coming together now. I only have one little facet to figure out before I can iron out the rest of the details. The first item I need to cross off my list is to figure out what ships are heading to America and if they are accepting passengers."

"However are you going to figure that out?"

"Oh, that's the easy part. I will just ask Liam," Lilliana proclaimed.

Gemma blinked several times before she asked, "Won't he find that suspicious?"

"Not at all," Lilliana said waving her hand. "He's constantly talking about the Marsden shipping line and its competitors. He just started to take over the business. Our father believes it's time for him to learn about his future inheritance."

"I see. When do you plan on getting the information out of him?"

"Tonight at the Silverton's ball. Father is making him escort me. I will make sure to have a friendly conversation with him in the carriage on our way."

"You have thought of everything. I'm sure it will work just the way you want it." A small smile grew on Gemma's face as she looked at Lilliana. "I just wish your plans didn't have to take you so far away from England. Why couldn't you have fallen in love with a nice earl or baron...or even a mere mister? Anything that might inspire you to stay where I have an actual possibility to visit you, chances are I'll never be able to travel to America to visit. Promise me you'll come back to see me."

"I promise to come back to see you. In the meantime, we'll keep in touch with lots and lots of letters. I want to know everything about your life and when you find the man of your dreams."

"Good. I suppose I should go. I'll see you tonight at the ball."

Gemma stood up and grabbed her pelisse. After she donned it, she walked over and gave Lilliana a quick hug. She watched as Gemma left the room and got up to walk back to the window to look at the rose garden. All she could do at this point was hope all of her plans went off without a hitch. Doubts clouded her mind as she knew from experience nothing ever went exactly as planned, and naught could be done to alleviate her anxiety. Lilliana decided to try and let it go. She turned and left the sitting room to find some kind of diversion. Perhaps a book would work to distract her thoughts away from any possible problems—thinking, or over thinking in her case, had always been her worst enemy. With a smile on her lips Lilliana strolled to the library. Dark feelings would not sink through and ruin her good mood. Preparation was the key to success. No one planned and schemed better than Lilliana Marsden.

A TREASURED LILY

DAWN BROWER

Dawn Brower

A Treasured Lily

A wise person told me that if I decided to write I needed to create a world that crossed over numerous books. I never set out to write and when I wrote my first book I never imagined the possibility of writing another book featuring those characters. My son is the reason I am continuing on and imagining ways to keep these characters alive. So this book and many more are because of him. Nathan thanks for inspiring me to write more, even if you are too young for me to allow you to read these books right now. Someday maybe you will. I love you.

I also want to acknowledge the usual suspects, my awesome beta readers: Christina S, Cheryl R, Capri B, and Amanda S. You gals rock!

"*I* just don't think it's a good idea."

"Nonsense." Lilliana Marsden looked up at her best friend, Lady Gemma Kemsley, and frowned. "It's a brilliant idea. My father is being unreasonable about allowing me to travel to America. The plantation in South Carolina is my inheritance. It's about time I claimed it."

"It's not going to work for you to just show up and claim it though. I don't get why you are in such a hurry. You know full well you won't inherit it until you marry." Gemma reached up and smoothed over her sanguine curls, tucking a loose strand behind her ear.

"Well, that's not entirely true." Lilliana's lips twitched into a cheeky smile; it helped to have a little insight into how her parents worked. Gemma didn't know how much she'd gotten away with over the years. Eavesdropping had become a habit of hers. A person could find out the most interesting things quite by accident. When she overheard her parent's most recent conversation she couldn't help the glee that filled her soul. Reining in her excitement had taken an enormous amount of restraint. She needed to leave England and start the life she envisioned for herself. One she had complete control over. Her parent's still hoped she would settle down and get married, but they didn't know her true reasons. "I stumbled across a bit of information that may help me to achieve my goal."

"I don't understand. Did you find a way to inherit it early?"

Lilliana got up, walked to the window of the sitting room, and pulled open the curtains. She stared out at the garden and pondered how to explain what she overheard, and exactly how it fit into her idea to get everything she wanted. Various shades of roses, red, orange, and white, scattered across the garden in a pattern that reminded Lilliana of a kaleidoscope. The garden remained one of the places that she turned to when she needed to reflect on what floated through her mind. It calmed her and made it possible for her to think rationally about any issue that arose in her life. Something about being surrounded by the plant life helped her to think and form her plans with a clear head. Lilliana needed to get Gemma to aid her in her quest to leave England. They worked their magic on her as she calmly let the curtain go and turned back towards her best friend.

"I don't *ever* plan on getting married. I told you that the day we met. My parents still insisted on a season or two. They believe everyone is capable of finding love. They don't understand they are a rarity."

A sting of pain stabbed through her heart, Lilliana rubbed her chest in an attempt to erase the phantom ache. After her disastrous first season, she knew quite well how unusual it was for a love match to exist within the ton. Her choices were lecherous old men and scheming vermin only after her money. There was one man though who made her want to believe he really loved her. She found out the hard way he only wanted to use her. She was thankful he didn't achieve his goal and Lilliana came out relatively unscathed, but the damage to her belief in love sat firmly in place.

"Most matches are made for business or political

reasons. It's all about money and there is no way I'm handing over mine to a male to control."

Gemma tilted her head and crinkled her nose in confusion. Lilliana knew she didn't get it. Her friend wanted to get married and have children. The two years difference in their ages showed when they discussed the possibility of matrimony. In time, Lilliana believed Gemma would look back on this conversation with clarity. In the midst of starting her first season and barely seventeen years old, Gemma still approached life with rose-colored glasses on. For a brief moment in time Lilliana had worn that same veil of hope; her parent's love inspired her enough to want to find it herself.

Reality came crashing in like a bolt of lightning and shattered every ounce of optimism she held within her. Lilliana realized finding love at the various parties hosted within London society equaled finding a mythical creature. The chances of finding a unicorn would be an easier feat. So she gave up on love and formed a new plan for her life.

"I still think you are being preposterous. Why are you so against marriage?" Gemma folded her arms across her chest and stared at Lilliana. Her eyes pinning her in place as she spoke. "That's what a lady is expected to do after all. I just don't understand how you plan on claiming your inheritance without the benefit of a husband to help you get it."

Lilliana could feel her lips twitch into a smile. Her mother often commented on how Lilliana received all her father's traits, even his less than desirable ones. William Thorston Marsden, fifth Viscount Torrington, had a way of getting what he wanted out of people. She admired that characteristic in her father and sought to emulate it. Still, she wished she had been lucky enough to get her mother's pale blonde hair instead of her father's dark curls. In Lilliana's mind, her twin brother, Liam, was blessed because he inherited her mother's coloring.

"I suppose I should explain it so you won't be left in the dark. I'll need your assistance after all."

Gemma got up from her seat and crossed to the window where Lilliana still stood. "You're my best friend. I'll help if I can, but I'm going to be honest and say I don't like this. I don't want to lose you. Please reconsider."

"I will miss you, but I need to find my own way. Please understand this is the best thing for me."

Gemma sighed and then pulled Lilliana into her arms for a hug. Lilliana wrapped her arms around her best friend. She had been curious about Gemma once she realized who she was. Lady Gemma Kemsley had been the girl her father wanted her brother to marry when they were younger. She sought out an introduction to get her measure and hadn't been disappointed in the young woman. They had only been friends for a few months, but in all her nineteen years she had never been close to another female her age. It didn't matter that a couple years separated their age; they were a different kind of soul mate. They appreciated each other on a level that no one else ever could or would.

"I'll try to understand. I really will, but I'm never going to like it. You are my only friend. I will always wish for you to be near me..." Gemma pulled away from Lilliana and clasped their hands together. "Tell me what I can do to help."

Lilliana knew she could count on Gemma. Elation filled her as she could envision how it would all work out. Now all she needed to do was give her all the details so she could do her part in the plan.

"I overheard my parents talking. I had no intention of listening until I heard my name spoken. I found out some interesting things that I never knew. Not the least being that Mama never intended to get married and Father had blackmailed her into agreeing to be his wife."

Gemma gasped. "What?"

"Makes you stop and question the validity of their love and all that doesn't it?"

Gemma's mouth hung open with shock radiating from her eyes. After a small pause while the information sank in she asked, "Why would he do such a thing?"

"Once upon a time Papa sailed his ship, the *Sea Rover*, as its pirate captain. Apparently he had a little feud with Mama's grandpere and she became the leverage he needed to enact his revenge. They came out of it okay, clearly as they are still together." Lilliana flipped her hand dismissively as she spoke. "The point is that Mama said that by the time I'm twenty if I still don't wish to wed, she planned on giving me the deed to the plantation in South Carolina."

Lilliana tried over and over to explain to her parents how much marriage was distasteful to her, without going into too much detail. If her father knew exactly how her heart had been bruised, he would have murderous intentions. The real issue was she didn't want anyone to know how naïve she had been. Now, she knew she could get what she wanted and nothing made her happier. Anxiety filled with equal swirls of excitement tumbled through her belly.

"That's still too long for me to wait. I won't be twenty until December and that is nine months away. What I want to do is sail there now and use my family position to gain control. My plans are not going to change just because nine months pass by."

"What good will that do? Without the deed securely in your control will they allow you to oversee the plantation? Isn't someone already there taking care of the property?" Gemma asked.

"There is an overseer yes. I'm hoping to convince him that the letter giving him orders to give me control got lost on the mail packet before my arrival. Come let's sit down in comfort as we work out the details." Lilliana grabbed Gemma's hand and led her to the settee. After they were seated she poured them both tea and handed a cup to her friend. Lilliana took a sip of tea before continuing their conversation. "I've thought a lot about what needs to be done. Even if the overseer doesn't believe I have control of the plantation no one has the authority to throw me off the property because it is owned by my family. If I have to wait, I'd rather do it in South Carolina."

Gemma nodded. "Okay, I suppose that makes sense. What do you need me to do?"

"Well the tricky part is leaving without letting my parents know. First, I need to find a ship sailing to America. Once I book passage I'm going to need a way to get my trunks on board without raising suspicion. I'm not worried about funds. I've been saving all my pin money for months now." Lilliana gave Gemma a smile. Surely she would see how she thought of every possible issue in her plan.

"So how do you plan on getting your trunks on board the ship?"

"That is where you come in. Once I know what ship I'm on, I'd like you to invite me to come stay with you in the country for a week." Lilliana set her teacup down and gave Gemma her full attention. She really needed Gemma to help her. If she didn't, her whole plan would fall apart. Her eyes pleaded with Gemma as she spoke, "My family won't question it because they know that our schedule is relaxed at the moment. It will give me a reason to pack a trunk or two and have them loaded onto a carriage. The carriage with your family crest on it that is."

"Oh, I understand. You will have the carriage drop you off at the docks and our servants will unload your trunks to be delivered to the ship. They won't have a reason to let your family know that you're boarding the ship. The servants will assume they already know." Gemma nodded her head in understanding.

"I knew you'd get it." Excitement filled Lilliana's voice. "It's all coming together now. I only have one little facet to figure out before I can iron out the rest of the details. The first item I need to cross off my list is to figure out what ships are heading to America and if they are accepting passengers."

"However are you going to figure that out?"

"Oh, that's the easy part. I will just ask Liam," Lilliana proclaimed.

Gemma blinked several times before she asked, "Won't he find that suspicious?"

"Not at all," Lilliana said waving her hand. "He's constantly talking about the Marsden shipping line and its competitors. He just started to take over the business. Our father believes it's time for him to learn about his future inheritance."

"I see. When do you plan on getting the information out of him?"

"Tonight at the Silverton's ball. Father is making him escort me. I will make sure to have a friendly conversation with him in the carriage on our way."

"You have thought of everything. I'm sure it will work just the way you want it." A small smile grew on Gemma's face as she looked at Lilliana. "I just wish your plans didn't have to take you so far away from England. Why couldn't you have fallen in love with a nice earl or baron...or even a mere mister? Anything that might inspire you to stay where I have an actual possibility to visit you, chances are I'll never be able to travel to America to visit. Promise me you'll come back to see me."

"I promise to come back to see you. In the meantime, we'll keep in touch with lots and lots of letters. I want to know everything about your life and when you find the man of your dreams."

"Good. I suppose I should go. I'll see you tonight at the ball."

Gemma stood up and grabbed her pelisse. After she donned it, she walked over and gave Lilliana a quick hug. She watched as Gemma left the room and got up to walk back to the window to look at the rose garden. All she could do at this point was hope all of her plans went off without a hitch. Doubts clouded her mind as she knew from experience nothing ever went exactly as planned, and naught could be done to alleviate her anxiety. Lilliana decided to try and let it go. She turned and left the sitting room to find some kind of diversion. Perhaps a book would work to distract her thoughts away from any possible problems—thinking, or over thinking in her case, had always been her worst enemy. With a smile on her lips Lilliana strolled to the library. Dark feelings would not sink through and ruin her good mood. Preparation was the key to success. No one planned and schemed better than Lilliana Marsden.

*R*andall Collins stepped out of a black open carriage and followed the Earl of Devon into his gentleman's club, Whites. Devon wanted to discuss business in a more dignified setting, hence the journey to his favorite club. Rand didn't much like overly pompous aristocrats, but Devon had an interest in a possible investment with his shipping company. If the meeting went as planned Rand would have a new investor and could expand his business.

"Ah, here we are, have a seat Collins and we'll discuss what is next for RandCo Shipping," The Earl said as he sat down in the nearest seat at the table. "And whether or not I want to give you some of my money to invest."

It grated on his nerves he had to seek investors to expand his business. Rand had a lot of big ideas and hoped the earl liked them enough to continue to invest in shipping company. He took the seat across from the earl and settled into discussing the future of his shipping company. With a small fleet of clippers at his disposal he did well enough for himself, but wanted to branch out into steamships for larger cargos and more reliable speeds.

"Did you have a chance to look over the papers with my proposal?" Rand asked.

"I did, and I admit my knowledge of shipping is rather limited. I hope you don't mind I invited someone that knows a bit more than I do to help me decipher some of the details. Viscount Torrington and his son should arrive soon." The Earl of Devon raised his head and scanned the room. He appeared to be scanning the room, as if looking for someone he invited to join them.

Irritation filled Rand's gut as he let the earl's words absorb deep into his mind. He clenched his fists tightly under the table, not wanting the man to see how much his words bothered him. Hell yes he minded, Devon could consult anyone he chose, it was his right after all to make sure he was doing the right thing for himself. However, he could have at least let Rand know they'd be meeting with someone else prior to arriving at the club. It was hard to be prepared for a meeting when all of the details hadn't been presented in advance. Before he could voice objection, two men walked in and took a seat at the table. One was as dark as the other was light. They bore a striking resemblance, in spite of the opposite coloring, that made Rand believe them to be closely related.

"Ah Torrington glad you and Liam could make it," Devon said. "This here is Randall Collins. He has grand ideas for steamships. What are your thoughts on the matter?"

As they had not been introduced, Rand gathered the older gentleman Devon spoke to was Torrington, the man he previously mentioned would be joining them. The upper class tended to refer to each other by their titles or last names. Rand couldn't wait until he could sail back to America. The higher born in English society had a snobbish attitude that he had trouble stomaching. Torrington nodded his head at both Rand and Devon before he started to speak, "Liam knows a bit more about steamships than I do. He has been looking into them for a while now to determine if they are worth investing in. I'm a clipper man, but I realize their days are numbered."

"I like the idea of steamships, but even they have their pitfalls. The coal needed to keep them running can be expensive. The cargo needs to bring in a more than fair price if a profit is to be made. They have their advantages, faster and more reliable travel. I think it's more economical for most cargo to continue to be brought over by clipper. Steamships are great for passengers and mail." The light haired man nodded at them as he sat up straight and looked Rand directly in the eye as he delivered his viewpoint.

It was obvious that Liam's beliefs were in direct opposition to his own. Rand clenched his hands into tight fists underneath the table as anger and frustration permeated his whole body. The boy probably had a point, although minute, Rand however did not want to deal in passenger ships. People made things messy. They could be demanding and irritating on a good day and damn abusive any other time. The chances of him being willing to start a passenger line bordered on slim to none.

"Is that the only good thing you can think of for steamships? What about cargo that requires a faster delivery? I know you English favor your tea. Steamships travel at faster speeds and allows for a swifter arrival. This means what you deem to be important cargo will arrive to its destination much sooner." He had to gain control of the conversation before these idiots talked Devon out of investing in his shipping line.

Steamships did make great passenger ships. The mail packets arrived much faster when they were placed on a ship powered by steam, but Rand had grander ideas. There were plenty of reasons to start investing in steamships. Those that began to do it sooner would have profits much sooner than those waiting to see if it worked. Sometimes it was worth it to take on a risky venture; although Rand didn't think it was as chancy as they were making it sound.

A bit of color formed on Liam's face. He clearly didn't like pointing out flaws in his estimation of the value of steamships. "You make a valid point, sir. Some cargo could benefit from the faster steamship. There is a clipper design that has been noted to bypass even a faster steamship. The record for the ship surpassed the fourteen knots of the steamship. That clipper managed to snatch up some of the tea trade. We had a few ships built around that design and they have worked wonderfully with any cargo that requires a more speedy arrival." Liam continued to glare at him as he spoke. His eyes crunched up in disapproval and his lips pursed into a thin line.

"Okay, I admit I'm just getting more confused the more these two gentlemen talk. Tell me straight Torrington, are steamships a good investment?" Devon asked.

"The short answer is yes, and no." Torrington grinned.

Torrington had an amused smile on his face as he watched his son sit back in displeasure. Apparently Liam's attitude entertained him or it could be the volley of their conversation back and forth, Rand didn't care to know what that something was though. He just wanted to derail them before they ruined his investment possibility. Damn them and their advice. If they kept talking about the negativities surrounding steamships they were going to talk the earl out of investing, and Rand would be right back where he started.

"That doesn't bloody help me." Devon threw his hands up in frustration.

"That's because there isn't an easy answer to your question. Any new venture is risky. All signs point to steamships eventually taking over. There are a few ships that are built to be powered by both steam and wind. We are having a few of those built to try out in our shipping line." Liam rested his hand on the table and tapped his forefinger on the polished wood as he explained, "The idea is that if coal runs out or becomes too expensive the option to use wind is still available and not all will be lost in the voyage. It will probably be a few years before we branch into a ship completely powered by steam."

"So you both do not believe steamships are the sound investment right now?" Heat began to dissipate through Rand as his anger reached a boiling point.

"In the future yes, but now it is still risky," Torrington said. "They are making a lot of progress in their designs, but they all have flaws. I'd go with what is a known quantity."

Rand unclenched his fists and wiped his sweaty palms over his thighs. His lips pursed in displeasure as he considered how to proceed. He couldn't erase the irritation from his voice as he spoke. "And yet you are still willing to try out a glorified clipper ship that could also be powered by steam?"

"Yes." Torrington continued with a bit of mockery in his voice, "I did say I leaned towards clippers at the beginning of the conversation."

Damned Englishman, and their perverse ways.

The conversation was spiraling out of control. Rand tried to steer the conversation in the direction he wanted, but they were relentless in their opinions. He curled his fingers into fists underneath the table and refrained from smashing them against the polished wood.

"I'll admit there is a certain beauty about clippers, but let's be realistic. The popularity of the ship has faded a lot over the past twenty years. The ship isn't seen in quite the same light as it used to be."

"So do you recommend investing or not?" Devon asked as he turned his attention once more on Torrington. "I need to give the man an answer."

Torrington looked at Devon and shrugged his shoulders. He looked him directly in the eyes as he spoke. "Honestly, it's up to you and how much of a risk you are willing to take with your money. It isn't a bad investment. No matter what, eventually you will make money." Torrington picked up his drink and took a quick swig. He set his glass back on the table and scanned the table before his eyes landed on the Earl. "To put it simply, Devon, it depends on the market and how well the cargo is managed. I did look over his plan and RandCo has been steadily gaining in capital. It just hasn't been at a rapid pace. Expanding at this juncture requires more money and it's not gaining enough on its own."

The more they opened their mouths the more irritated Rand became. He couldn't believe the gall of these men. They were talking around him instead of including him in the conversation. He had to force his way into it in order to be heard. He built RandCo all on his own. Yes, the progress had crawled at the pace of a snail, but the growth remained true. It might take him longer than he wanted it to, but he could continue to do it on his own. He'd be damned if he remained sitting here taking their distain and disapproval.

Rand forced his way into the conversation. "Good of you to give the stamp of approval on my business, Ol' Chap. Why don't I save you all the time and just say that the offer is off the table. I don't especially like being discussed like I'm not here."

Liam began, "We didn't mean to imply—"

Rand interrupted, "Save it. You act like I don't know a lick about business. I built this company all on my own without your expert advice. I can continue to assemble it without your money too, Devon. I admit the boost probably would have made expanding easier. I just don't like the strings that extra help apparently comes with."

He looked over and found Torrington studying him as if trying to ascertain his origin. He must not have a lot of experience dealing with Americans. He knew he could be a bit brash and defensive at times, but he had no desire to change.

"A bit hot-headed, aren't you." Torrington raised his eyebrows at him and a quirky smile lifted at the corners of his mouth.

"A product of where I happened to be raised, I suppose." Rand shrugged.

Torrington laughed before saying, "In America? Yeah, I suppose that could be the explanation. From my experience most of you could take a bit of lessons on diplomacy."

"And you all could learn to be more accepting of the differences in all men," Rand retorted.

"Down puppy. I meant no offense. My wife happens to be American. She can be a bit...stubborn at times. Don't do anything rash," Torrington reasoned.

Rand had to admit that little tidbit amused him some. Torrington's wife must be an exceptional woman to put up with his arrogance on a daily basis. It would be interesting to meet her and get a more in depth look at her character. "Your wife's American?

What state did she hail from? Maybe I know her family."

"Doubtful as they all died a number of years ago. Her plantation is being run by an overseer at present. It's located in Charleston, South Carolina."

"I never knew that," Devon stated.

"Yes, we're lucky it survived the War Between the States. She left shortly before the war broke out and sailed to France to live with her grandpere," Torrington explained.

"How ever did your plantation manage to survive the war?" Rand had to admit that he found it interesting that they had a plantation in Charleston that survived the war. A lot of the plantations had been burned to the ground by the Union army.

"Luck mostly." Torrington leaned back in his chair. "The union army decided to use it as a hospital. My wife, Pia, told her overseer to remain as neutral as possible and that allowed for a certain amount of leniency from both sides of the conflict."

"Well if we're done discussing business how about a bit of pleasure?" Devon asked.

"What do you have in mind?" Torrington questioned as he leaned forward and rested his hands on the table. "I have plans with my wife this evening and can't be drawn into anything too extensive."

"How about a game of whist?" Devon asked.

"I have to be back in a couple hours to take Lily to that ball." Liam looked at his father as he spoke.

Torrington nodded. "Good point. Lily has a temper and she isn't afraid to use it. Best if you're not late. Why don't you take the carriage home and send it back for me."

"I can always give you a lift back, Torrington," Devon offered. "Although I'm supposed to go to that blasted ball tonight too. Gemma is expecting me to escort her."

"As much as I hate to admit it, I think we'll have to attempt more amusing pursuits at a later date. Maybe tomorrow night?" Torrington looked to Devon for confirmation.

"Splendid idea." Devon nodded his affirmation. He turned towards Rand and asked, "Collins, you want to go to the ball?"

"Can't say I've ever been to a ball before. Sounds fun. I have a few days before I sail back home. It could be a nice diversion." Rand had been watching them discuss their options for entertainment. It resembled a pugilist in the ring; they volleyed shots back and forth at each other and danced around any real issues. If he hadn't been so irritated, he'd be a bit more fascinated by their way of speaking to each other. He never had any desire to go to a ball before, but he could add it to his once in a lifetime experiences.

"Good, good. Then just come with me to my townhouse. My valet can help you get ready and you can help me escort my daughter, Gemma."

Rand got up to follow the earl out of his club. He nodded at Torrington and Liam. "Nice meeting you gentlemen. Perhaps we'll see more of each other before I depart."

Pompous jerks. His real wishes didn't even come close to wanting to see them ever again. He knew he'd see them at the ball later that evening, but hoped it would be the last time he ever laid eyes on them. They single-handedly made him restructure his whole plan for expanding his business. He didn't hold them in any high esteem. The meeting did not go as he intended it to. These men and their grand ideas, or lack thereof, had made sure of that. No, what he felt for them bordered on hate. He had to deal with uppity men who believed they were better than him his whole life. A person didn't grow up in an orphanage without having some lasting internal scars. The emotional distress the high class brought out was deep rooted and he couldn't let go of it easily. In his experience they didn't give a damn for anyone, but themselves. These individuals were not different. If he never saw them again he might be able to forget their existence.

CHAPTER 3

*L*illiana sat down at her vanity table and put the finishing touches on her hair. She did very well getting herself ready without a maid of her own. Having to depend on anyone for assistance went against all of her ideals. She had been ordering dresses that were easy to put on herself since before her come out ball three years prior. It had taken her a while to learn how to do her own hair, but like anything she put her mind to she excelled at it. Today, she wrapped her ebony curls partially up in a chignon with a few curls falling down to frame her face. Satisfied with her handiwork, Lilliana stood up and stepped into black satin shoes. She stopped wearing light colors when she decided never to marry. Young girls wore pastels. While they didn't have much choice in the matter, she certainly did.

Society dictated that if a lady remained unmarried they needed to appear more demure. One of the ways to convey that distinction to the world was in the color of their dresses. A year ago Lilliana decided she that she would no longer wear such hideous colors. White and pink did nothing for her complexion. She needed bolder colors that enhanced her looks. So she convinced her mother to allow her to wear something more suited for her. After a long heated debate she won and had more flattering colors for her wardrobe. She reached down and smoothed the skirt of her cobalt ball gown. The blue gown enhanced the color of her eyes and enhanced their appeal. She had fallen in love with the color and fabric when she visited the modiste a few weeks ago. It made her happy to be able to finally show off the creation at a ball.

Lilliana loved to dress up and attend parties. It made her feel special and beautiful. Not to mention how fun it was to be able to dance and laugh with her friend, Gemma. She may not want a husband, but she still knew how to enjoy herself within the expectations set by the ton.

Lilliana grabbed her gloves and left the room. She walked down the stairs just as her brother walked in the door.

"Oh good, you're ready to go," Liam said.

"Did you doubt I would be?" Lilliana raised her eyebrows at her brother. "I'm always prompt and you know it."

They were twins, not that you could tell by looking at them. They each had very distinct features. Lilliana looked at Liam noting how much his coloring favored their mother. She couldn't help wishing once again she favored her mother instead of her father. They may each take after a different parent, but one thing remained true; a Marsden didn't take it well when someone ordered them around. Liam had a more diplomatic personality, but even he had bursts of temper. Liam managed to hold on and fight battles he believed were worth the energy needed to expend in order to win them. When he happened to be in a rage though, it was best to clear the room because he exploded when he couldn't hold his anger in.

"I'm aware of your tenacious attitude. I'm always prepared for a battle when I have to deal with you," Liam declared.

"Nonsense. I'm the epitome of graciousness." Lilliana flashed Liam a wholly wicked, gamine smile.

At her pronouncement Liam began to laugh. His chuckles bounced over the walls and boomed loudly throughout the entrance hall. The color of his face became bright red as he gasped for breath. Lilliana moved past him to wear her pelisse hung by the door. Early spring in London still held a chill, and she didn't want to be cold as they traveled to the ball. After she had the pelisse securely around her shoulders, she turned back to her brother. His laugher slowed down to a light gurgle as if he attempted to rein it in.

"I don't see what you find so funny, little brother."

"You are never gracious. You're a demanding wench, and you know it," Liam retorted.

Ignoring him, Lilliana strolled towards the entranceway. They walked out of the front door and into the awaiting carriage. Lilliana waited for her brother to be seated before she replied to his taunt. No reason not to be comfortable for the upcoming disagreement.

"No need to be mean, I can be nice. " Lilliana tilted her head. "If it serves my purpose."

"Lily dear, you don't do nice. You scheme and cajole your way into everything. No worries, I love you and wouldn't have you any other way. It's part of your charm." Liam flashed her a smile that mirrored hers. He could look positively wicked at times.

"You're just trying to suck up now for acting like a bird-wit."

"Awe, that's a bit harsh. I'm never thoughtless. You know that," Liam told her.

"Then explain your actions just now?" Lilliana raised her eyebrows in question."'Cause you generally don't act like an arse."

"I met an interesting American today. His comments grated on me a bit."

Lilliana's interest piqued at his comment. She couldn't tip her hand too much, or he'd latch on to her questioning and ask some relentless ones of his own. They were fairly close and often sensed things about each other. Liam knew her too well and probably would figure out before anyone else what her actual plans were. She couldn't allow that to happen for any reason. He would do everything he could to stop her from traveling to South Carolina.

Besides leaving Gemma, she would miss Liam a great deal. If anyone could persuade her to abandon her plans, it was her brother. So she began her questions remaining as neutral as possible.

"What did he do to irritate you so much?"

"I can't pinpoint it exactly. I think it was basically centered around his attitude. He had a penchant for rudeness."

"Sounds like an interesting chap. Any chance I can meet him?" Lilliana inquired.

"For what purpose? You aren't going to start some kind of feud with him because he was annoying, are you?" Liam questioned.

"Please." Lilliana raised her eyebrows. "What kind of person do you take me for?"

"The kind that enjoys trouble a bit too much."

Liam did have a point—she enjoyed getting people riled. She often said things just to see what kind of reaction she could get out to them. It amused her to no end how often they fell for it. This time though she really did want to meet the American. He must have arrived in England by way of ship and chances were he'd know the next ship sailing back home.

"You know me too well. I don't like people that aggravate my family in any way." Lilliana agreed.

"No worries, he didn't bother me that much," Liam replied, "but if you really want to meet him then you will have a chance tonight."

"Really? Why is that?"

This was going rather easy. Almost too effortless, and maybe she should take that into consideration, but Lilliana believed in taking risks. She needed to know why he was going to be at the ball. Any information about him would be useful in gaining his trust and help in obtaining the necessary sailing schedule.

"He is the guest of the Earl of Devon. He is attending the ball tonight with his family."

"Oh, poor Gemma."

"What the bloody hell does Gemma have to do with it?" Liam inquired.

"Well, isn't it obvious? As the guest of her father she'll have to put up with his rotten attitude more than we will." Lilliana explained.

"I'm sure your friend will be just fine. If not, you will come to her rescue like you always do."

"I don't get why you don't like her that much. She is the sweetest girl. You should try and get to know her a bit."

Lilliana could see Liam's frustration as he ran his hands over his face. No doubt learning the business had started to take its toll on him. She knew their father could be demanding and expected a lot out of his children. Perhaps she should go a bit easier on him. His stress levels had taken an all-time high when he started to take on more responsibility. He needed to learn it all so that one day he'd be in a position to take control.

Lilliana wanted to believe her parents were infallible, but she knew that someday they would no longer be with them. Their father realized it all too well. He lost his parents at a young age and hadn't been prepared to run the business on his own. So for that reason he started to teach Liam everything he needed to know as early as possible. Viscount Torrington didn't want his son to be taken by surprise with the responsibility of the estate and many businesses in his holdings.

"I'm sure she is delightful. I don't have time for her kind of amiable right now." Liam stared at her with derision in his eyes as the sarcastic reply left his lips. Something about Gemma bothered him, but Lilliana didn't know what. He always seemed to want to avoid her and he made every attempt to do so.

"What's that supposed to mean?" Lilliana asked. She sat up and stared at her brother anger simmering through her, making her cheeks feel heated. It offended her that he found Gemma so unworthy.

"Don't take that tone with me. Nothing against

her, but you know she wants to get married. I see the stars in her eyes and I'm not that guy. I wish she'd quit looking at me like that. It will be a number of years before I even consider getting leg-shackled."

Oh, she got it all right. Her friend didn't compare to his expectations, and somehow he had gotten the notion she sought his attention. Maybe he saw something she didn't when looking at Gemma or it could be he was projecting his own ideas onto her friend. It might not have anything specifically to do with Gemma, but more what she represented to him. Liam had a lot on his mind and marriage didn't top his list of priorities. Lilliana didn't think that Gemma had set her sights on any one in particular. Sure, her brother exhibited a handsome face, but even Gemma had to realize his youth played a part in his reluctance to get married.

"I'm sure you're wrong about her. Yes, she does want to get married. She looks at everyone. You're around me a lot as my chaperone and she'd be a fool not to notice you. Nothing more than that." Lilliana flipped her hand nonchalantly. "I know you have your own resentments, but you have to remember she didn't have anything to do with what our two fathers originally planned. Besides, she hasn't settled on anyone just yet." Lilliana looked into his eyes pinning him with a glare. "Be nice."

The carriage stopped, and Lilliana looked up to see a footman holding the door open. They finally arrived at the Silverton ball. It was now time to start putting her plan in motion.

"I'm not going to argue with you, Lily. Let's try to have some fun at this function tonight," Liam suggested.

Lilliana smiled at his offer of peace. "I don't want to argue any more than you do. Let's go inside and see who's in town to enjoy this ball." She planned on having lots of fun at the social gathering. The first thing she wanted to do involved garnering an introduction to her brother's American foe.

They stepped out of the carriage and walked up the steps to enter the Silverton residence. Lady Silverton always hosted the best balls each season; Lilliana hoped that this one proved to be just as wonderful as the ones she had attended in the past. She knew at the very least she'd be a step further in her plans to go to America by the end of the ball. She hoped that the man she sought out could answer all of her questions.

"By the way what is the name of the American that you didn't like too much?" Lilliana asked.

"Why? I thought you decided to leave him be?" Liam asked.

"I never agreed to any such thing. I need to make sure he is an okay fellow to be around Gemma."

"Ah I see, I suppose that makes a bit of sense. His name is Randall Collins."

"Good to know. I like to have as much information as possible before I meet someone."

"I'm surprised you're not interrogating me for more details."

"Why? Is there something else I should know?"

"Nothing I can think of. I doubt you will have to worry very much though," Liam replied.

"Don't concern yourself with what I worry about, but why do you believe I won't have to?" she asked.

"He owns his own shipping line. He said he only planned on being in England a few more days before he set sail for home."

That had to be the best news that she'd hear that night. Lilliana carefully schooled her face to remain blank. She didn't want to give away how much his statement excited her. He owned his own ships! Surely she could talk him into allowing her passage on one of them. Lilliana wanted to rub her hands together with glee, but knew the action would only raise more questions. It took everything she had to physically restrain herself from making her hands do the motions.

"Oh good. Maybe I'll leave the man alone then."

"Somehow I doubt you will," Liam muttered.

"You have no faith in me."

"I have lots of confidence in you," Liam told her. "I just also happen to know you too well."

"I know." She sighed. "If you want you can go find one of your friends to talk to, I'll be fine. I'm going to probably be with Gemma all night anyway."

They walked into the ballroom after they were announced. Liam scanned the room and spotted someone he wanted to talk to. He nodded at them and strolled over to their side. Lilliana scoured the ballroom looking for her best friend. Drat, it looks like they haven't arrived yet. She'd have to bide her time and remain calm until she got her chance to accost Randall Collins for information. She walked to a chair and sat to await their arrival. She tapped her fingers on the arm of the chair. Many people believed that patience was a virtue, but the concept escaped Lilliana. She never did understand why she should be made to wait. Perhaps her actions could be construed as spoiled, but she liked to think of them as exacting and necessary. The night would be long if she had to sit here anxious for the Devon party to arrive. The American captain held the final detail to tie it all together. He needed to arrive and soon. If his ship held the capabilities to transport her to her desired destination, she'd unleash all her charm on the man. He wouldn't know what hit him. Lilliana always got what she wanted.

CHAPTER 4

"*A*h we're here," the Earl of Devon said. "The worst part about these functions is waiting in line to get out of the carriage."

Rand agreed with the earl's assessment. Nothing compared to the atrocious confinement he'd been subjected to with the earl who talked too much and his daughter who could barely string two words together.

"Well at least we can finally get out of the carriage and stretch our legs," Rand said.

They each stepped out of the carriage and walked up the steps. Rand followed the earl and his daughter as they entered the residence. So far he believed the choice to attend the ball ranked near the top of his list of his worst decisions. He hoped his opinion of the situation proved to be wrong once he actually made it inside and experienced the event itself. After the announcement of their arrival, they walked down into the elaborate ballroom. It appeared as if anyone and everyone had shown up for the ball. The possibility they were amongst the last to arrive occurred to Rand as he tried to follow the earl and his daughter through the crowd. Once they got to the far side of the ballroom, they stopped walking and turned to look at the guests dancing on the ballroom floor.

"Quite the turnout, isn't it?" a voice asked from behind Rand. He turned to see a beautiful woman with black curls floating around her heart-shaped face. Her full lips formed a crimson bow as they tilted up into a pleasant smile. For a brief moment he stood still, stunned at her appearance. In those brief moments he realized the lovely young woman came over to speak to the earl's daughter.

"Oh good, I thought it would prove impossible to find you in the crush of people here." Gemma gave the girl a quick hug.

A lighthearted laugh floated from within her and it seared Rand's soul. The night improved considerably with her appearance. Maybe the decision to come hadn't been the worst one he'd ever made after all...

"You doubt me?" she asked. "What is it with people doubting my abilities tonight, first my brother, and now you. Have faith in me please."

"Of course not! I would never doubt you. It just took us forever to arrive. I despaired at the idea I might not be able to spend any time with you. Have you danced yet?" Gemma inquired.

"Yes, I have danced. You know my card doesn't stay empty for very long, I have lots of names on my card. It's nearly full." She waved her card at Gemma with a triumphant grin on her face.

Rand stood there waiting for the forgetful chit to introduce him to her lovely friend. He hoped to add his name to her dance card before it filled up. By her last statement he believed he would be too late unless he acted fast, he prayed she would agree to add his name to her card. Her eyes glanced over and locked with his.

"Do I know you?" she asked.

"Oh how rude of me. I'm sorry I should have introduced you." Gemma apologized.

Yeah, she should have. Her youth exploded out of her every time she opened her mouth. Hopefully she matured as she got older. Otherwise her future husband may have an annoying female to deal with. She didn't matter to him though, his eyes remained glued on her friend.

"Mr. Randall Collins." Gemma gestured toward him. "Please meet Miss Lilliana Marsden."

Finally a name to go with the beautiful creature! It suited her perfectly. Her features rivaled any lily he had ever had the pleasure to see. Indeed, she was an elegant flower expertly cultivated and pleasing to be around. He really needed to hold her in his arms even for a brief moment. The introductions were made perhaps now he could entertain the possibility of dancing with her.

"Nice to meet you, Miss Marsden," he said.

"The pleasure is all mine, Mr. Collins," Lilliana replied. "You're not from around here are you?"

"No I'm not, I'm actually from America. South Carolina to be exact," Rand explained.

"Really? That's interesting. Lilliana has ties to South Carolina." Gemma jumped into the conversation as she relayed that interesting tidbit of information.

Rand turned his attention to Gemma and stared at her with little interest. He had forgotten the little mouse still stood by them. As soon as he had Lilliana's attention, Gemma became nonexistent.

Her father had abandoned them both a while ago; Rand had no clue where the earl had disappeared too.

"I didn't know that, but of course we did just meet," Rand replied. "Where in South Carolina do you have ties?" Rand turned his attention back to the enchanting Lilliana.

"Charleston. Do you reside near there?" she responded.

"I actually reside in a nearby town, Beaufort."

"Oh, that's lovely. I have only visited South Carolina once. We sailed over when I was a child to check on the property held by my family. I'd like to see it again someday." Lilliana's voice had a whimsical tone as she spoke. A faraway expression clouded her eyes as she appeared deep in thought. After a few moments she shook her head and gave her attention back to Rand. "Are you sailing back soon?" she asked.

"In a few days I am heading home," he replied. "There hasn't been a whole lot in England to inspire me to stay."

"Nonsense." Lilliana smiled. "There's a lot in England that is absolutely stunning. You're just not inclined to give it a chance."

Rand found himself smiling back at her,

absolutely enchanted. A more charming female did not exist, at least one he had ever met. He must dance with her soon. Rand really needed to garner any chance he could to touch her, no matter how brief.

"I heard you say that your dance card had yet to be filled. Any chance I can add my name to it?" he requested.

"Oh." Lilliana looked at her card and chewed on her bottom lip. "I don't know I had hoped to spend some time with Gemma."

"Please." His eyes begged her to accept.

"Oh, all right, let's see. I suppose you can have the next dance. It's a waltz. Is that okay?"

"I have no problem with that," he agreed.

A half-smile formed on his face. He couldn't have been happier with the outcome if he tried, and a waltz would allow him to touch her more that he had hoped to. He couldn't wait to hold her in his arms and have her full attention.

"Gemma, you don't mind, do you?" she turned and asked her friend. "Maybe you can find a dance partner too."

As if on cue a male walked up behind Lilliana and said, "Are you staying out of trouble, imp?"

Rand looked up to see his nemesis from the

earlier business meeting standing by Lilliana. He had no clue who Liam actually addressed with his statement until Lilliana spoke.

"Oh bother," Lilliana's annoyance came to the surface with her statement. "I'm being good. Go find someone else to interrogate." Lilliana grabbed his arm to prevent him from leaving. "No better yet stay. You can dance with Gemma. She needs a partner for the next dance."

Liam looked disturbed at the idea of dancing with Gemma. Not that Rand could blame him either. Given the choice he'd choose Lilliana every time. The little mouse seemed to become even more demure in his the presence of Liam Marsden. She withdrew and appeared both happy and frustrated to have him in her presence. If Rand had more time he would probably wonder why she was displaying such a huge contradiction, but at that particular moment he really didn't care.

"Uh...sure, I guess I can."

"You don't have to." Gemma leaped into the conversation to dismiss the idea. "I know you don't like to dance."

"No, it's okay. I want to," Liam said.

Rand didn't believe him for a minute. He concluded Liam only placated the girl. Not for a second did he think the young man actually *wanted* to dance with Lady Gemma. A look of fear crossed over Liam's features before he masked it with a more congenial expression. He didn't care though because he got what he wanted out of the situation. Lilliana Marsden would soon be in his arms. Rand only thing he cared about getting her there.

Lilliana stepped up and placed a kiss on Liam's cheek just as the sounds of the music of the current dance ended. She had a bright smile on her face and her eyes glowed with happiness. "Oh, that's fantastic. I knew I could count on you."

Rand felt irritation grow inside of him at the sight of Liam, but he let it go as soon as Lilliana turned towards him and held out her hand for him to take in his. This was what he had been waiting for since the moment he turned to see her for the first time.

"I suppose that means it's time for the next dance," Rand stated.

"You're going to dance with him?" Liam scowled. "I'm not sure that's a good idea."

"I don't care what your opinion is, Liam," Lilliana said. "I want to dance and Mr. Collins offered. Go dance with Gemma and quit being a brooding chaperone."

He glared at her, but then turned towards Gemma and took her hands. Rand still holding Lilliana's hand in the crook of his arm led her out to the dance floor. Gemma and Liam followed them, and they began the waltz. Lilliana danced beautifully in his arms. She had a light step and floated around the ballroom floor.

"Can I ask you a question?" Inquisitiveness reflected in her eyes as she stared directly into his. She mesmerized him and held his attention captive with her own.

"You can ask me anything."

"Is it possible for me to sail back to South Carolina with you?"

"Pardon me?" Rand stared at her with befuddlement.

"I want to go live on our plantation in Charleston. My father is being difficult about it. I decided I would have to take matters into my own hands," Lilliana explained.

In that moment he realized exactly who she happened to be related to. It all clicked into place as he saw Liam dance by with Gemma in his arms. Lilliana Marsden and Liam were brother and sister. So that made her the daughter of Viscount Torrington. Rand knew he would regret it if he allowed her on his ship. The little he garnered about the man while he sat before him in the business meeting earlier told him a lot about the man. He had very high expectations and little time for dimwits. No doubt he would kill him for taking his daughter away from him. Liam, her devoted brother, would help his father accomplish the task.

"I'm not so sure that is a good idea." He looked down at her with wariness in his eyes. "Your father is a force of nature and your brother isn't far behind him."

"I don't care. I'm capable of making my own decisions."

"And you expect me to take on their wrath?" Amusement laced his voice. "I'm not sure I'm up to these lofty expectations you have for me."

"Absolutely." She wrinkled her nose up at him. "I think you're more than up for what I'm asking of you."

"So you actually want me to help you run away from home?"

"Well, when you put it like that... Yes, I do."

He would be every kind of fool to go along with her idea, yet he wanted to. If he took her with him he might have a possibility of winning her over. In England he didn't stand a chance in hell of getting her to accept him as her own. As soon as he laid eyes on her he knew he wanted her. The more he talked with her the more he liked the idea of holding on to her forever. As foolish as her idea appeared to be Rand knew it also happened to be the only opportunity he may get of actually having her.

"I suppose you have all of the necessary details worked out," he replied. "I'm not likely to have your male relations storm my ship and demand you back before we depart am I?"

"Trust me. I'm good at strategies. You just happen to be the last detail I needed to make it all work the way I wanted."

"Trust has nothing to do with it." Rand laughed. "It has more to do with self-preservation. I happen to fancy breathing."

"Don't be ridiculous," Lilliana retorted. "There isn't any reason to be so dramatic. My father isn't likely to kill you."

"Right. Because he is the personification of civility."

He watched her blink several times as his words sank in. How bad of a temper did Viscount Torrington actually have? Rand watched as she mulled over his words. Perhaps he had misunderstood the viscount. His impression of the man suggested he had a violent side. One he had no problem showing to the world if he deemed it necessary.

"Father does have a temper, but I still believe you have nothing to worry about," Lilliana explained.

"You said I happened to be the final detail in your plans." Rand sighed. "Were you waiting for me to show up?"

What were the chances the chit new of his existence before their introduction? No, it wasn't likely as he hadn't been in England that long.

"Not exactly, I had no clue you existed before today," she told him. "These plans have been in the works for a few weeks now."

"And yet I'm the very thing you need to make it all work. How is that possible?"

"Simple really, I need someone with a ship that is willing to transport me. I am hoping that person is you."

He wondered how far he could push her. The decision to give into her and take her on his ship had already been made. Lilliana just didn't know he already decided to let her come back to America with him, but only because it worked in his own plans.

"What do I get for my trouble?" he asked. "I'd be risking quite a lot to assist you with your scheme."

"What do you want? Money? I certainly can afford to pay for my passage."

Rand's lips rose into a cocky smile. He desired a lot from her, but at this point only one thing would do as payment. Would the lovely lady be willing to give it to him? He had nothing to lose and only one way to find out.

"How about a kiss?"

Lilliana looked stunned as she stared unblinkingly at him, and then just as suddenly she stopped dancing right in the middle of the dance floor. Her face flushed a pretty shade of pink as she began to move to the music again with him in the lead.

"How forward of you. I'm not sure I like your idea of compensation."

"It's a small thing, one little kiss. To be given to me at a time of my choosing." He leaned in close to her and whispered in her ear. "Are you afraid?"

Lilliana's breath sucked deep into her chest, and he could feel her slowly exhale it in little pants. Her pulse raced on her wrist beneath the palm of his hand and thrummed a small beat as he held it firmly in his grasp. A blush formed on her cheeks turning them a nice shade of pink, and her lips parted in anticipation. Her body's reactions suggested she had an interest in kissing him also. Would she take the bait and give him what he desired? He needed her to accept the proposal. Once she did he'd have her sailing with him in a few short days.

"All right, you have a deal," she agreed.

"Excellent. I will send information on where you can board the ship. I look forward to our voyage together."

He led her back to the side of the room when the dance ended and stopped next to her brother and Gemma. She looked up at him and smiled before turning her attention back to her friend. Rand nodded at Liam and sauntered away. He had some preparations to make before he could welcome her on his ship. Tonight, it looked like he was going to be preparing his ship to sail a tad earlier than he originally planned. Oh, but what an extraordinary reason to go through the hassle of making the trip a bit prematurely. He couldn't wait to have Lilliana Marsden on his ship, and in his world.

*L*illiana couldn't believe how easy everything started to fall into place. A note from Randall Collins arrived early that morning. His plans to leave had changed slightly. Instead of three days, his ship would sail back to North Carolina the next day. Excitement filled her as she realized it had all worked out as she planned. Randall Collins, with his unruly dark brown hair and mischievous hazel eyes, took her breath away. She didn't want to agree to a kiss as payment, but at the same time she anticipated it. He stirred feelings in her that she didn't know how to explain. So she decided to push it out of her mind. A lot needed to be done before she could leave with him.

She sent a note to Gemma to come visit her for

tea so she could wrap up that little detail. Gemma needed to be made aware of when her invitation to visit happened to be taking place. She also needed to get permission from her parents to stay a week or two at the Earl of Devon's country estate. Her father would be the hardest to persuade, so he sat on the top of her list of things to accomplish that day. She left her bedroom and walked down the stairs to his study. No time like the present to get that little tidbit checked of her to do list.

"Are you busy?" She knocked on the side of the doorframe and walked into her father's study.

Viscount Torrington sat behind his desk with a bunch of papers scattered across the top of it. His long dark hair tapered at the nape of his neck, but a riotous strand escaped and folded over the top of his forehead. His head rose at the sound of her voice and his blue eyes twinkled with delight.

"For my favorite daughter? Absolutely not." Her father rose to greet her.

"I'm your only daughter." A tiny giggle escaped her mouth as she crossed the room to give him a hug.

"That's a good thing too," he retorted. "I don't know if I could've handled two of you."

"Of course you could have." Lilliana gave him a mischievous grin. "I'm the essence of all that is good."

"Are you trying to trick me?" Viscount Torrington laughed. "I'm made of sterner stuff than those other fools you walk all over. What do I owe the pleasure of this visit?"

"Nothing much really, Gemma has to go back to her family's country estate for a week or two. She invited me to join her. It's my hope you'll allow me to go."

"I don't know if that's the best idea right now, Lily. Things are a bit busy around here at the moment," he explained.

"That's exactly why you should allow me to visit. Liam is busy learning the business. You can't expect him to keep escorting me to these functions. It's only the little season anyway. I don't need to go and it'll be nice to spend time with Gemma."

"What does your mother have to say?" he asked.

"I haven't spoken to her yet. I figured I'd approach you first. Please Daddy, let me go." Lilliana used her most coaxing voice on her father. She stuck her bottom lip out in a mock pout and batted her eyelashes at him expectantly.

"Thor, are you busy?" They turned as they heard a voice from behind them. "Oh, I didn't know you were in here Lily."

Her mother either had the worst timing or the

best. Lady Torrington strolled into the room with a questioning look on her face. Her pale blonde hair was perfectly coifed without a hair out of place, and her emerald green gown rustled as she made her way across the room to join her husband and daughter. Lilliana took a moment to envy her mother's beauty and wished once again she had been blessed with her coloring. Sometimes she hated her brother for getting the lucky genes. She could very well deter her father from allowing her to go to Gemma's. If only she had more time to talk to him before her mother interrupted. She needed to convince her father to allow her to visit Gemma's country estate. Her mother's timing may have interrupted her plans, but maybe she could salvage it somehow.

"Hello Mama," Lilliana said. "I stopped in to ask Father's permission to visit with Gemma at her family's country estate for a week."

"Oh? And when were you going to ask me?" her mother asked.

"After I finished talking with Father," Lilliana said.

"Pia, I just asked her if she already spoke with you," her father said. "I think it would be okay for her to have a small visit. As long as she isn't gone more than a week."

Lilliana could feel elation soaring through her. She rocked on her heels and hugged herself with joy. Apparently that small amount of time had been enough to convince her father to allow her to go. Thank God for small favors. She needed to be on that ship in the morning.

"I suppose that would be fine," her mother said. "When will you be leaving?"

"Tomorrow morning. The earl's carriage is going to stop by and pick me up. It's short notice I know, it's why I'm asking now so I can get my trunks packed."

"All right, I don't like that you are leaving so fast, but I guess I'm find it to be acceptable. Our social functions are pretty slim right now anyway," her mother said.

Lilliana threw her arms around her mother in a fierce hug. She loved her parents dearly, but they tended to be a bit overprotective. It shamed her to know that her leaving would hurt them, but she had to leave, her happiness depended on it. She truly believed she belonged in South Carolina.

"Thank you, Mama. I need the break and some quiet time with Gemma."

"What I don't get a hug?" her father asked.

"You already got a hug," Lilliana teased.

"What I don't rate a second one?" He raised his eyebrows at her statement.

"Of course you do," Lilliana said as she turned to wrap her arms around her father. "You deserve more hugs than I could ever give you, Daddy."

Her father squeezed her tightly in his embrace. Nothing compared to a hug from her father. It made her feel safe and loved. She meant what she told him. She could never give or receive enough hugs from him.

"Okay princess, I have work to do and some things to discuss with your mother. Go get packing or you'll never be ready to leave on time."

"I love you two, you really are the best parents, and you are right, I have a lot to do. Gemma is coming for tea soon as well."

Lilliana left the room with a huge smile on her face. The talk had gone a lot better than she hoped. Gemma would arrive any minute and she needed to pack. She doubted sleep would be easy tonight with all the excitement. As she entered the hall she heard the front door open and Gemma stepped inside. Gemma looked over at her and strolled to her side.

"Oh good, you're here," she said as she walked over to give her friend a hug. "Although I've already ordered tea and scones. Let's go into the sitting room and talk."

Gemma followed Lilliana into the sitting room, removed her pelisse and set it on a chair, and then sat on the settee. She turned and gave her full attention to her best friend.

"So what's the urgency?" she asked.

"He's leaving tomorrow. I need you to have the carriage bring me to the ship in the morning," Lilliana explained. "Everything will have to be stepped up a day. Can you manage it?"

"Of course," Gemma agreed. "It's a small thing to arrange to have one of our carriages pick you up in the morning. Are you sure you want to do this? I have to ask one final time."

"Yes, I do. I told you how much I needed to leave."

"I know, but Mr. Collins isn't exactly what I expected you to sail away with. He's a very handsome man. I don't want you to do anything you might regret later."

"Nonsense. I can handle Mr. Collins, besides I don't plan on getting married. Maybe a little fling is something I should consider."

"What?" Gemma's sanguine curls fell over her face as her emerald eyes widened in shock.

"Why shouldn't I know what passion is like? I don't need to save my virtue for my future husband if I don't plan on having one," Lilliana explained.

"There can be other ramifications of finding out what passion is besides losing your virtue, Lily."

"I'm aware of that. I didn't say I decided to experience yet, I'm only considering it. I need to make sure I'm okay with the possible complications first."

"Good, at least you are stopping to think about it first. I don't want you to make a mistake."

"I don't believe in mistakes. Everything we do is a life lesson. It is through those so-called mistakes that we learn and grow. If I decide to give myself to Mr. Collins, it will be a wonderful thing. I refuse to think of it as a possible error in judgment."

"I know you are going to do whatever you choose to do. I just hope that it's the right decision for your continued happiness. I only want what is best for you."

"I know you do." Lilliana acknowledged. "I'm truly going to miss you."

"I know, but you need to do this." Gemma's eyes held a hint of sadness in them as she gazed at her.

They turned when a maid brought in a tray with the tea and scones Lilliana had ordered. She carried the tray over to them and placed it on a table beside them.

"Do you need me to pour miss?" the maid asked.

"No, I can handle it. Thank you, Melly."

Melly curtsied and walked out of the room. Lilliana turned toward the tea and poured some into two cups and handed one to Gemma.

"Now that the details are settled, let's talk about a lighter subject." Lilliana said.

"What did you have in mind?"

"Oh, I don't know anything. What do you think of this weather we are having? Scorching hot one day and cold and rainy the next"

"That's England for you." Gemma said with a laugh.

The mood lightened and Lilliana sat back on the settee. She needed to enjoy one last afternoon with Gemma before she no longer could. She needed the memory to take with her and hold tight. As much as she needed to leave, it also occurred to her that she'd be entirely alone in her new home. If she could take Gemma with her, she would have included it in her scheme. It's too bad it couldn't be done, because Gemma's friendship held a special place in her heart.

CHAPTER 6

*A*fter Rand had time to think about this foolhardy plan he realized the sooner he left the better. He trusted Lilliana to have all the details set, but he didn't hold a lot of conviction that her father would not get wind his daughter's plans. If it had any chance of working they needed to leave with all due haste. So after he left the ball he went to his ship and ordered the preparations to set sail. After that he only had one problem left, he had a whole day to kill and no idea what to do with himself.

The day had been excruciating for him. He found himself pacing the length of the ship most of the day in anticipation of her arrival. Sleep failed to arrive that night and made him cranky while he waited for the sun to rise. In his note he told her to arrive to set sail after the sun had risen in the sky. It made him happy to realize she knew the importance of punctuality as he watched the Earl of Devon's carriage arrive at the docks. As she stepped out of the carriage, she raised her hands block out the sun as she got a look at his ship. Rand turned and motioned two deck hands to follow him as he wandered down the gangplank to greet her.

"A couple crew members are going to load your trunks on the ship," he told her. "We set sail in less than an hour."

"Good. I don't want to wait to set sail. I'm glad we are leaving immediately."

"If you follow me I'll show you where you'll be staying during the voyage."

Lilliana followed him onto the ship and below deck to the cabin she'd be residing in the length of the journey to South Carolina. The cabin was small, but he hoped she'd make do with the sparse conditions. Especially, since it happened to be the only cabin available for her use. He watched her walk into the room and take off her pelisse. She set it on the table and turned toward him.

"Thank you for allowing me to sail with you, Mr. Collins."

"Please call me, Rand."

"I'm not sure that's wise. It's entirely too informal," Lilliana responded.

"My ship's a rather informal venue." With a smile he continued, "Trust me, it's easier if you acquiesce to my request."

He watched as she mulled over his words. Rand hoped she gave in and called him by his given name. He ached to hear his name pass through her lips. Little informalities had to start somewhere. Giving her permission to use his given name helped to ease her slowly into his strategy of lulling her to his will. He had a plan of his own and he intended to succeed.

"All right," she said with a sigh. "If you insist, I will call you Rand. I still think it's a bad idea though."

"Duly noted, but I'm glad you are willing to give it a try regardless."

"I suppose if I'm to call you Rand, you must call me Lily. Only my closest friends and family do."

"I'm honored to be amongst that small circle of people. If you'll excuse me, I have much to do before we depart," Rand replied.

"Rand wait; I have one question before you leave."

He turned back when he heard his name; a

shudder rolled over him at the sound. The more she said it the easier it appeared to come out of her mouth. He loved hearing it and hoped to hear her say it for the rest of his life. It breathed life into him where none had previously existed.

"What do you need to know?"

"It's about the bargain we made."

He could see the hesitation in her words. Clearly she had been thinking about the payment that they agreed upon. Good, he wanted her to think about him kissing her and often, because he intended to do it more than she knew or expected him to.

"You mean the kiss you agreed to let me have," he responded.

"Yes. See I had more time to think about it..."

"I hope you are not going to go back on our bargain. It's not too late for you to go home."

"I have no intention of going back on our bargain. I'd like to modify it slightly, if you are willing."

"Okay, you have piqued my interest. How would you like to change our deal?" Rand asked.

"I make no excuses for my innocence. My upbringing demanded no less. What I'd like to do is rectify that with your help."

Surprised, he responded, "Are you asking me to take your innocence?" That couldn't be right, and yet he felt every inch of his body preparing to teach her everything she wanted to know. He hoped to God that she meant it because he wanted to be the only one she'd ever know. Lilliana belonged to him and in time she would realize it.

"I'm not sure exactly what I am asking of you. I just get this feeling when I'm close to you. I don't ever plan on getting married so..." her words trailed off. She started to pace in the small room her anxiety starting to show.

"You figure I'm as good as anyone in showing you what passion is all about," he finished for her.

Rand's stomach dropped as her words sank in. The pain, a sucker punch, he hadn't been expecting. At first he had no idea how to respond to her because her words were still floating through his brain. Never marry? He would work on changing her mind. As much as he wanted to teach her everything she desired. Rand knew if he did she'd never consider being his wife. There would be no reason to. She'd get all she wanted out of him and toss him aside in time. That didn't mean he couldn't seduce her to his way of thinking without actually sealing the deal.

"Yes," she said nodding in his direction. "I know its risqué, but I feel I can trust you."

"You shouldn't trust me Lily."

She stopped and stared at him as if she actually saw him for the first time. Her gaze rolled over him starting at his feet and resting at his eyes. With the intake of her breath he knew she saw the strength of desire in his eyes. She just didn't know the full extent of what he wanted to do with and to her. She'd find out one day, but not as soon as she liked.

"Regardless I do. Please consider what I'm asking."

"No."

"Why not?"

"Because you don't know what you are asking of me. I don't heel to commands," he countered.

"I don't understand. What do you want from me?"

"It's simple enough Lily." He crossed the short distance of the room, pulled her into his arms, and whispered in her ear. "I want everything."

"Then give me what I want." Lilliana's face was flushed, and her breaths came out in short pants.

"No. Things will go at a pace I set. I will not give into your demands."

"Why must you be so obstinate? You want me. Take what I'm offering you," she pleaded.

"Maybe I will, maybe I won't. In the meantime, I will take the kiss you owe me."

Rand tilted her head and leaned down capturing her lips with his. A small sound of surprise came out of her mouth, and he took advantage of its opening. He touched her tongue with his, and she innocently followed his lead. Their tongues intertwined as he gently glided his over hers. His lips caressed hers as he learned her taste. Her hands wound around his neck and her fingers ran with abandon through his hair. Rand lifted his lips and trailed them over her cheeks and chin in light kisses. He drew back and looked at her half closed eyes. When they fluttered open, he saw a hazy desire filling the blue depths, a need matching his. He placed a quick kiss on her forehead before he let her go. If he didn't put some distance between them, he wouldn't be able to stop. He would need to move slowly, if he intended to win her forever.

"That's enough for now. I must go." With a half-smile on his face he said, "Think of me while I'm gone." He turned and left before she could answer him.

That had gone a lot better than he planned. He didn't have any doubts about winning her. When he wanted something bad enough, Rand never lost. Winning Lilliana would be an enormous battle, and he hoped her own nature would work against her belief that marriage didn't work for her. In the meantime, he had a ship to get ready to sail and no time to lose. He marched up on deck to get going before he lost something he treasured more than his own life. Lilliana Marsden now belonged to him. Damn anyone if they tried to take her away from him.

As he reached the top of the deck he saw Lilliana trunks ready to be taken below deck at a later time. Rand walked to the stern of the ship and located his bosun and first mate.

"Is the ship ready to set sail?"

"Yes, Captain," his bosun answered. "Sal and Jim are going to take the lady's trunks to her cabin. Do you want us to lift the anchor now?"

"Yes. It's time to go home," he told them. "The sooner we get there to better. Give the order."

"Aye, Aye Captain" the bosun said and left to follow Rand's orders.

"Do you need us to do anything else before we leave Captain?" the first mate asked.

"No, we don't have any cargo this trip. Just make sure the navigation goes well. We have a good wind and should be out to sea soon. I'll be in my cabin if you need me. You're in charge for the time being."

Rand walked back below deck to his cabin. He

passed the closed door of Lily's cabin and for a brief moment considered knocking on it and kissing her senseless again. Deciding against it he continued on to his cabin. No reason to rock the boat just yet. A good seduction took time.

CHAPTER 7

*S*everal hours later, Lilliana stood in the middle of her cabin and crossed her arms over her chest. A mere kiss left her with feelings she never experienced before with anyone else. Rand told her to think about him, and she thought about nothing else. Phantom tingles grazed across the tops of her lips and she could almost feel the slight pressure of Rand's as they caressed her. She ran her fingers across her lips, trying to understand the emotions swirling inside of her. In her first season, she had allowed one of her many beaus to kiss her. It hadn't stirred any emotions within her, and so she tossed it aside as something she didn't really care to experience again. Perhaps she had dismissed kissing too soon. Rand clearly knew what he was doing, and Lilliana realized with the right person doing the kissing it could be quite enjoyable. It now held an appeal it never had before.

Rand generated the most wonderful feelings, and she wanted to find out where they all would lead. Perhaps he had been right in denying her idea of a more clandestine affair right away. A challenge just made things a bit more interesting. After his kiss, Lilliana knew she wanted to explore all of her options, and she intended to get her way. Plans could be adjusted to reflect necessary changes.

Marriage and forever had never been on her agenda. That desire hadn't really changed, but she had a small thought that perhaps she wouldn't mind having Rand around long term. She now desired him in a way she hadn't needed anyone else. Lilliana started to scheme in her head how to make him hers. Her life would be exceedingly different with him by her side. Perhaps she could talk him into living with her permanently without the benefit of marriage.

Her ideals adapted to include him in every part of her life. Rand could help her run the plantation in South Carolina. So far he appeared to be a good man, when he hadn't jumped at her offer she learned what she needed to know about the depth of his character. He told her not to trust him, but clearly she could. The man hadn't wanted to take advantage of her and refused to take her innocence. She just needed to find a way to get him around to her way of thinking.

A knock on the door brought her out of her thoughts. She strolled to the door and opened it. She found Rand leaning against the doorframe with a cocky smile on his face.

"Did you miss me?"

He wore an overconfident smile on his handsome chiseled face. His brown hair looked a bit ruffled from working topside of the ship. It caused Lily to want to run her fingers through his hair and feel it for herself. He stood before her as if expecting her to give into the whims crossing through her mind. Cocky bastard believed he had won her over already. Okay he had, but he didn't need to know that just yet. If they had a chance, some boundaries had to be set up and established in advance. She garnered that much watching her parents over the years. Her father knew exactly how far he could push her mother before her she exploded with temper.

"Not at all." Lilliana brushed him aside. "I've

been too busy to give you a second thought. Are you here for a reason?"

"Busy really? Doing what exactly?" he inquired.

"I started writing some correspondence I'll need to mail once I arrive in South Carolina. I'm going to have to let my parents know where I am eventually. I didn't dare leave anything at home to make them aware of my intentions."

"Probably a wise decision on your part. How will you explain to them your decision to leave?" Rand asked.

"I'll tell them the truth. They know I've wanted to live on the plantation for over a year now. I loved it when we visited as a child. I grew up in England, but South Carolina calls to my soul."

"Then why all the subterfuge?" Rand raised his eyebrow questionably.

Lilliana raised her left eyebrow at his question. "I don't know what you mean."

"You know exactly what I mean. If you love the property as much as you say why deny you the opportunity to visit. What are you not telling me?"

"Ah I see your point. Technically I'm not supposed to visit without one of my parents with me. I didn't want to give them a chance to deny me the opportunity to go. I have the better part of a year until I'm old enough to gain the majority to go on my own. Father didn't want to let his only daughter go off to another country just yet. He was adamant about my staying home as long as possible. We had many arguments about the issue."

"I can't say I blame him. If I had a daughter I'd probably be a bit overprotective myself."

Lilliana shrugged her shoulders and turned away from him. "Yes, well there's overprotective and then there's smothering. Father tends to lean towards the latter."

"Most fathers are," he said. "At least the good ones."

Lilliana turned back around and face him. "Probably, I just know how my father is. I love him, but he can be a bit...relentless at times. Probably stems from his pirating days."

"Wait, what did you say?" Rand asked with a stunned expression on his face.

"Oh, I must have forgotten to mention that to you. My father used to sail his ship the *Sea Rover* as Pirate Thor Williams. It's how my parents met."

"But he's a viscount." Rand's bafflement at her pronouncement was evident in his words.

"And he used to be a pirate. What's your point?"

"That it just doesn't make sense. How can a member of the English aristocracy have been a pirate?" He raised his hands showcasing his frustration.

"I'm not sure on the details." Lilliana shrugged. "They are a bit sketchy. It had something to do with my mother's grandpere and attempted murder. Suffice to say he had a long road back to claiming his title."

Rand began to rub his temples. Lilliana knew she had to tell him about her father's past. The possibility of him getting his own ship ready and coming after them remained high in her concerns. As far as she knew a faster ship than the *Sea Rover* didn't exist. Her father had been excited to make the necessary modifications to make the ship faster than in his pirate days. She hoped they had a good head start before he realized she'd boarded a ship headed to America.

"You are going to be the death of me," he exclaimed. "How long do we have?"

"I don't know what you mean?" Lilliana faked innocence at his remark.

"I mean how long before your ex-pirate father comes after you?"

"Um, well, I'm not sure. I guess it depends on

how long it takes him to realize I am not spending the week at the country estate of the Earl of Devon."

"I give it a day tops before he is getting his ship ready to set sail after us."

"I'm afraid you may be right," she agreed. "At some point they will see Gemma out in society and question my whereabouts. The only good news is that it'll take a while to get the *Sea Rover* ready to set sail. I happen to have overheard him say he planned to careen his ship. The rest of the fleet owned by Marsden Shipping is elsewhere earning their keep. We may have a while before he has access to a ship capable of coming after us."

"Really? How advantageous for you. No wonder you wanted to get on a ship heading for America as soon as possible," Rand retorted.

"I told you I had a plan."

"Indeed you did I just didn't realize how extensive the details were."

"I have always believed the details are what made the best schemes possible," Lilliana said. "I'm good at plotting and planning."

"I noticed," Rand said with a half-smile.

"You're not mad at me are you?" Lilliana leaned into him and attempted to cajole him into a more relaxed state.

Rand raised his eyebrow at her questioning her methods, but allowed her to lean her body farther into his. "Not at all, dear. I may have to readjust our course, but I think I can manage to evade your pirate father."

"He isn't a pirate anymore."

"My apologies, your *former* pirate father."

With a petulant smile she said, "You should apologize. He's reformed, mostly."

"Lilliana, dear I'll say one thing about you, things are never dull with you around."

So far things were going as planned. She adjusted the details to include winning over Rand, and he currently fell in line with each one. When she decided she needed him in her life, she realized she'd have to tell him all the family's dirty secrets. He'd taken the fact her father had been a pirate rather well in her estimation. Now to step up her plan to get what she wanted. She got a little taste of desire and craved more. She began to rub her hands across his broad chest and massaged her fingertips into his well-toned muscles. When she noticed his breathing change, she looked up into his eyes to get his full attention.

"Did you stop by for any particular reason?" she asked coyly.

He leaned down and his mouth grazed her ear. Lilliana shivered as his breath caressed her neck. He whispered, "I have many reasons for stopping in to see you."

"Name one," she replied.

"I'd like to kiss you again."

"What's stopping you?" Lilliana had trouble breathing. The pace of her heart quickened, and she became heated from being near him.

"The fact that you want it as much as I do." Rand took a step back. "I believe you are a closet wanton."

"I believe you just insulted me," Lilliana retorted.

"I would never do any such thing. I adore you. However, you are in a hurry to lose your innocence. I'm not sure you realize what you are ready to throw away. I'm trying to be a gentleman."

"Nonsense, I know exactly what I'm offering you. I never asked you to play the part of gentleman. Why not just give in? You want me as much as I want you."

"Your pirate father for one. If he catches up to us I'd like to say I left you unspoiled. It could very well preserve my life." Rand folded his hands over his chest as he looked at her.

"I don't believe you. My father has nothing to do with your intentions towards me."

"Maybe you're right, but what if you're wrong? Nevertheless, when or if I decide to make love to you it will be my decision. You've already given me consent to try. I'd rather it be at a moment of my choosing."

"I think you are being unreasonable." Lilliana pushed her bottom lip out into a pout at his refusal to give in to her demands.

"And I think you are acting like a spoiled brat."

Spoiled brat? How dare he? *That man doesn't know a lick about me and he referred to me as a brat and a wanton. Maybe I should just give him exactly what he believes me to be.* She stalked over to him and threw her arms around him, pulling his head down. Her lips crushed his breathing life into her frustrations. With each movement the constant turmoil of her emotions bled into the kiss, their tongues dueling for control. Lilliana pulled her tongue back in her mouth and bit down on his bottom lip. She kissed away the soreness with a gentle sweep of her lips to soothe the ache she created. Rand pulled her into his embrace, and her hands roamed through his hair to bring his head closer to hers. Rand groaned and put his arms around her so he could deepen the kiss. Finally, he was acting in a way that would lead to what she desired from him. After what seemed an eternity, Rand wrenched himself away from her and put some distance between them.

"Damn you woman. You drive me insane."

"Thank you, I do try." An impish smile formed on her face as desire flowed through her.

He laughed and continued to back away from her. It made her feel powerful to know the kiss had rattled him to the core. Yes, she believed that every one of her plans progressed nicely.

"I think I may have taken on more than I can handle," he said.

"Oh, you don't think you can handle little ol' me?"

"Not tonight imp. I only came down to invite you to dinner. You distracted me from my original purpose."

"Backing away in defeat then?"

"You can win this little skirmish love." He smiled. "But I promise you, I'll win the war."

"I guess we'll see about that." She gave him a searing look as she said, "I've never lost before and I don't intend to now."

"Well then its time you learned how to take defeat with graciousness."

"Grace is my middle name." She gave him a devilish smile. "I personify it."

"Touché my dear," he said. "I'll give you that much. Let's agree to disagree at this point. I need to eat, I'm famished."

"So am I, but not for food," she replied.

He groaned as he turned around and started to walk out of the cabin. After he crossed the threshold, he turned back around and looked at her. Her words had the desired outcome; Rand appeared to be struggling to get his emotions under control.

"If you decide you're hungry for real food, come up to the galley. I'm heading there now. Perhaps I'll see you later."

"Only if you choose to visit me in my cabin again." She threw the words at him to see what kind of reaction she could continue to garner from him. Battling with words was something she did rather well.

"I bid you goodnight," he said and walked away.

That little encounter had definitely gone in her favor, although he left a bit quicker than she would have liked. He called their battle of wills a war. When she told him she didn't intend to lose she meant it. If he wanted a war then he had one and he better be prepared for anything. In her limited experience she knew that everything happened to be fair involving desire and war. This confrontation of his included both and she planned on using everything in her arsenal to triumph. Lilliana liked nothing better than winning; after all she happened to be good at it.

CHAPTER 8

*R*and walked along the deck and took a
deep breath. The more time he spent in
the lovely imp's company the more power he lost
over the situation. Stopping by to invite her to dinner
a week ago had been a strain on his control. He
needed to rein things in a bit. Never in his wildest
dreams did he imagine a woman like her existed.
Lilliana Marsden's reckless behavior stirred his own.
The trip back home would be his undoing. He didn't
believe he could resist the entire three weeks it
would take to reach port. In order to keep his hands
off of her he had done everything to avoid her.
Retreat did not look good on him. Taking a step back
made it possible for him to look at things with more

clarity. He now had a plan of action and he intended to implement it soon.

"Have you been avoiding me?"

Rand could almost feel Lilliana standing behind him. He leaned on the ship railing to look out at the turquoise waves as they rolled across the ocean. He figured out she didn't really like being ignored and deliberately pretended he hadn't heard her. Keeping his gaze forward, he waited for her to explode.

"Damn you, answer me." The palm of her hand met his back with a resounding *thud*, leaving a trail of sharp tingles in its place.

He turned his head and looked over his shoulder. His gaze traveled over her from top to bottom. He noticed that she had not donned a gown, but had instead put on breeches and a tunic draped in a cuffed red jacket. He had to stop himself from growling in approval. In the sunlight, he could see the outline of her breasts beneath the white blouse. The breeches fit her perfectly, and he got a good view of her legs and hips. He ached to ask her to spin for him so he could also see how they fit her derriere. Instead he kept to his plan of indifference and acted like her presence didn't matter to him.

"Can I help you?" he asked.

"Yes, you can give me your attention."

"I didn't realize that attending to you had been made a requirement of allowing you to travel aboard my ship. I apologize if I am slacking in my duties," he said with a droll smile.

"Don't be absurd. I never demanded that you give me all of your attention. But I'm bored and I hoped you might want to spend some time with me." Her bottom lip lifted into a pout as she folder her arms across her pert breasts.

"I'm kind of busy right now. I doubt I'll be able to spend any time with you."

"Doing what? Ascertaining if the ocean might dry up this century?" Sarcasm dripped from every word.

"No need to get testy with me, dear," he said absentmindedly. "I am just taking a small break to enjoy the view. I love how the sun looks as it rises on the horizon."

"So what do you have to do that is taking all of your time?" she demanded.

"Oh little things, you know like sailing this ship. I'm to take over from the first mate in a few minutes," he explained. "Unless you'd rather I leave it to fate and let the ship roam wherever it wants to."

He couldn't help needling her. Her face flushed, and her eyes became a stormy blue; she was lovelier when anger overtook her features. He liked it almost as much as when her face glowed with passion. If he couldn't see his favorite expression on her face, he'd take the look of rage instead. At least it mirrored desire a little bit.

"Don't be ridiculous," she retorted. "I understand the necessity of steering the ship. I just didn't realize that you actually had a part in it."

Rand shrugged his shoulders at her response. "Well, I am the captain of the ship. It stands to reason I'd have something to do with how it is run."

"Oh, I thought you just owned the ship. You actually captain it as well?"

"I do on this one. The other ships in my line have captains I've hired to work with my company."

She walked past him to lean on the railing, stopping to look out at the wide expanse of the ocean. Rand got a chance to look at her from behind. He knew that he'd enjoy that particular view while she wore trousers, and the vision before Rand did not disappoint him. His hands itched to touch her, so he took a step back before he gave in to temptation. She turned around and looked up at him.

"So you leave often to sail your own ship?" she asked.

"I don't stay home that often. I haven't had a reason to," he replied.

"Do you even have a home of your own?"

"No, not really. I stay at a boarding house when I find myself in South Carolina. I didn't see the point of building a home when I'm rarely there. I make my living by sailing. I usually stick around long enough to do some accounting and once it's completed I order the ship ready to go out again."

"It sounds like a lonely existence," she said.

"I didn't notice it. I kept busy and I made money. It's all that mattered to me."

"You don't want a family of your own?"

"No. I didn't think I'd make a good husband. So I believed I made the right choice in devoting my life to building my shipping company," he responded.

"I don't believe you."

"What is there to doubt?" he asked. "My inability to make some woman happy or that I enjoyed my so called lonely existence?"

She stared at him as if trying to dissect his meaning. How could he explain to her that until he met her nothing else mattered? He found purpose in building his business. He had no family and no one that depended on him. That only left one thing for him to do with his life. He had plenty of ambition to spare, and he focused all of his energy creating something for him to believe in.

"I doubt both. I know you are capable of making a woman happy if you set your mind to it. No one enjoys a lonely existence. Why have you punished yourself with the belief you are better off alone?"

"I have no family. I don't know what it's like to be surrounded by people that love you. I'm not punishing myself. I'm living the only way I know how," Rand explained.

"How long have you been alone, Rand?"

"All my life. I never knew my parents. I grew up in an orphanage. I ran away when I turned ten and got a job on the first sailing vessel that would hire me. They told me my mother died giving birth to me and no one knew who my father could be. My mother named me before she took her last breath. No one could afford to keep me so they dropped me off at the nearest church. That is how I ended up in a home for boys."

"Have you ever considered finding your father?" she asked.

"No. I don't even know where to look. The only thing I have to go on is my mother's name. That doesn't exactly tell me who my father might have been."

"If you don't mind me asking, what is her name?"

"Emily Collins," he told her. "But as I said it doesn't help trace down my wayward father."

"I'm sorry," Lilliana replied. "I didn't mean to bring up something so sad. I'm glad you told me though. It explains why you are so comfortable being alone."

"You have no reason to be sorry, Lily. It is what it is. I don't have a problem talking about it. You are incredibly lucky to have parents who love you. Remember that when they come after you because you know they will."

"I do know it. No matter how much I don't want them to, they will. I know they worry about me. I only hope that once they see me they will let me stay," she said with resignation in her voice.

"Good. It will be easier if you realize that," he muttered. "I will leave you with that to think about. I need to relieve the first mate now."

"Can I come with you?" she asked. "I promise I won't bother you. Well at least too much. I'm just tired of my own company and you are the only person I know on this ship."

He thought about what her company would be like as he stood at the helm of his ship. Once the picture formed in his mind he couldn't let it go. He couldn't avoid her forever if he hoped to get her to want to stay with him. He figured he could fight his desire for her if he had something to keep his hands busy. There would be no harm in allowing her to keep him company as he kept the ship on course. His hands would remain damn near tied to the helm allowing him to refrain from giving into his baser instincts.

"Yeah," he murmured. "I don't mind if you keep me company. Follow me."

He turned away from her and began to stroll toward the wheel that steered the ship. As he approached, he saw the first mate keeping it steady and on course. He didn't know for sure if Lilliana followed him, but he figured she must have considering she asked to keep him company.

"I'm here to relieve you. Go get some sleep so you can take over later on this evening," he told his first mate.

"Aye, Aye Captain. I'm mighty tired. I'll see you later. Good day miss."

Rand turned and watched as the first mate bowed his head to Lilliana. She returned the gesture before joining him at the helm. She sat down on the deck, crossed the legs, and rested her back on the mast near the helm. Her hands rested on the deck as she leaned back to look at the sky.

"What is running through your mind?" he asked her.

"Have you ever looked at clouds and thought they reminded you of something?"

"No, I can't say I have."

"My brother and I used to play this game as children. We would lie down on the ground and watch as the big fluffy clouds floated by us. Sometimes they reminded of us of things in our lives: a bunny, a flower, or even a horse drawn carriage. It became one of our favorite games. When I looked up at the sky I remembered what a great childhood I had."

"Are you feeling a little homesick?"

"No not at all. I just wished you had even an ounce of what I had growing up. I had two adoring parents and you didn't even have one."

"I told you not to feel sorry for me, Lily. I'm content with how my life turned out."

"That doesn't mean that you shouldn't strive for more from life, Rand. You deserve everything, happiness included. You're a good man and you should have a little joy," she told him.

"I promise you I will," he said with a cocky smile. "It's just a work in progress."

"Good," she said with an impish smile. "In the meantime, I'll do my part in ensuring you continue to work on it."

He laughed and turned his attention back to keeping the ship on course. They sat in silence for an hour before she got up and stretched her legs. She walked over to him, wrapped her arms around his waist, and rested her head on his back. Rand enjoyed the feel of her arms wound around him. He could almost hear his heart drumming in his ears as it began to beat faster. He closed his eyes and absorbed the feeling. If he could he would turn around and hug her close to him, but he had to keep his attention on the helm of the ship.

In that moment he knew he loved her, because with her arms enveloping he let himself feel for the first time in his life. Rand had been alone his whole life. He didn't depend on anyone and didn't look to anyone else to fulfill any of his needs. Lilliana made him want things he never knew he wanted. With her he could feel himself lighten inside. He thought he didn't want anyone in his life until her. That need had been buried deep inside of him a long time ago.

"As fun as this has been I'm kind of tired. I'm

going to go lay down in my cabin. If you want me you know where to find me," she told him.

Rand nodded in agreement. "That I do."

He watched for a moment as she traipsed across the deck. Enjoying the view of her derriere in breeches one last time, he hoped she continued to dress in a similar fashion the rest of the voyage. He let out a small breath of relief once he could no longer see her. He had managed to keep his hands to himself and have a pleasant conversation with her. He only had to make it another two weeks and get her safely tucked away at her family plantation.

CHAPTER 9

*L*ily walked out of her cabin and up to the deck. Rand hadn't openly admitted to it but she knew that he had been avoiding her. Once she tracked him down he at least allowed her to keep him company. She hoped to further her agenda and get him to see how an affair would benefit them both. To be honest, she wanted more than an affair—she wanted him to be her lover for life. Marriage still seemed too risky of an endeavor for her, but the more time she spent with Rand the more she knew she needed him in her life. Her plans now included him at her side. She just had to find a way to make that happen.

She roamed aimlessly along the deck and stared out into the ocean pondering what the next step in her plan should be. Seduction could hold the key to achieving her goal. Perhaps it was time to discover where the captain slept. She could ambush him in his cabin and let things take their natural course. Rand had said if he wanted her he would do it at a time of his choosing, but so far that time had not taken place. Lilliana was beginning to get restless waiting for him to make a move. She did not do well sitting idly by waiting for something to happen. Her nature leaned more towards taking action and seeing what happened afterward.

Not watching where her feet took her she ran into a deck hand and fell back on her derriere. She braced herself with her hands and looked up into a pair of brown eyes and a concerned frown.

"I'm sorry miss. I didn't mean to knock you down," he apologized.

"No it's not your fault..." She realized she didn't know his name. She stared at him a bit bewildered; Lilliana hadn't bothered to get to know anyone on board the ship. It gave her an idea on what to do to not only gain Rand's attention, but also help to alleviate some of her boredom.

"Sal," the deck hand told her.

"What?" Did he just say something about sailing?

"My name is Sal, miss."

"Oh. I feel silly now. I thought you were talking about the sails."

"I never thought about that actually. Sal is just a nickname."

"Really? What's your actual name?"

"Salvatorio," he said with a grimace. "It's a bit long, but it's a family name."

"I kind of like it." She smiled. "Sal perhaps you can help me with something."

"I will if I can, but first let me help you up."

He held out his hand and Lilliana gave him hers. Sal helped pull her up so she stood beside him.

"Thank you."

"You're welcome. What can I help you with?" he asked.

"I'm going a bit stir crazy. Do you happen to play any card games?"

"I'm fairly good at whist. I could get a couple of other men to play a game with you. A few of us have some free time right now," Sal replied.

"Oh splendid. I just need to retrieve my cards from my trunk. Where would you like to meet?"

"We can meet in the galley. We have a couple hours before the next meal. After that we are back on duty."

"Good. I shall see you soon then." Lilliana nodded and walked off.

When she reached her cabin she dug through the trunk for her cards. She didn't think Rand would like the idea of her playing cards and entertaining some of the crew. The only thing she had uncertainty about was how to get him to realize she was embroiled in a game of whist with some of his deck hands. She hoped that he would just stumble upon them, and she could get both of her agendas accomplished. Locating the cards, she put them in the pocket of her trousers and skipped up toward meet them in the galley. She sashayed as she made her way to the galley with a huge smile on her face. When she entered the room she saw three men sitting at the table. Sal she knew from her little accident on the deck.

"Good you are all here. Introduce me to your friends, Sal," she demanded.

"This guy here with the hook nose is Jimmy and the scary looking one is Georgie." Sal introduced her to his two shipmates.

She raised her eyebrows at him. "Scary?"

"I'm harmless, I can't help how big I am," Georgie explained.

"All right then. Let's get started. I'll cut the cards

first to see who we partner up with." Lilliana began to shuffle the cards as she spoke. She cut the cars and drew a seven. The men followed suit and cut the deck to reveal a card. Sal drew an eight, Georgie a jack, and Jimmy a king.

"It looks like I'm partners with Sal. Do you mind if I deal first?" Lilliana asked.

"No, I don't see any reason why not." Georgie replied. The other two murmured their consent as well.

Lilliana sat down and began to shuffle the cards with dexterous hands. She placed them to her left to let Georgie cut them. She picked them back up and started to deal thirteen cards face down to each of them. After dealing all the cards, she flipped the top one over to reveal the trump.

"Hearts are trump gentlemen. Let's begin." She told them.

With a laugh they grabbed their cards and began to play in earnest. They played a grueling game for an hour before Rand found them. Sal and Lilliana were ahead, but barely. She was so engrossed in the game she hadn't realized he had walked in until he spoke.

"What are you up to?" Rand demanded.

She looked up into his eyes and smiled. "I think that's fairly obvious. We are playing Whist."

"Not a good idea. Time to break this game up. Sal, Jimmy, Georgie go see the bosun and report for duty."

"But we have an hour until..." Sal began to say.

Rand interrupted, "Don't argue. If you want to keep your position once we reach port you will follow my orders."

The three of them got up and walked away grumbling as they left the room.

"Was that necessary? We were having fun." Lilliana's voice filled with anger.

"Yes. I don't believe these men will over step any boundaries, but I happen to know that you want to lose that innocence of yours. I won't have you tempting them into doing something to jeopardize their livelihoods."

"Don't be ridiculous. I had no intention of propositioning any of them. I do have standards."

"Do you? You damn near accosted me the first day on the ship. How am I to know exactly what you will or will not do?"

"That's not fair. You are the only man I have ever asked that. I truly believed you would make a wonderful lover. Apparently I need to once again readjust my views. Clearly I was mistaken on your worthiness."

"Oh, so now I'm not good enough?" he asked. "Does that mean you are going to find another one of the men and ask them help you lose your innocence?"

Rand's face began to get red with each word he enunciated. His eyes shot daggers in her direction as he folded his arms across his chest.

"Maybe I should. You don't want me so what difference does it make who I give myself to?" Lilliana glared at him.

"I never said I didn't want you."

"Well, you sure fooled me. You keep avoiding me and definitely turn down every offer I make to you. You win, I give up."

Lilliana got up to storm away, but Rand grabbed her hand and spun her into his arms. She tilted her head to look up into his eyes. The lines of his mouth were tight as he pressed them together and stared at her.

"You can't give up. I won't allow it."

"It's not up to you to allow anything, Rand. You have no right to dictate to me."

He ignored her word and with tenderness lowered his lips to hers. This kiss was different as he coaxed her into yielding to him. Slow and gentle he caressed her in such a way her anger evaporated. A different kind of passion took its place. Heat spread through her and the kiss took on another level. It didn't take long before she ran her hands through his hair and pulled him closer to her. The kiss overtook them as they battled for control. Determined to win, Lilliana took a different strategy. In this war between them he had stepped back and took control of the situation. He always had the upper hand. That needed to change if she wanted to win. So as much as she enjoyed the kiss she knew it needed to end. In order for her to get him where she wanted him he needed to chase her. This game needed to change, and she knew how to make that happen. She pulled away from him and took a step away to gain some distance.

"You don't get to do that whenever you want, Rand. I rescind my offer. I don't want to be your lover anymore." She licked her lips. "The kisses have been enjoyable, but this just isn't working for me. Maybe you're right; I need to look into finding someone else to introduce me to the art of love making."

She saw the dumbstruck look on his face before she turned and walked away. Maybe now things would go her way. She hoped she didn't miscalculate in her scheme and he didn't do the opposite; her intention was to present him with a challenge. All she could do now was sit back and wait to see if he took the bait.

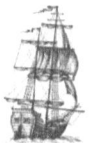

*R*and stood there and watched Lily walk away. Her beautiful derriere displayed nicely in her trousers. He wanted to cup her ass in his hands and pull her back into his arms. The more he saw her wearing men's attire the more he desired her. *Who am I kidding? I will want her no matter what she is wearing.* Damned if he didn't understand what the hell just happened between them? That kiss amped up things, and he wanted to strip all of her clothes off and just give in to her demands. He should be glad she halted things when she did, but all it did was leave him confused. No way in hell was he going to allow her to find another lover. If he had to give in to her demands first and convince her around to marriage he would. That plan didn't sit too well with him though. He wanted her to believe marriage between them was a good thing. Passion could be fleeting, and he wanted more than that with her. He needed her to love him as much as he had grown to love her.

He scrubbed his hands over his face and weighed his options. Perhaps avoiding her wasn't the best idea. Clearly she didn't want him to keep his hands off of her so he would just give her want she wanted. Short of the actual act that is, he still believed it was best to wait before making love to her. He believed they could be happy together and wanted Lilliana to be his wife. The best way to start changing her mind was to give her a little taste of what that future could hold. Once she started to crave him and what he could do for her it wouldn't take much for the rest of it to follow. With that idea in his head he decided to pay her a visit in her cabin. *Don't want me anymore? Well we will just see about that.*

Rand sauntered out of the galley and down to Lilliana's cabin. He rapped lightly on her door and waited for her to open it. When she did he couldn't help the slight intake of breath at the sight of her. Her hair was floating down her back in endless black waves. She still wore her trousers and tunic. Her blue eyes shined as she looked up at him.

"What do you want Rand? I thought we settled everything."

"You may have, but I'm not nearly done with you."

"Well that's a shame because as far as I'm concerned there isn't anything else between us. You can leave now."

She started to shut the door, but he stopped it with his hand. He pushed the door open and strode inside of her cabin. He shut the door with a quiet click behind him and turned the lock.

"What are you doing?" Lilliana asked.

"I believe we have a few things to discuss."

He stalked toward her. She took a few steps back to retreat from him. Tripping over her feet, she almost fell. Rand caught her, pulling her into his arms.

"This isn't a good idea." Lilliana said. Her breaths came out in small pants. A rosy glow started to form on her cheeks, and her eyes became glassy. All he did was hold her and rub her back gently with his fingers. He wanted her to become accustomed to his arms wrapped around her. They did need to talk before he demonstrated what he came to her cabin for.

"I'm tired of good ideas. I think it's time I did

something I wanted for a change. Starting with how much I want you. I refuse to let you give up on me...on us."

"I already told you..."

"You will not find another lover. You're mine."

"I belong to no one. You best realize that now," Lilliana said with conviction.

"No. You do. You belong to me. And I will tell you exactly why."

"Oh do tell this should be interesting," her reply scathing.

"Because no one else will ever be your equal and because I also belong to you. We are a pair and we belong together. No one else will do for me anymore than any other man will be for you. Stop fighting it."

"Right. Cause I'm the one that's been hiding and avoiding you."

"I'm done. I give up. You said I won, how could I have won, if I don't have you? I'm here and I will show you what it can be like between us."

"You're going to make love to me now?"

He could hear the surprise in her voice and he smiled. "Not exactly. We are going to take this slow. Passion done right is savored. I plan on enjoying every inch of you until you beg for mercy."

"I don't beg."

"You will," he promised.

Pushing her hair aside he caressed her cheek with his lips. Light kisses feathered across her forehead and nose to finally rest on her lips. He tasted her lips with his. Lilliana moaned and pressed her body against him and rubbed her breasts against his chest. He could feel himself harden as her hands roamed across his back. Reaching under her shirt his hand found her breast, and he pinched her nipple between his thumb and finger. He wanted to feel her everywhere. Spinning them around he pressed her against the door and lifted her up.

"Wrap your legs around my waist," he ordered.

Once he had her in the position he wanted, he lifted her shirt and placed his mouth on one of her rosy nipples, and Lilliana groaned with pleasure. He licked and raked his teeth over them until they were pebbled like tiny red berries. He started to rain kisses along her neck and then nibbled on her ear lobe. Her hands pulled at his hair and yanked the silky strands back so she could place her mouth on his. He swung her around, walked her over to the bed, and laid her down. Taking a step back he could see her face flushed with desire and heavy pants leaving her mouth. She sat there staring at him.

"What are you waiting for? Join me."

"No. This is all we are doing tonight. I told you I'm taking my time."

She picked up the nearest object and hurled it at him. It happened to be a heavy book, and he barely dodged before it smacked him in the head instead hitting the wall behind him with a loud bang.

"You are the most frustrating man. Just go before I cause you bodily harm. I hate you."

"No you don't," he said with a laugh. "That's why you're so frustrated. We will continue this at a later time. There are a few things I want from you before we take that final step."

"Too bad. You're not getting them"

"Oh I will. You will gladly give them to me too."

"No, not a chance in hell," she shouted.

"Oh yes, love. I will leave you now. We will table this discussion for when we make port. We should be arriving in South Carolina sometime tomorrow. Good night."

Rand turned and left her to think about his parting words. He would get her to agree to marry him when they arrived. She might not love him yet, but she would. He was willing to settle on passion for now.

CHAPTER 11

*T*he afternoon sun shined brightly in the sky and beamed down on top of her with brilliance and warmth. Lilliana looked out at the approaching land mass from the deck of the ship. When she decided to shirk her parent's mandates and travel to South Carolina she had never envisioned a journey quite like the one experienced for the past three weeks. Spending time with Rand and getting to know him had been a torturous experience. The man made her feel things she never wanted to feel before. She didn't believe loving any man was a good choice, but here she was letting that unwanted emotion wash over her. Still she didn't want anything of a permanent nature from him. She may have foolishly fallen in love with him, but her views on anything long term hadn't changed. Marriage was still out of the picture for her.

Rand's visit to her cabin the night before had left her hot and needy. She did everything she could think of to get him to succumb to her way of thinking. Nothing in her arsenal had worked in her favor and it might be time to concede defeat. Rand had an agenda of his own and it didn't mesh with hers. Now they were approaching the port of Charleston. Soon she'd be separated from him, never to see his handsome features again. He hadn't given in and become her lover, but perhaps there was a way to still make that happen.

He said he wanted to discuss something with her once they docked at port. There had to be a way to get him to agree to an affair, but she hadn't thought of a means of accomplishing that feat. So with a heavy heart she sighed the closer the ship came to port. No, this journey hadn't gone has she planned at all.

"Why do you look so sad?" she heard Rand say from behind her. "You're almost to your desired destination."

"I don't know what's bothering me. I feel like something good has ended." She wrapped her arms around herself as if to ward off a chill. "'There's this feeling of dread that has taken root deep down in my soul."

"It doesn't have to," he whispered in her ear.

She turned around to look into his eyes. Lilliana could see the same anxiety reflected back at her. Rand wanted her, and it appeared like he had some idea on how to make that happen.

"I suppose not," she said.

"I've been meaning to ask you something."

"What's that?"

She had always been a very curious person. Rand needed to get on with whatever he wanted to discuss with her. This hot and cold nonsense was starting to get on her nerves. He needed to just give in already or let her go.

"How do you plan on getting yourself and your trunks to the plantation?"

That's all he had to ask her? Disappointment flowed through her as she let his words crash through her heart. He hadn't wanted to find a way to spend time together. That didn't mean she couldn't find a way to make it happen. Lilliana had a strong will and determination that rivaled any army general. Never had she failed to achieve a goal she set for herself, yet she couldn't help feeling rejected.

"Oh that," she said without enthusiasm. "I sent a

letter on the mail packet before we left, letting them know of my arrival. If everything went as it should the overseer will have a carriage waiting to transport me."

"What will you do if the letter didn't arrive in time?" he asked.

"I don't know, I'm sure I'll think of something."

"Because you always do," he said with sarcasm in his voice.

"Precisely. I can take care of myself."

She watched as he rubbed his temples in frustration. Lilliana knew that she could be a bit vexing and understood his actions. Being aware of her faults did not endear her to his dilemma though; she had her own issues to deal with. Her nature did not allow her to give him any relief. He would need to find a way to work through his aggravation all on his own.

"All right," he finally said. "Let me know if the carriages arrives or not."

"Fine."

"I mean it Lily. I want to know either way so I can see you off."

"Because you care so much about my welfare," she said sarcastically.

"Are you trying to make me angry?" he asked. "I

do care about you and you know that. I also want to have a discussion with you before you run off, but I have a few things to take care of before I can have a proper conversation."

"I am just in a mood." Lilliana explained, "I won't run off without talking to you before I leave."

"I need to get back to my crew and help them with the ship. Do you need anything before I leave?" he asked. "Will you be all right if I leave you alone here?"

"Of course, don't be silly. I already told you I could take care of myself. It's not like I'm about to jump ship or something. Go do what needs to be done to dock the ship. I have a plantation to get to later today."

"Okay. I will find you later. Do not leave without seeing me first, promise me."

"I won't, I promise."

If she truly had to say goodbye, she wanted something to remember him by. A kiss she would never forget. They had already kissed a few times but, Lilliana knew she would never tire of kissing Rand. After the first one it had become her favorite activity. If another man kissed her, she knew it would not inspire the same feelings that Rand's did. No man would make her feel quite the same way.

Lilliana enjoyed watching Rand stroll along deck giving orders to his crew members. He had an authoritative tone in his voice, and they all jumped at his commands. She missed him already and their separation hadn't happened yet. However would she get by knowing she wouldn't see him each morning? A sting of pain hit her chest at the thought of never seeing him again. She couldn't explain the feeling in her chest. Could it be love? Did she go and allow herself to fall in love with Rand? Surely she hadn't been that stupid.

The ship docked at the port in Charleston, and they dropped the anchor. Once they secured the vessel Lilliana only had to wait for them to bring her chests from below. She had already meticulously packed her belongings securely in her trunks. Lilliana scanned the dock to see if anyone from the plantation had arrived to retrieve her. She wanted to get to her new home as soon as possible. No carriages appeared to be anywhere near the wharf. Her heart sank with the realization that she would need to find another mode of transportation to her family's plantation.

Either the letter hadn't made it to the plantation or they didn't have any real idea when the ship was expected to dock. She had only given them an estimation of when her arrival would be. Depending on the wind available ship speeds varied making it difficult to determine an exact time a ship might dock at port. Still even with only a broad idea of when to expect her they should still be waiting for her. The overseer would know to account for the variations and make the necessary adjustments. It might be an inconvenience to come and check each day, but that was one of his duties. That must mean the missive she sent got lost or delayed somewhere along the way.

"Did your transport arrive?"

She turned to see Rand standing behind her. Sometimes she thought he had the worst timing, or perhaps the best. He always seemed to appear when she needed his assistance most. After all she wouldn't have been able to sail to Charleston without his aid. It looked like she would now need him to help her find a way to her plantation.

"No. It looks like my message may have been waylaid," she replied.

"Don't worry about it. I had a feeling that this might happen. I will ensure you make it to your destination. It just might take a bit longer than you planned."

"How much longer?" she asked.

"A night perhaps, I will have to arrange for a carriage to take you to your plantation. In order to do that, I'll have to go to shore and hire one for the journey. I'm unsure how long that will take and I still have a few things to do on board the ship. You are welcome to stay aboard in your cabin or I can escort you to a local inn. If it's possible to take you this evening I will make sure you get there."

"No, don't rush on my account. I can handle one more night on board the ship if you don't mind. I think I'd prefer to stay in my cabin. At least I know what to expect from the accommodations."

It also might give her another opportunity to have Rand as a lover. He wanted to discuss something with her perhaps that was his plan all along.

"Good." He nodded in approval. "I would feel better knowing you are safely on board the ship. You never know what you will find in an inn."

"Thank you for helping me. I know you don't have to."

"Yes, I do. I would never forgive myself if something happened to you, Lily. Your well-being is very important to me."

"I suppose I should make myself comfortable in my cabin. I had hoped to go on land and see a little more of the country I am to call home," she said whimsically.

"If you are willing to stand my company I can take you on a small tour of Charleston when I go to arrange for a carriage. We will have to walk and will only be able to see the downtown area, but I think you will enjoy it. There is nothing like Southern hospitality."

"I'd like that very much," Lilliana said with a small smile on her face.

"Good be ready in an hour and we will go to shore. While we are out we can stop some place for a meal and finally have that conversation. There's something I want to ask you."

"What?"

"Not now Lily, later will come soon enough."

"All right. Come get me in my cabin when you are ready to depart," she told him.

He nodded in assent and walked off to finish whatever a captain needed to once they docked at a port. She admired his handsome face and commanding presence and couldn't wait to spend the afternoon with him strolling along Charleston's streets. Maybe somewhere along the way she would figure out how to spend more time with him. Of course that could be the very thing he wished to discuss with her. She had no idea what his plans included. Hopefully he had something in mind that would allow them to see each other again. Rand may be planning to sail again very soon. Lilliana wanted him to stay with her long enough for them to become lovers, finding a way to make that happen eluded her. No time to worry about what may or may not happen. Lilliana did have one thing to look forward to and focusing on the positive had always been instinctive for her. For now she would go down to her cabin and rest for the upcoming adventure. She had a new town to learn and fall in love with.

CHAPTER 12

*T*he culmination of Rand's life summed up to one thing, loneliness. That realization hit him hard when he discussed it with Lilliana while they were out at sea. Before Lily he had been blind to the reality his life had become. She breathed life into him. He hoped the journey from England to North Carolina had endeared her to him. He believed she wanted him, but was that enough for her to agree to be with him forever? She was an intrinsic part of what he wanted for his life. She held all of his wishes and dreams in the palm of her hands. He knew she wanted to live on the plantation, and he would do whatever it took to make that desire a certainty for her. So with nervousness coursing through his veins he approached her cabin door and knocked on it.

"Come in," she called from behind the door.

Rand walked inside at her bidding. She was sitting on her bed reading a book. Her black curls were falling loosely around her shoulders. Lilliana looked up at him, her blue eyes beaming with questions.

"It could have been anyone knocking. You should have at least gotten up to see who decided to rap at your door," he scolded her.

"It only could've been you. I didn't have expectations for anyone else to call on me." Lilliana shrugged and set the book down next to her. "You didn't have to knock you know. You have an open invitation to visit me any time you like."

Did she still believe that propositioning him would work? He would seriously like to take her up on her offer of just a liaison, but he wanted so much more. He hadn't planned on discussing what he wanted until later. She needed to understand that a love affair would never happen between them. Lilliana deserved everything he had to offer her. He just needed her to accept what he proposed for their future.

"Yeah, I believe you said something similar before," he replied.

"I've been waiting for you for what seems like forever," Lilliana exclaimed. "Why do you keep resisting? We are friends, right? I think that will make us the best lovers because we understand each other."

"No, becoming your lover will make us more than friends. I doubt we could remain anything resembling friendship once the affair ended. If you want to be just friends I suggest you forego the idea we become lovers. It's not something that can be separated. That kind of relationship changes things. I'd want more and you would too. You just don't realize it because of your innocence. Make up your mind one or the other because I refuse to only be your friend. I want a hell of a lot more than that from you."

"Perhaps you could define what constitutes more for you? I don't know how much I'm willing to give."

"More means everything a man could want from a woman. Probably more than even that. I want you to belong to me in every possible way."

Lilliana stood up and walked over to him. She placed her hand on his chest and looked up into his eyes. Her eyes pleaded with him, and it broke his heart that he couldn't be what she wanted him to be. She must understand how it needed to be in order for them to have any chance of a decent relationship. He offered her all of himself and he desired the same from her.

"That may be a bit more than I want. What you are asking of me scares me more than I can express with mere words. I don't give control over easy. If there is a person I could do that with, it would be you. I'm just not so sure I am capable of allowing you to have that much power over me." Lilliana took a few steps away from him putting some distance between them as she spoke.

"I need you Lily. I don't want to change you. I happen to like you the way you are. If you want me, even a little, I need you to take a chance. There is no maybe in this situation. It's all or nothing."

"So I either agree to go along with your plan or you leave me to what? Forget I ever existed? Are you capable of doing that? I don't know if I could ever erase you from my memories. I like you, Rand. A lot more that I thought I could possibly ever like a man. Generally they are worthless to me. Most of them see dollar signs when they look at me."

"And you think I'm like them?" he asked bewildered. "First off, they are all fools if they only see you as a way to gain extra funds. You are the most beautiful woman I've ever met. I see you as a woman not a way to pad my finances."

"Don't act so offended, I meant what I said. I'm very fond of you. I didn't mean to imply you only saw money when you looked at me. I'm just stating how my beaus of the past have viewed me. You are the only male outside of my father and brother that I respect," she told him. "I want you to understand that you are the only male, outside of my family, I could ever possibly trust."

"I see."

"No, I don't think that you do. You mean an awful lot to me Randall Collins. I really do want to attempt more with you. I just don't see that we need to go beyond what I am offering you."

The conversation had derailed, and it looked like he needed to put it back on track.

"I had hoped to convince you that being with me would be not only the best thing for me, but also for you," he replied.

"What do you mean?"

He could hear the anxiety in her voice as the words left her mouth. Lilliana paced through the room and wrung her fingers together. She frowned, and her forehead crinkled up with confusion. Even though this escalated his plans he knew that he had to lay everything out for her—a decision had to be made. If they had a chance of moving forward, he needed her to agree to everything.

"I want to ask you something. I have been thinking about it for a while now," he began. "I know that we both had a different idea of what our future would hold, but I like to think that all changed on our journey."

Lilliana's forehead creased with uncertainty. She remained silent for several seconds before she responded.

"I suppose on some level that is true. What is it that you want to ask me?"

"I think we both have a certain amount of affection for each other. I believe we work well together and could potentially make each other very happy. What I mean is...what I want to ask you..." Rand said his voice shaking and cracked with emotion.

Why did he find it so hard to get the words out? Could he make it any harder on himself? She just stood there in front of him patiently waiting and he stumbled over his words. He just needed to say them and believe she would give him the answer he desired.

"Will you please marry me?" He breathed a sigh of relief as he finally managed to get the words out.

"You want me to be your wife?"

"With all my heart."

Lilliana crossed the distance of the room and stopped directly in front of him. She looked into his eyes and searched for something. He didn't know what, he just knew she was trying to figure him out and appeared to think the answer might reveal itself on his face.

"Why?" she finally asked.

"I thought I explained about the fondness I have for you and how well we are together. We have a spark between us that is dying to ignite. Please consent to be my wife, Lily. I can't just be your lover or your friend. I need all of you."

"You really believe we can make it work?" Lilliana asked. "Because I never intended on getting married. I explained that to you. Why would I have changed my mind? I wanted a lover not a husband."

"I honestly do. I think that we have a better chance than most at making a marriage work," he replied.

"I need more convincing. I don't believe marriage is for me. I need a reason that will make me want to tie myself to you."

She needed more convincing? How did she expect him to convince her? Rand stared at her for several minutes as he weighed his options. He reached down and picked up her hand and pulled her closer to him. With her hand still encased in his, he placed it over his heart and wrapped his free arm around her waist. His heart beat rapidly as he stared into the depths of her blue eyes. Her tongue darted out, and she licked her pink lips, wetting them in expectation. Rand placed his lips on hers and began to kiss her, coaxing her mouth open with fine tuned passion. Lily's free hand began to roam through his hair, tousling it with eager frenzy. He put a small amount of distance between them and began a trail of feather light kisses over her cheeks and down the arch of her neck. A soft moan vibrated against her throat as he caressed it with his lips. Her pulse raced beneath his fingers, and he couldn't tell the difference between the beats of her heart against his drumming rapidly in his ears. Passion ignited fast between them. Their shared ecstasy was never in doubt, only whether or not they would share it for a lifetime.

Rand needed her to agree to be his wife. He hoped that by giving her a small taste she would see that they were meant to be. That this thing between them wouldn't go away after a few times of loving each other. They needed forever to explore each other and the desire that built each time they came together. He released her and backed up a little bit to look her directly in the eyes. They were still flushed with unspoken yearning. He took a deep breath and told her his view on their situation.

"It's time to make a decision. I already explained I require everything from you. I want to wake up each morning by your side and know that you're mine. I want the privilege of making love to you whenever I want and knowing you want that too. If you don't agree to marriage we won't have that. Do you really only want one night? Wouldn't it be so much better to have every night in each other's arms?"

"That does hold some appeal but why would we need to get married to have that. We can still do that without marriage."

"And what if we have children? Do you want them to grow up with that stigma? No. I want it all. Please agree to marry me."

"What about your ships? You said I'd have every night but not if you go off sailing for months at a time."

"I don't plan on sailing again once we are

married. There are plenty of men who would love to earn a decent wage and captain my ships for me. I can run the business from here in Charleston and stay with you." Rand caressed her back with his hand. "I used to think the business was all I wanted. Everything I believed about myself changed when I met you. Together we could do anything."

"All right," she said. "You do have a point."

"So, is that a yes?"

"Yes, I will marry you."

Rand pulled her into his arms and held her for a long moment before he felt he could let her go. Leaning down he kissed her forehead and again lightly on her lips as relief pour through his veins. Now that she agreed to marry him, he needed to make it official.

"Good, I'm glad you agree. While we are out we can get married."

"Are you in some kind of hurry? Why do we need to get married so fast?" she asked.

"I don't want to give you a chance to change your mind. Plus I'd like to arrive at your plantation as your husband. Once we get there I want to start our lives together and build something worth keeping forever. I don't see any reason not to begin to make that happen immediately."

"I suppose that makes sense," she said.

"Good, come with me and let's make it official."

Rand grabbed her hand in his and pulled her out of the cabin. They walked up to the deck of the ship and strolled down the gangplank onto the dock. As they roamed the streets of downtown Charleston, Rand couldn't help thinking about the happiness filling him to the brim. She had actually agreed to marry him. For a brief moment, he believed she might say no. That moment of apprehension had made him react with a bit of spontaneity. When he asked her to be his wife his original intention centered around waiting and doing everything right. He panicked and demanded an immediate ceremony for fear she might change her mind. He didn't want to take any chances that she might, with Lily anything was possible. Rand had one goal and it was to make Lily his wife. He didn't have time to worry about anything else, including how her parents would react to their sudden marriage. Viscount Torrington would put him through hell for marrying his daughter without prior permission to do so.

It didn't take them long to find the local church. The church had four long white columns in front of tall burnt red doors. The inside of the chapel had simple designs. It lacked decorations, but had detailed stained glass windows. A man with white hair dressed in the robes of a clergy knelt at the altar lost in prayer. Rand didn't want to disturb him so he led Lily toward a pew and waiting for him to finish his worship. After several minutes he stood up and realized they sat in the pews. He walked over to them and nodded to both of them.

"I am Reverend Thomas," he said. "How can I help you two?"

"We were hoping that you would be willing to marry us," Rand said.

"Certainly," the man agreed. "Did you have a special time in mind?"

"Actually we want to get married right now," Lilliana murmured.

"Really? Is there a reason you two are in a hurry?" he asked.

"Just want to start our lives together. We don't see any reason to wait," Rand responded.

"I guess I can accommodate you. We will need two witnesses," the reverend said. "Do you have anyone in mind?"

"We don't know anyone here in Charleston. We only arrived on my ship this afternoon," Rand explained.

"Well a couple of my parishioners are due to

arrive any minute. We can ask them if they would be willing to stand as witnesses," he said.

"That would be lovely," Lilliana said with a smile.

"In the meantime, why don't you tell me a bit about yourselves? What are your names?"

After Rand gave the reverend their names, they heard a couple walk into the church. They all turned their attention to the new arrivals. An older couple walked up the aisle and stopped by the pew that Rand and Lily were sitting in.

"Jamieson, Eliza glad to see the two of you," the reverend said with a nod.

"We're glad to see you as well Reverend Thomas." Jamieson nodded at him. "Eliza and I are here for our monthly meeting to help the less fortunate in our community."

"Yes, before we begin I'd appreciate your assistance with another matter," the reverend told him.

"What can we do to help?" Eliza asked.

"These two young people wish to get married," the reverend responded. "Would you be willing to stand as witnesses while I perform the ceremony?"

"Oh, how wonderful. I'd be happy to," Eliza smiled.

"I will as well," Jamieson agreed.

"Perfect we have everything we need to begin if the two of you are ready." The reverend looked at Lilliana and Rand.

"We are more than ready." Rand folded Lilliana's hand within his own. "Please begin the ceremony Reverend Thomas."

"Follow me to the altar," he told them.

Lilliana and Rand got out of the pew and walked, still holding hands, up to where the reverend stood. He opened the Bible and began the ceremony to make them husband and wife. The simple wedding appealed to Rand. He liked that they were about to start their lives together without any more complications. They would still have to deal with Lilliana's family at some point, but he wouldn't have changed anything.

"You may kiss your bride," the reverend said to close the ceremony.

Rand pulled Lily into his arms and pressed his lips to hers. The kiss was simple and sweet—nothing like he wanted to do. He had a fierce desire for his beautiful bride, but he knew he couldn't give into those temptations yet. As soon as he got her back to his ship he could have her in every way he wanted. Rand had waited this long, surely he could wait a few more hours to make her completely his. He lifted his lips off of hers and raised his face to look into her eyes. A smile of happiness showed across her extraordinary face. In that moment any doubts he had fell away.

"Are you ready to leave Mrs. Collins?" he asked.

"I am more than ready Mr. Collins."

Rand turned towards Jamieson, Eliza, and Reverend Thomas.

"Thank you all for making sure we were able to have a wedding today. We are forever in your debt." He nodded in their general direction as he spoke.

"Think nothing of it young man. It's nice to see two young people in love and ready to take on the world," the reverend said.

"Nevertheless we appreciate your willingness to perform the ceremony on such short notice. Perhaps we will see you on Sundays for mass." Lilliana smiled at him.

"You are more than welcome to join our congregation," the reverend told them.

"Good day to everyone my wife and I are going to find someplace for a nice dinner."

"Best of luck to you both," the reverend said.

Rand and Lily turned and walked out of the church. Never once did they let go of each other's hands. They found a quiet place to have dinner and patiently waited for to take the next step in their growing relationship. They were now man and wife, and Rand couldn't have planned it all better if he had tried. Lilliana glowed, and he felt himself basking in it as they spent a few quiet moments just enjoying each other's company.

a beautiful and enormous feeling swept over Lilliana as she looked at her husband. She shouldn't be surprised by how he made her feel, but every time she looked into his eyes a new thrill rolled through her. She should have expected him to want marriage, but it hadn't really crossed her mind. The more they discussed it the more it had made sense to her. It had taken her a while to admit it to herself, but Lilliana knew she loved Rand. As wonderful as the emotions coursing through her were they didn't compare to the fear of rejection. He hadn't once mentioned his own feelings. Telling him would be a risk, but surely it was worth it.

No matter how many times she let that thought roll through her mind she still had trouble believing it. A husband, she actually had willingly tied herself to someone else forever. For a person that never intended to be anyone's wife so far she found it incredibly easy to be Rand's. Admittedly they had only been husband and wife less than two hours, but everything between them had a natural and oh so right feel to it. Rand hadn't said anything about love in his proposal, and it bothered a small part of her. She needed to know that he loved her, but she would wait until he knew it as much as she did. Forcing him to say the words would take away the joy of them. They wed and for now that had to be enough.

They finished eating their meal and left to procure a coach to take them to the plantation the next day. A small bubble of excitement continued to well inside of her at the thought of them being together in every way possible. She wanted him so much. Nothing could ever change how much she loved him.

"Ah if it isn't the two newlyweds themselves," a male voice said from directly behind them said with a laugh.

Rand and Lily turned to see the witnesses from their wedding directly behind them.

"Jamieson, Eliza," Rand nodded. "We didn't expect to see you two again so soon."

"We just finished our meeting with Reverend Thomas," Eliza smiled.

"It went well, I expect," Lilliana said.

"It did indeed, "Jamieson agreed. "If I am not being to forward, can I ask you a question?"

"Of course," Rand said. "What do you want to know?"

"Well your wife looks mighty familiar to me. Where to you hail from?" Jamieson asked.

"Lily is late of London, England. She's traveling to live at her mother's plantation," Rand replied.

"Actually now it's mine." Lilliana grinned.

"What?" Rand looked surprised.

"It's my dowry. Didn't I mention that?"

"No dear, you failed to inform me of that little bit of knowledge."

"Well now you know," she said with a shrug.

"Oh, I see the resemblance, now," Jamieson said. "You are the daughter of the Viscount Torrington."

Lilliana looked up at him with shock on her face. She didn't think anyone would make the connection from her to her parents. Somehow this man knew not only them, but her relationship with them.

"You know my parents?" she asked.

"I would think so. I am the overseer of the

plantation after all. I've worked for your father for years," he replied.

"How serendipitous and quite convenient," Rand said. "We were just looking to hire a carriage to take us to the plantation. Perhaps you can assist us."

"We did get a letter in the post today that Miss Marsden would be arriving shortly. It didn't mention a husband," he said.

"Well as you know that bit was last minute. You did witness the wedding after all. Its Mrs. Collins now," Lilliana told him.

"Indeed we did." Jamieson nodded. "Eliza is the housekeeper at the plantation and also my wife."

"It will be wonderful to have someone living in that big house again," Eliza beamed. "When are you planning on arriving at the plantation?"

"As soon as possible," Lilliana said. "As my husband said, we're looking for a carriage. I have a couple trunks that need to be transported from Rand's ship."

"We can help you with that. We brought a carriage to town. We can meet you at your ship. If you are ready to come tonight you can travel back with us," Jamieson said.

"Oh, that's wonderful. We thought we would have to sleep on the ship again tonight. I'd much prefer a bed that didn't rock quite so much," Lilliana said looking pleased. A joyous smile lit up her face.

"My ship is docked at the port. We can walk back there now and meet you to load the trunks onto your carriage."

"A solid plan young man. We will meet you there shortly," Jamieson answered.

Lilliana and Rand started to walk back to his ship. Once there, Rand began to order a couple of his deck hands to get Lily's trunks ready to be taken to the awaiting carriage. Lilliana leaned on the railing of the ship and surveyed her surroundings. Nothing about the day had gone as she imagined it. She found herself wed and heading off to her plantation to start her life anew.

"Are you ready to go see your plantation, dear," Rand said from behind her.

Lilliana smiled as she turned and wrapped her arms around him. She rested her head on his shoulder and for a brief moment just enjoyed the feel of his arms wrapped around her.

"Yes," she told him. "I feel like I've been waiting forever to get to where I am right now."

"We haven't arrived just yet."

"I know, but we will soon. This journey has been about more than reaching the plantation. It's also about me and what I want out of life. Thanks to you I'm realizing all of my dreams. I owe you so much."

"You don't owe me anything," he said with a shake of his head. "You have it all mixed up. It's I that owes you."

"We will have to agree to disagree," she responded.

"I have a feeling we will be doing that a lot in our lifetime."

"You may have a point," she said with a laugh. "But for now let's go to the plantation. I would like to arrive before nightfall."

"I would as well."

"Which reminds me. Did something about Jamieson seem familiar to you?" Lilliana said.

"Not particularly," Rand said.

"I don't know what it is just yet, but he reminds me of someone. I'll figure it out when I've had more time to think about. With all the excitement of the day my mind can't stay focused on one thing."

"I'm sure you will." He leaned down and placed a soft kiss on her forehead. "Let's go join them in their carriage."

"All right," she said.

Lilliana walked down to meet Jamieson and Eliza at the carriage. Once they arrived Lilliana took a moment to observe them. They were an older couple around her parent's age. "Have you been taking care of the plantation the entire time that my parents have been married?" Lilliana asked them.

"I took over shortly after your parents were married," Jamieson told her. "I used to work with your father."

"Please tell me you didn't sail with him in his pirate days," Rand exclaimed.

"Actually I used to be his first mate," Jamieson said.

Lilliana heard Rand groan at Jamieson's admission. She really didn't see why. So what if Jamieson used to be the first mate on her father's ship. That didn't make him a bad person, but perhaps she was a bit biased. She adored her father and didn't think that the fact he used to be a pirate detracted from his lovable nature.

"Oh that's wonderful. You will have to tell me some stories from when you two sailed together." Lilliana asserted.

"Well, I must admit the most interesting one involved your mother." Jamieson explained.

"I know he kidnapped her. Father used to tell us the story of how they met as a bedtime story."

"Are you serious?" Rand asked baffled.

"Of course I am. I wouldn't joke about such a thing. Their story had a very romantic element to it," Lilliana told him.

"He kidnapped her!" Rand shouted.

"What's your point?" Lilliana asked. "It led to them falling in love. You do realize I wouldn't exist if that hadn't happened."

"I do." He sighed. "That doesn't make what he did right."

"Perhaps not, but my father would never hurt my mother." She folded her hands over her chest, staring into his eyes. "Everyone is human Rand. We are all capable of making mistakes. He owned up to his and my mother forgave him. It isn't our place to judge."

"You're right, of course. I just can't wrap my head around it."

The carriage rattled along the narrow road as they talked. The journey toward the plantation amounted to a few miles outside of Charleston. Talking as they traveled helped the journey go faster, making it seem like it only took minutes to arrive.

"Well lad, the little lady is right. Thor loves Pia. That fact became evident pretty fast to the crew. If you take out the things you find atrocious it did have a romantic feel to it," Jamieson told him.

"I will have to take your word for it," Rand replied.

"Jamieson, have we met before?" Lillian asked.

"Only once, when you were about five or six years old. Your parents traveled to make sure that the plantation's assets were okay after the end of the war. You all stayed for a few months. Your mother was a bit reluctant to leave. You liked it so much that was when she declared it would be part of your dowry."

"I didn't know that. My parents never told me why they made it part of my dowry," Lilliana said. "You seem so familiar to me though, I don't think that brief meeting would have left an impression."

"No ma'am I doubt it would have. I barely saw you on that visit. I spent most of my time with your parents making sure they had all the information they sought."

She couldn't put her finger on what was so familiar about him. Lilliana was determined to figure it all out. Spending time with Jamieson and Eliza on the plantation would help her ferret out the mystery. She had time to figure out why he was so recognizable to her. Perhaps it was just because she had met him before, but she doubted it.

CHAPTER 14

The carriage pulled to a stop in front of a large plantation house with four large white columns encasing the entranceway. The house was entirely white with large windows and two large green front doors. A wide staircase led to the porch and entranceway. Rand could see why his wife wanted to live in the plantation home. It was a piece of beautiful architecture with a rich history. The fact that it had survived the war was an amazing feat. He couldn't wait to start his new life in this home with Lilliana.

Jamieson hopped down from the carriage once it was at a complete stop. First he helped Eliza down from the carriage, and then he began to reach for the trunks strapped down to the back of the carriage.

Rand helped Lily from the carriage and turned to speak to Jamieson.

"I can help you with those," Rand said.

"If you are willing to help me get these up to your room I'll be much obliged."

"Most of this stuff does belong to my wife. I'd be an awful cur to leave it for you to do alone."

"I'd understand if you wanted to get settled in right away. I'm sure the journey here was quite lengthy. I appreciate your help." Jamieson nodded at Rand in appreciation.

"The faster we get these unloaded to sooner we can all relax. I'm sure you'll appreciate a little extra time to unwind."

"I do indeed. Let's get these trunks inside," Jamieson proposed. "It'll be dark soon."

Jamieson reached over and pulled the straps off of the trunks and began drag it over so it would be easier to lift. Rand stepped over by the other side. They each stood by their chosen side, lifted, and walked the trunk indoors. Rand let Jamieson lead him up the stairs to the room he would share with his wife. Once they reached the room they set the trunk by bed and went to retrieve the other trunk.

"Those trunks are a lot heavier than they look,"

Jamieson said once the trunks were delivered to their room.

"I have no idea what she has in any of them." Rand laughed and wiped a bead of sweat off his brow. "I am not sure I want to know either."

"Can't say I blame you. Sometimes it's best to be left in the dark."

Rand laughed again. "You may be right there."

"I am, trust me. I've been married twice and I learned the hard way not to question certain things in a woman's boudoir."

"What happened to your first wife?" Rand asked. "If I'm not being too personal that is."

"No, no it's okay. It's been a lot of years since my first wife died. I gave up on the domestic side of things after I lost her and our child. It took a lot for me to get back on my feet. Thor played a huge part in making me want to live again. Meeting Eliza made me realize I could allow myself to be happy. My wife, I loved her dearly, and I know she wouldn't have wanted me to throw my life away because she died."

"I'm so sorry. That had to be very difficult for you. I'm sorry I made you relive it even for a small moment. I couldn't imagine what I'd do if I lost Lily."

"I hope it doesn't come to that." Jamieson's face

became solemn. His eyes took on a darker hue as he frowned.

Rand hoped speaking of his deceased wife and child wouldn't leave him in a melancholy mood for the rest of the night. He hated that he may have caused him any misery. Unfortunately he could relate on a small level. Growing up as an orphan gave him firsthand knowledge to the wretchedness of losing a family member. He never wanted to experience that heartache ever again. At the sound of Jamieson's voice he snapped back to the present. He couldn't let the despair of the past wrap its way around his heart again.

"Let's go downstairs. It's time for dinner and I'm sure Eliza has a wonderful meal prepared for us," Jamieson said.

The two of them left the bedroom and strolled down the stairs. Rand followed Jamieson to the dining room. They went inside the room to find Lily laughing at something Eliza had said. She looked up at him and her smile grew brighter. She motioned for him to come closer and take the seat next to her.

"Is everything all taken care of?"

"Yes. The trunks are stored up in our room."

"Good. I can unpack tomorrow," she said.

"That's a scary thought. Those trunks were quite heavy."

"I had to take what I deemed important. I don't plan on returning to England anytime soon." She shrugged.

"Yes. I can see why taking things that you needed and deemed important would top your list. If there is anything you need that you didn't bring with you please let me know."

"I don't need you to provide for me, Rand. I can take care of myself."

"I know you can, but you're my wife now. It's my privilege to see to your wants and needs. I look forward to it all."

"It feels a bit controlling to me." Lily's left eyebrow lifted widening it so the blue of her eye was more noticeable. Her cheeks flushed a pretty shade of pink as she pressed her lips together forming an appealing pucker.

"I didn't mean it to be. Forgive me?"

"You're forgiven." Lilliana leaned over and wrapped her arms around him to give him a quick hug. "I know you didn't mean it the way it sounded. Sit down and eat something. I'd like to start our first night as husband and wife on a good note."

He intended to have a beautiful wedding night

with her. He had an idea on how he could make it both beautiful and wonderful. With a firm plan set in his head he sat back to enjoy the meal.

"It looks like you have prepared a lovely meal, Eliza," Rand said.

"It does indeed," Lilliana said. "If you don't mind me asking what do you call all of this?"

"We eat a light meal in the evenings. Our big meals are usually served at noon. This is just a simple meal of corn bread, frizzled beef, stewed fruits, and oyster pie." Eliza replied.

"It all looks delicious," Lilliana said. "I can't wait to sample everything."

"We also have tea or milk if you'd like," Eliza offered.

"I'll have some tea please. I haven't had a decent cup in ages."

Rand laughed. "She acts like the crossing over on my ship deprived her of the niceties in life."

"Nonsense, I had a lovely time aboard your ship. I just haven't had tea since the morning we left England," Lilliana replied. "I'm quite looking forward to a nice cup of it. If it's not too much trouble that is."

"You should know Mrs. Collins..." Jamieson began to say.

"Lily, please," she interrupted. "You've worked

with my father. You can call me by my given name. My closest friends and family call me Lily. I insist you do as well."

"Lily," Jamieson began, "I received a letter from your father. I just got a chance to look over today's post."

Rand stopped eating and looked up as Jamieson spoke. It couldn't be good news he had to impart. Viscount Torrington had to be out for blood since Lilliana ran away from home. He would be in his crosshairs for assisting her in her act of defiance. Something he was not looking forward to, but knew it would be a necessary evil if he wanted to make peace with the man.

"That doesn't surprise me," Lilliana said. "What did he say?"

"He is coming for a visit. He mentioned that you might show up before him and I needed to make sure you didn't leave before he arrived."

Lilliana laughed before saying, "Why ever would he think I'd leave? I told him in the letter I left for him and mother I planned on residing here."

"Wait a minute you left them a letter? You didn't tell me that," Rand exclaimed.

"I didn't?" Lilliana answered. "I swear I mentioned it."

Rand rubbed his temples as he let her words wash over him. How could she have forgotten to mention that little tidbit to him? Didn't she believe he had a right to know something so important? "No dear, I'd have remembered you telling me that you left your ex-pirate father a letter telling him you had run away from home. In fact, you said earlier that you intended to write them once you arrived at the plantation."

"Hmmm...well I guess I do remember saying that. I didn't know how you would take it. It's not important really. I gave it to Gemma to give them once they realized I hadn't gone to stay at her country estate." Lilliana paused and looked him in the eye. "I had to do it, you know that."

"Yes, I do. I'd have just preferred knowing that you had." Rand sighed.

"Oh I see, you think I deliberately left you in the dark? Which I suppose you are right about. I had intended on letting you know at some point though. It slipped my mind. Whenever you are around me I tend to forget important matters, for more desirable ones. In my defense you never once asked for any details on what I had in the works."

"You are right once again, I didn't ask, because I really didn't care at the time," Rand agreed.

Lilliana flashed him a brilliant smile.

"I did say we would have to deal with your parents at some point."

"Indeed you did," Lilliana looked over and asked, "Jamieson, did my father give you any idea when they might arrive?"

"I'd give it a rough estimate of within a day of your arrival to a week depending on the weather for their crossing."

A day? That wasn't nearly enough time to prepare for the arrival of his wife's parents. "So it's a possibility for them to show up sometime tomorrow." Rand sat back in his chair and awaited a response to his question.

"It is," Jamieson agreed.

"We will just have to make sure we are ready for their arrival. I'm sure Torrington will want my head when he arrives," Rand replied. He folded his hands under the table and began clenching and unclenching them. He didn't want her parents to dislike him, but he didn't regret marrying Lily.

"I'm not likely to let him kill you, lad," Jamison replied.

"Nor I, as I rather like your head where it is," Lilliana agreed. "I really don't think you need to worry though, they will be happy I decided to get married. They have been pushing me towards matrimony for a while now."

"I have to agree with you. I'm rather attached to my head myself." Rand nodded at his wife. "I have to disagree with you though; we have plenty to be worried about. I know if my daughter married some random man I'd be out for blood. Just be prepared for the worst."

"I'd rather not dwell on it to much. Let's make plans for something fun instead." Lilliana said changing the subject.

He didn't want to cause Lily any stress so for her sake he would attempt to let it go. He knew she was being too nonchalant about it though.

"You could go horseback riding and learn the land you inherited," Eliza suggested.

"That's a lovely idea. Do you have horses here that we can ride tomorrow?" Lilliana asked.

"Yes, there are a few in the stable suitable for riding. I can help you when you are ready to leave," Jamieson replied.

"After breakfast we can go for a ride. Does that work for you Rand?"

"I think it's a fine idea."

"Wonderful. It will be nice to be able to ride a horse again."

"There you go picking on my ship again," Rand said with a laugh.

Lilliana stuck her tongue out at him with a playful laugh in return.

"I have fond memories of your ship. I am not the one picking on it."

"I know, dear. I'm just giving you a hard time." Rand moved to get up. "If you will excuse me, I'm tired and going to go rest in my room."

"I can come up with you," Lilliana said.

Rand stiffened at her offer to join him, but he didn't want her to come along with him just yet. He had plans for their special night. He would welcome her willingly later on, eagerly.

"No, finish your meal. Join me later. I'm not going anywhere, I promise."

Rand left them in the dining room and bounced up the stairs to the room he shared with Lily. He had an idea on how to make their first night together as husband and wife unforgettable. He needed a few things and everything would be perfect. Lilliana deserved the best and he intended to make sure she had it.

CHAPTER 15

*L*illiana sat as long as she could with Jamieson and Eliza, trying her best to enjoy the food before her. It all tasted like grains of sand. What she wanted was to join her husband in their room. The food did nothing to quench her needs. Only Rand would be able to accomplish that. She had no idea what Rand was up to, but she intended to find out.

"If you will excuse me, it's time I retired. It has been a long day." Her patience had its limitations and she found herself at the edge of them as she looked over her supper companions.

"Of course, have a good night. We'll see you at breakfast," Eliza said.

Lilliana nodded at both of them as she got up from the table. She walked out of the room and with a slow gait strolled up the stairs. The staircase was wide and open with plush red velvet cascading down each step. The baluster and newels were burnt mahogany, polished to a perfect shine. The hallway wove down an intricate path that led to several bedrooms. She remembered where hers was because she loved it so much. It was located at the end of the hall on the left. The room was decorated in a mint green and browns. It reminded her of a decadent forest.

When she reached her destination she opened the door and gasped in surprise. The illumination from all of the candles bathed the room with a soft glow. Lilliana looked up and saw her husband's desire filled gaze. He had removed some of his clothing and sauntered to her side in his bare feet. Lilliana stared into his eyes as he reached up and caressed her face with one of his hand. His other arm wound around her waist and pulled her toward him.

"I've been waiting for you."

"I'm here now," she said as she licked her lips. "If you had given me a clue I'd have been here sooner."

"I don't mind. The best things are worth waiting for."

"You say the sweetest things," she whispered.

"I don't. I say what I mean." He placed a small kiss on her neck. "I feel like I've been waiting for you my whole life."

"You don't need to wait anymore. I'm here, take everything you want."

"I intend to. Now that I have you exactly where I want you, I am going to take my time...and savor every inch of you."

He leaned down and pressed his lips over hers in a light kiss. Lilliana released a small breath filled with anticipation; Rand pressed his lips more firmly to hers. He tasted wonderful, like honey and cinnamon. She let her tongue duel with his for control. Their passion escalated the longer they kissed. Lilliana raised her arms and wrapped them around his neck and pulled him closer to her.

He pulled away and looked down at her. Lilliana bit down on her swollen lip and moaned. If he didn't start giving her what she needed she had no problem forcing him to her way of thinking.

"Take it easy, love," he whispered as his lips caressed her ear. "We have all night to explore each other."

"I need so much..."

"So do I, but it will be so much better if we take our time."

"I don't want to. Please Rand."

She ran her hands through his hair and pulled his head towards hers. Their passion ignited full force. Lips, tongues, and teeth battled to get the upper hand. He turned her around and pressed her against the wall; Rand unlatched every hook of her dress and pulled it down. She didn't wear a corset so she stood before him in only her chemise and pantalettes. She could feel his body towering over her as his hands roamed her body. He continued to place little kisses along her neck and shoulders.

"I'm going to take every last stitch of clothing off of you now, Lily." His breath hot on her ears as he whispered, "Then I'm going to taste you everywhere."

She felt herself grow wet between her legs at his words. His words evoked so many different tumultuous emotions inside of her. Her skin was sensitive to his touch; every place his hands roamed she grew hotter, needier, and more desperate to see what he would do next. Rand peeled the rest of her clothing of as fast as possible and turned her back around to face him. He took a step back and let his gaze roam over her nude body. Lilliana's body heated to a scorching flame under his direct scrutiny.

Looking boldly into his eyes she reached up and cupped both of her breasts in her own hands and pinched her nipples. She saw him gasp with a sharp intake of breath and slowly release it. Her desire escalated the longer he watched her.

She wanted to reach out and touch him; more importantly she wanted him to remove the rest of his clothing so she could look at his gorgeous body.

"You are stunning and you're mine."

He took a step closer to her and reached out to touch her naked body. His hands roamed over her naked breasts and plumped her nipples between his fingers. They became stiff from his ministrations, and he drew one of the nipples inside of his mouth. His tongue roamed over it and brought a long drawn out moan from her mouth.

"Please Rand, I need you."

"And I will give it to you, love. Together we will do and feel so much tonight."

He pulled her with him to the bed and laid her down with gentleness on the soft mattress. His gaze caressed her again before he lay down next to her on the bed. His hands trailed over her belly and brushed over the curls between her legs. His nimble fingers found her center as they rubbed her tender flesh. Lilliana ached so much and needed him to be inside of her. She didn't understand why he didn't make her his. He seemed to be moving too slow for her and, she had no clue how to make him go any faster. She didn't know what to expect having never made love to man before, but Rand made her want and need everything he did with her. Every sensation trailing over her body made her ache for him in so many ways.

He changed positions and crawled over top of her. He lowered his face between her legs and pushed her legs further apart. She didn't know what he intended until his lips kissed the nub between her legs. She would have squeezed his head with her legs if he hadn't been holding them in place. His tongue rolled over her sensitive flesh and she screamed.

"So beautiful," he said before he lowered his head again and started to lick her core.

The more he licked the tighter her body got in anticipation. Rand's gaze held hers for a moment as he watched something wonderful build within of her, a pressure so deep that at any moment an explosion would occur. She couldn't help being frightened by the intensity while secretly hoping for something more. He continued his relentless strokes of his tongue on her hypersensitive center. She didn't know what happened inside of her but she knew if he didn't stop she'd burst from all of the sensations. Her intuition proved right as she ruptured from the inside out. Her body quaked with uncontrollable spasms, and she screamed with each new ripple of pleasure outpouring from her body. Nothing had ever compared to what he just made her feel. She wanted to feel it again.

She looked up through hazy eyes as he undressed. Finally she would be able to see his beautiful body. Once all of his clothes were removed, he joined her on the bed again. His shoulders, chest, and arms were rippling with well-defined muscle. Light patches of hair dusted his chest and trailed down to his stomach. She looked at his thick manhood and wanted to wrap her hands around it. She couldn't help but wonder how it would fit inside of her. Every inch of him appeared too large, and she feared her body wouldn't be able to accommodate him. She really wanted to try though because she had a need building up inside of her. One she knew only he could fill.

"I think you are ready for me now," he said.

"I've always been ready for you."

"I know and we're going to do things a little differently," he whispered. "Do you trust me?"

"Always."

He rolled her on her side with her derriere facing him. He lifted her leg, pulled it over his hip and with slow thrusts started to enter her from behind. Her tight channel didn't want to let him in, but she desperately needed to feel all of him inside of her. She leaned back as he slid himself inside of her one slow inch at a time. When he reached her barrier he stopped for a moment to allow her body time to adjust, and then pushed fully inside of her. Lily's heart filled with so much love to have him joined with her. Even the brief sting of pain was worth it to know how it would feel to have him deep inside of her. She never thought she could feel so much emotion welling up inside of her. A small tear formed in the corner of her eye as her own happiness overwhelmed her. Rand waited for as she became accustomed to being filled by him, and once the ache left she started to move against him. Having him inside of her was beyond her wildest imagination. The completeness made her feel whole and part of him.

"Easy love. There is no need to rush."

"Please, Rand. Love me."

"I do, I am."

He continued to push himself in to her until he filled her completely. The completeness of his filling her had been amazing, but it didn't compare to his strokes caressing her channel. The different feelings he caused as he thrust himself in an out of her couldn't be explained. As he rocked himself inside of her, he also caressed her with his hands and lips. He pinched her nipples and rubbed them with the palm of his hands. A thousand tiny sensations roared through her body, and she knew she would explode at any minute. Just before her body detonated he leaned down and absorbed her scream with his mouth. Her core squeezed him, and she felt his seed burst within her. He wrapped his arms around her and groaned as he kissed her wild abandon.

"Lily, you undo me," he said as he trailed light kisses over her forehead and cheek.

"No more than you do me."

He slowly pulled himself out of her. Emptiness overcame her at the loss of him. She wanted more and as soon as possible. The reality of loving him had far surpassed anything in her wildest dreams. Rand got out of bed and blew out any candles still lit then crawled back in bed tugging the covers over top of them. He left a lantern lit on the bedside table to extinguish itself as the fuel burned out. He pulled Lily into his arms and held onto her as if his life depended on it.

Lilliana couldn't sleep. Emotions filled her to the brim in a turbulent fashion. She had trouble stilling them long enough to relax and fall to sleep. She could hear Rand's even breaths as he slept beside her. She wondered how he could remain so calm as her own emotions jumped all over the place. Lilliana needed him to know how much he meant to her.

"Rand, are you asleep?" she asked quietly.

No answer came from him. She found it incredulous he could sleep at a time like this.

"I guess you are," she said as she snuggled closer to him. "If you were awake I'd tell you how much you mean to me. I'd let you know that you changed me. I know that you don't love me yet, but I can love you enough for the both of us. In time I know you will love me too. You just need to allow yourself to feel it. I can wait for you."

She closed her eyes and took a deep breath.

"I can wait because you are worth waiting for. I just wish you stayed awake to allow me to say this all to you. I'm going to do it again when you will actually hear me." She caressed his cheeks lightly with the tip of her fingers. "I don't mind telling you I love you a million times."

With a smile on her lips she opened her eyes to gaze at his handsome face. Yes, she could and would do whatever it took to make him feel how much she loved him. For now she would lose herself in some much needed sleep. The morning would arrive soon enough and she could tell him that fact over breakfast if needed.

CHAPTER 16

*R*and held Lilliana tight. He heard every word she said the night before. He just hadn't known how to respond to them. Rand no longer had a lonely feeling roaming through his soul. Lilliana's confession had meant so much to him. She had given him a gift he didn't think he could ever return. He didn't feel worthy of her love, but he was selfish and would not refuse it. He needed her and would never let her go. Lilliana fit into his life perfectly—in a way he never knew he needed. She gave him a new purpose, and he intended to make sure she never regretted gifting him with her love. After she fell asleep, he watched her all night. A more beautiful sight didn't exist for him. His wife had sneaked into his heart and seized it when he let his guard down. She owned his soul.

While his gaze remained on her she rolled over and opened her eyes. "Good morning," she said and rubbed her eyes with her hands.

"Good morning to you beautiful." He gave her a quick kiss. "Are you ready to start your day?"

"Can't we just stay in bed all day, I can think of a few things we can do," she said coyly.

"Well I never said we had to get out of bed just yet." Rand kissed her again.

She wound her arms around his neck as he deepened the kiss. When he lifted her leg around his hip, he could feel her wetness stroke his shaft. The need to be inside her grew as his cock hardened. He trailed kisses down her neck and he pushed himself inside of her. She moaned with pleasure. With slow strokes, he slid in and out of her tight channel until her breaths became heavy on his shoulder. She bit his ear and licked away the pain.

"You feel so wonderful inside of me," she said with a groan. "Give me more Rand. I need it."

At her words he began to move harder and faster inside of her. A squeal of pleasure filled the room as he rolled Lily on her back and raised her hips under his hands. She wrapped her legs around his waist and held him tight against her. He rode her hard until she screamed as her orgasm rolled over her. He followed her into bliss a short time after her.

Rand held her tight in his arms when each wave of pleasure reached in and grabbed a hold of his soul. He rolled them onto their sides with heavy breaths coming out of his mouth. His breathing started to slow down and even out as his body became more relaxed. He didn't think loving her could get any better, but this time the pleasure had been even more intense than the first time.

"Darling, I do believe you have found your calling."

"And what's that?" she asked with boldness in her voice. Her fingers trailed lightly down his back.

"Loving me," he said and kissed her forehead.

"Always."

"I hate to say it, but I do believe we need to start moving now."

"Must we?"

"Yes, Jamieson and Eliza are expecting us for breakfast and we did make plans to go horseback riding. Unless you have changed your mind about getting a look at this land you inherited."

"I do want to go horseback riding. So let's start the day."

"Good. Let's get moving. I'm famished."

"So am I," she said with a laugh. "And yes, for food."

They got up and quickly got dressed. Rand grabbed Lily's hand as they strolled down the stairs into the dining room. Eliza and Jamieson were already seated at the table. Jamieson had a paper spread out in his arms as he read it. Eliza sipped from her cup as she gazed at nothing in front of her.

"Good morning," Lilliana said them both.

Jamieson closed his paper and looked over at the two of them as they sat down at the table. Rand nodded to him.

"I trust you both slept well," Jamieson said.

"Indeed we did," Lilliana said as a small blush grew on her cheeks.

It did his heart good to see that his wife could be embarrassed. He believed her brazen attitude overflowed every aspect of her life.

"Can I get you two any coffee or tea?" Eliza asked. "We have a small breakfast bar and we serve ourselves. There are hard-boiled eggs, sausages, and toast. A variety of jams as well as some scones if you like."

"I'd like some tea," Lilliana answered.

"What about you, Mr. Collins?"

"Coffee, and please call me Rand. I don't see why we should remain formal."

"Thank you," she said with kindness. "I don't see any reason either. I will get your drinks and be back soon."

He watched as she left the room. Eliza was a kind woman. He liked to think his mother would have been like her.

"Would you like me to make a plate for you?" he asked Lilliana.

"Oh, that would be lovely, thank you."

"Anything in particular you want?"

"A bit of everything," she said with a laugh. "I did tell you I'm famished remember."

Rand got up to make a plate for himself and Lilliana. As she requested he put a little bit of everything on her plate before he set it in front of her. He decided he would do the same for himself as he finished filling up his own plate. He sat down at the table and took a bite of toast as he looked over at his wife.

"Are you still planning on taking a couple of horses out today?" Jamieson asked.

"Yes we are. After we finish breakfast if that's still all right." Lily said.

"Of course it is. Technically you do own them after all."

"I guess I do. I hadn't thought of that," she answered.

"When you are finished, I will walk out to the stable with you and show you which horses are good for riding," Jamieson said.

They ate in silence as Rand watched Lilliana eat everything he had put on her plate. She really had worked up an appetite. Once she finished eating she dabbed her mouth with her napkin and looked over at him.

"What?" she asked.

"Nothing, just admiring my wife."

"We'll I'm done eating and want to go riding. Are you finished?"

"Eating? Absolutely."

"Well I guess we are ready to go investigate that stable of horses," Lilliana proclaimed.

"If you'll follow me I will show them to you," Jamieson replied.

A door slammed and a loud noise rumbled through the house followed by an equally thunderous bellow.

"Lilliana Marsden, where are you!"

"I think your parents have arrived." Jamieson said

with a tilt of his head. "I believe that bellow was your father."

They looked up as they saw Viscount Torrington storm into the room followed by a woman that Rand assumed was his wife and Lily's mother. Viscount Torrington's face was so red it bordered on being purple. If Rand were a coward he would try to slink out the door, and out of harm's way. He didn't back down from anyone and he planned on staying married to Lily for the rest of his life. If he had one hope it would be a very long life. He could have gone a while without dealing with her father, but it looked as if he didn't have much choice in the matter.

"Young lady we have some things to discuss." Torrington glared at Lily as the words roared from within him.

"Are you hungry father? We were just enjoying breakfast. Please have a seat," Lily replied with a cajoling voice.

Rand suppressed the urge to roll his eyes at Lily and her father. Did she really believe treating him like a child in the throes of a temper tantrum would work?

"Don't try to placate me young lady. You deliberately disobeyed and lied to us. You will answer for your indiscretions." Torrington practically bellowed the words at her.

Rand's lips formed a thin line of displeasure. He understood Torrington's irritation, but he couldn't and wouldn't allow him to lay a hand on her. Lily was his to protect now. "Well, I can't allow you to punish her. Please have a seat Viscount Torrington so we can discuss the situation like civilized people." Maybe if he reasoned with her father they could handle the situation as peacefully as possible.

Torrington turned and glared at Rand. Up until that point his attention had been solely focused on Lilliana. He knew that he would have to face him eventually, and it looked like it was time to do so. Rand had no regrets even if it looked like the man intended to beat him to a bloody pulp.

"I think I understand now." Torrington stormed over to Rand's side of the table and leaned on one of the chairs. "You are the one I need to hold responsible. Why did you kidnap my daughter, Mr. Collins? Did my interpretation of your business make you that mad? I don't take those actions lightly."

Rand should have known that the viscount was entirely too calm as he stood there talking to him. He believed the man capable of reasoning, but he should have factored in Lilliana's importance to him. If he had a daughter he would have been capable of murdering the poor sot that ran away with her. He didn't blame the man for his feelings on the matter. However the fist that planted in his face and knocking him out he did find fault with. *The blasted man hadn't even let me explain anything* was his last thought before blackness took over and he fell unconscious.

CHAPTER 17

*L*illiana jumped out of her chair and ran around the table to kneel before Rand's crumpled body sprawled out on the floor. At first she had remained rooted in her seat in horror watching her father's fist meet Rand's face. It was only after her mind could process the scene before her she was able to act. A scream to match her dismay erupted from her mouth before she rushed to her husband's side. Now she patted his cheek lightly to see if she could get him to wake up without any success.

"Jamieson, we need to get him upstairs." Lilliana gasped. "I don't know how long he is going to be out."

"I can certainly help. Thor, you are going to need to help me, he isn't a small lad."

"Damned if I do. I think he's exactly where he belongs."

Lilliana turned and glared at her father. His only reaction was to shrug without care. Her father may believe Rand belonged on the floor, but it was only because he didn't really know him. In his mind he kidnapped her forcing her to accompany him to South Carolina.

"Don't be an arse. He likely deserved to be pummeled a bit for running off with your daughter, but he is now her husband. You need to respect that." Jamieson spoke up to her father.

"In fact, I don't. I plan on murdering the thieving bastard as soon as he wakes up. He clearly had a death wish and I'm happy to oblige," Torrington replied.

Lilliana could see from the expression on her father's face he meant every word he said. She had to find a way to reason with him. The blame belonged squarely on her shoulders, not Rand's. The decision to run away had been made long before she had met him. She needed to make him understand how much she loved Rand. She adored her father, but she was not going to allow him to harm her husband. No matter what it took she would make sure her father understood he couldn't come between her and the man she loved.

"Daddy, I can't allow you to hurt him any more than you have. Please understand this decision was mine to make, not yours. I belong here with my husband." She walked over to him and placed her hands in his. She looked up into his eyes and showed every ounce of emotion rolling through her in one look. Lilliana pleaded and demanded with her eyes for her father to understand what she wanted from him. If he couldn't hear her words she wanted him to see what his actions would do to her. "I need your help. Can you try to recognize that and assist Jamieson to take him up to the bedroom?"

"Fine. I will help him, but then you and I are going to have a long overdue talk."

Lilliana turned to Jamieson and said, "Can I trust you to make sure no harm comes to him while you both take him upstairs?"

"You have my word, the lad will arrive safely. " Jamieson nodded at her father. "I will make sure he comes back down with me after we settle him in your room."

"I'm not going to do him any harm." He glared down at Rand's unconscious body. "Not until he is awake at least."

He walked over and grabbed Rand's head and heaved upward as Jamieson grabbed his feet. She noticed that even though her father had agreed to help carry Rand he didn't do it with any kind of care to his well-being. It irritated Lilliana to watch him be so disrespectful to her new husband. She would just have to take Jamieson at his word. He would make sure her father didn't hurt him. Once they came back down she would make sure her father understood what would happen if he did anything at all to her husband. She would never speak to him again if he marred him in any way.

"I think we need to talk before your father comes back down."

Lilliana turned to look at her mother. She had barely noticed her arrival after her father forced his way into the dining room. Breakfast was completely ruined. She had lost her appetite anyway when she watched Rand fall from his chair and hit the ground with a loud thud.

"I think you may be right. I've made a mess of things," Lilliana said with a sigh.

"Darling, that is the understatement of the year." Her mother rolled her eyes as she pushed a strand of her pale blonde hair behind her ear. "You didn't have to deal with your father for the past three weeks. I don't think I've seen him this mad since my grandpere tried to murder him."

"Your grandpere actually did that? I thought that was just something you made up to make the story sound more daring."

"Yes, he did and don't change the subject. You need to explain yourself. Why did you run off? Did meeting that man cause you to lose your mind?" her mother asked.

"No of course not. Don't be ridiculous. I didn't leave because of Rand. He just made it possible for me to get what I wanted."

"Then explain this all to me. Why did you marry him? I know you were against marriage."

"I'm not allowed to fall in love? I didn't leave because of him. I left because I wanted to live here. You were just not listening to me. So I made the necessary arrangements to get what I wanted. Rand just agreed to transport me." Lilliana walked over to her mother and grasped her hands within in her own. "He's an amazing man, Mama. I'm not saying that just because I love him. He protected me and made sure I had everything I needed. Even when I threw myself at him he refused me. He's a good choice and I stand by it."

"Well you don't have to convince me. It's your

father that isn't likely to believe you. It might take a little bit to make him understand, but I will try to help you."

"Thank you. I am sorry that I worried you. I tried to alleviate that."

"When you have children of your own someday you will realize a mere letter isn't reassuring enough. Parents always worry about their children. It's a responsibility that never goes away."

"I need to check up on him," Lilliana said.

"Your father isn't likely to let you near him until he has words with you. I've never seen him so irate and scared at the same time. Thor always seems to have things under control. Let him have his say first. I'm sure your husband will be fine in the meantime."

"I suppose you're right. I will wait." Lilliana looked over at the open doorway. "However, I'm not going to let him scream at me while my husband needs me. I will give him a moment of time to say his piece, but if I think Rand needs me the conversation is over."

Right after those words left her mouth Thor breezed in followed by Jamieson. He still wore a thunderous expression on his face. His lips pursed in displeasure, and his eyes narrowed to tiny slits as he focused his attention on her once again.

"Now that I've tossed the rubbish into another room, you and I are going to have a little discussion on mistruths and nearly giving your parents heart palpitations."

"I already apologized to mom. I'm extending it to you as well. You know I didn't mean to make you worry about me. This is where I want to be. I'm sorry, Daddy, but this is where I belong."

"You wouldn't be here if not for that upstart American. I can't believe you married him. We can rectify that when we get home."

"Are you listening to me at all? I'm not going back to England. Not now and probably not for a long time. I married Rand of my own free will. Nothing you say will make me want to leave him. I love him and I'm staying here as his wife."

"I'll tell you how I will rectify it. I will make sure the bloody bastard is no longer breathing."

Lilliana flinched as those words left her father's mouth. How could he threaten the man she loved? Didn't he want her to fall in love and get married? Both her parents kept pushing her toward that end, and now he doesn't like the result? No, her father would understand he couldn't dictate to her any longer, and he would never lay a hand on her husband again.

"You will do no such thing. Rand hasn't had an easy life. You are not going to make it any more miserable. He grew up alone in an orphanage. His mother died giving birth to him. He told me he knows next to nothing about his parents. I know it pains him that he didn't know anything about her except her name."

"Your daughter has a point, Thor. You need..."

Her father interrupted Jamieson, "I don't need to do a bloody thing. You have no idea what I went through when I found out she hopped a ship with him. I've never been so scared in my life."

"I think I understand that kind of pain better than anyone," Jamieson replied quietly.

She heard her father groan so she turned her attention back to him. He had a perplexed look on his face as he watched Jamieson.

"I'm so sorry—I wasn't thinking. I know you experienced a loss that would cripple even the strongest man."

Lilliana bobbed her head back and forth between the two of them. "I don't understand what you are talking about."

"I lost my first wife, Emily, and our child. She died giving birth to him. The poor boy wasn't breathing when he came out. I lost everything in one moment and wasn't even there to see them both through it."

"Emily? How interesting, that's Rand's mother's name," Lily replied deep in thought. She couldn't help wondering if there was a connection. Could there be? No, Jamieson said they both died. She grabbed Jamieson's arm and gained his full attention. "I don't mean to pry, but is there maybe a possibility—"

Her father turned toward Jamieson and asked, "Do you know what she is talking about?"

"Are you suggesting what I think you are? How could that even be possible?"

Lilliana wasn't sure if she hoped she was right, or if she prayed she was wrong. She could see pain in every inch of Jamieson's features. "What was your Emily's full name?"

"Before we married it was Emily—" Jamieson paused for a second and rubbed his hand over his face, "Good God, how did I not see it?"

"See what?" her father asked.

"Her name was Emily Collins...they both share the same name. Do you think they did it on purpose? Gave him her family name to hide him from me?"

Her father shook his head and shrugged. "I'm not sure, Jamieson. I don't have the answers you seek, but surely this is a good thing. You have a son."

"Only a few decades too late," bitterness laced Jamieson's voice.

All this information was a little too much for her to take in. Jamieson was Rand's father. No wonder he seemed so familiar to her. Lilliana stared at him for several moments. She took in all of his features and mannerisms. The more she looked at him the clarity of it all became firmer inside of her head. She knew why Jamieson seemed so familiar to her. It should have been obvious from the start. He reminded her of her own husband. It all made sense now that she had all of the information. How was she going to tell her husband about this? It was all so —extraordinary.

"Who do you think hid him from you?" Lilliana asked.

Her father placed a hand on Jamison's shoulder, giving him support. Her father knew something she didn't. He must have been privy to this story. They were close; they sailed on a ship together. Jamieson must have shared the details with him.

"Her damn family. When they found out she was pregnant they disowned her. I arrived after she had given birth to him. They told me she died and that the baby never even had its first breath. How could they have lied to me?" Jamieson crinkled up as pain poured out of his eyes. A small sound of pain fell from his lips before he spoke again. "I grieved so much that it led me to signing on to work with Thor on his ship. Nothing could have kept me in Beaufort after that. No one knew she was really my wife and wouldn't tell me anything. Told me it was a family affair. I didn't much see the point in fighting them. I believed I had nothing left to live for."

"Rand is your son. Why would they do that to their own grandchild? They may have hated you, but Emily was still their daughter," Lilliana said bewildered.

"Not everyone sees things in the same way. She ruined herself by getting involved with me. They believed her soiled goods. I don't know why they lied about my son dying. I would ask them if they were still alive. That is if I could stop myself from strangling them."

"I get why this information is interesting to Jamieson, but explain to me why you even care Father."

Lilliana understood why Jamieson was a bit emotional at the news, but her father seemed equally overwhelmed. Not too long ago he was out to murder her husband. Something that still irked her.

"I can't very well murder my friend's only child. Especially as he just found out he existed, now can I?"

"Oh, I see how you are. You can murder my husband, but not your friend's son. That is some convoluted logic." Lilliana's blood boiled at his statement. She clenched her hands into tight fists and restrained herself from hitting her own father.

"I have to agree with her there, Thor. That doesn't make much sense to me," her mother interjected as she walked into the room.

Lilliana turned to look at her mother. At least she had one reasonable person on her side. "Thanks Mother, though I could have used your support a lot sooner."

Her mother waved her hand in dismissal. "I came in when I was needed. Have you settled everything?"

"Father was just going to explain why it made a difference that Rand is now Jamieson's son, not just my lowly husband." Lilliana glared at her father. "I'm not so sure we've settled anything."

"You didn't watch him suffer when he believed they both had died. It's personal and I also understand what it's like to be a father now." Her father folded his arms over his chest. "Although I can't kill him, it doesn't mean I can't maim him a bit. He did abduct my daughter."

Jamieson frowned and said, "Well from what I understand of the situation she left rather willingly. You can't harass the lad for helping her out. Besides it isn't like you didn't do a little kidnapping in your day."

"He does have a point dear," Pia agreed.

If the situation wasn't completely ludicrous Lilliana would laugh. How had things gotten so far out of hand? She hoped Rand took the news all right that he had a father. It probably wouldn't help having to deal with her father as well. It would be some pretty difficult news to swallow on top of all the chaos already in their lives. At least her father wouldn't murder him now. She still thought it was absurd he only decided against that action because Jamieson believed Rand to be his son.

"Well, you two keep discussing this nonsense. I'm going to go check on my husband."

With those words Lilliana stormed out of the room to go check on Rand. Maybe he was awake now and she could spend some time with him. He did say he would take her horseback riding around the plantation. Of course that might be asking a bit too much, she would let him decide what he was capable of doing. If all he wanted was to go for a sedate walk she'd do it. She was just grateful to have him in her life. Maybe that would be a good way for them to get away from the madness that had overtaken everyone.

CHAPTER 18

*R*and woke up in his room with a splitting headache courtesy of his new father-in-law. When his head cleared he walked down the stairs to confront him. No way did he intend to leave Lilliana to fight his battles for him. When he reached the doorway he overheard them discussing his mother. Everyone always said you never heard anything good when you eavesdropped. He learned that lesson the hard way. Rand tromped away from his wife—and his father.

With the earth-shattering news—Jamieson being his father—dropped on him, he needed to get away and think. Rand practically ran out the front door to gain some distance between him and his newfound family. The only thing he thought about as he strolled away from the house was how much his life changed in such a short period of time. He didn't notice where his feet led him; he just kept prodding along until he couldn't take another step. When he finally took notice of his surroundings he saw a large oak tree looming in front of him. Its branches blew in the breeze as the leaves whistled with each movement.

His breaths became shallow as he swallowed that truth with a heavy reluctance. He never expected to find the man who helped create him. So many emotions rushed through him he couldn't pinpoint which one to hold onto. He needed to get back to the house and be there for his wife. He knew he acted like a coward by walking away. Closing himself off and not dealing with the issue wouldn't solve anything. He should have stayed and faced his demons instead of running at the first sign of adversity.

Jamieson seemed like a good man, aside from working as a pirate's right hand man. If what he said held true then he didn't know of his existence. Rand couldn't hold him accountable for the actions of someone else. He should give him a chance to be the father he never had. Easier said than done, in his opinion at least, years of believed abandonment were hard to let go of. He knew Jamieson said he thought he died. Rand heard all of the details; it was just hard for him to process. He wanted to believe everything he heard, but it all had a surreal feeling to it.

He had more than himself to think of now. With a heavy heart he started back toward the house. Lilliana depended on him, and he couldn't let his own inner turmoil get the best of him. As he walked back up the plantation steps, Lilliana exited the house and stopped with the door open. She stared at him for several minutes before she stepped forward and wrapped her arms around him.

"I'm so sorry. My father shouldn't have hit you."

"I don't blame him, Lily, he should be protective of his daughter."

"Still. He could have at least listened first before reacting." Lilliana frowned.

"I don't want to talk about it. I just want to hold you for a little while."

"There is something I should tell you..."

"I already know."

She was going to tell him about Jamieson. He didn't want to discuss his newfound father with her. He wanted to forget he had overheard the conversation.

"You do? How?"

"I overheard part of the conversation. It was a little bit to take in. It's why I'm outside. I needed the fresh air. To think," he said in a quiet tone.

"I see. I'm at a loss on how to respond. I thought you were out here because of me and my father. Instead it has to do with the news about yours. How does it make you feel?"

"I don't feel like talking about it. Why don't we go for a ride instead. It is what we planned before your father rudely interrupted us."

"Shouldn't we ask Jamieson..."

"Ask me what?"

They turned to see Jamieson standing in the open doorway. Rand wanted to walk away again. He didn't want to deal with him and what the man could mean for him. He did want to make his wife happy so he tried to put a smile on his face just for her, even though smiling made his face hurt.

"We are looking to go horseback riding." Rand said.

"Ah, I'd hoped to talk to you. I went looking and you were not in your room."

He wanted to give him a chance, but he hadn't had enough time to process it all. Jamieson may mean well—he just couldn't handle his well meaning emotional responses at the moment ."I'm not much in the mood to talk right now."

"It's kind of important, son."

"Don't call me that. I'm not your son," Rand replied scathingly.

"Rand!" Lilliana's shock evident on her face. "I don't think you need to be so rude to Jamieson. He is only trying to reach out to you and talk."

"You know?" Jamieson asked.

"That you believe you are my father? Yes. It doesn't make it true," Rand said.

"If your mother is—was Emily Collins, then yes, I am your father," Jamieson said with conviction.

Rand stood and looked at the man for the first time and took him in. Jamieson's features resembled his in a lot of ways, and he carried himself with an air of authority. Looking him over it didn't surprise him as much to realize that the man claimed to be his father.

"I know you think this is some kind of miracle. I'm not so blind to the ramifications of this mess. I'm not going to hug you and say I'm glad you are my long lost dad. I'm not made like that. I can't just accept you and be okay with years of perceived abandonment."

"No one is expecting you to... Just give it some time." Lilliana wrapped him in a tight embrace.

"Just show us the horses. I can't deal with this right now."

"I can do that," Jamieson agreed.

They strolled to the barn, and Jamieson led them to two horses in stalls next to each other. They were beautiful well-mannered animals.

"The chestnut is named Max and the white filly we call Sally. They are both good horses and are great for riding. Do you require a side saddle?"

"No, I don't ride side saddle," Lilly told him. "I have a skirt made just for riding astride, it splits down the middle. I made sure to wear it when I got dressed this morning anticipating going horseback riding."

"Good, I don't much care for the side saddle, it's dangerous," Jamieson replied.

"My father agrees and never allowed me to learn how to ride with one."

"I'll help you two get the horses saddled so you can be on your way."

Jamieson opened the stall and threw a saddle up on one of the horses. Lilliana stood to the side as Rand put the saddle on the other horse. Once both horses were prepared, they mounted them and rode them out of the barn. Lilliana's laugh of delight filled the air as she brought the horse to a light canter. Rand caught up to her quickly and kept up with the pace she set.

"I think we should talk about what happened," Lilliana said.

"I'm not ready to think of him as my father, Lily. Don't push it."

"You really need to give him a chance, but it's your decision I won't push."

"Thank you for supporting me."

"I'm your wife. It's what I'm supposed to do." She smiled. "How about a race?"

He started to tell her to no, but she took off at a fast gallop before he could get the words out. He knew she was only trying to lighten his mood, but he deemed a horse race too dangerous. No way would he put her life at risk by galloping their horses at full speed.

"Slow down Lily," Rand called.

His heart thundered in his chest as she sped in front of him. He wanted to reach out and stop her, but it was physically impossible. Rand could feel the color draining from his face with each bit of distance that grew between them.

She didn't hear him call out to her. Lilliana kept her horse's pace at a fast gallop. Rand raced to catch up to her, but she had gained a terrifying lead. She turned her head to look back at him, and with her attention divided she didn't see the tree branch directly in her path. She turned a moment too late, and Rand screamed as she flew from the horse. Her body hit the ground with a loud *thud*. He stopped his horse and jumped off of it racing to her side. Fear like he never knew before spread though his body. He couldn't lose her, not when he just found her, not ever. A tear began to form in his eye and fell down his cheek as he knelt beside her still body. Pain began to seep into his heart at the thought of losing her.

"Oh Lily, please be okay," he said pulling her into his arms. "I love you, I can't lose you when I just found you."

He stood and carried her back to the house trying not to jostle her. His fear was palpable and deep rooted inside of him. He had never been so afraid in his life. When he saw her flying from the horse all of his worst nightmares came to life.

"Quick someone help me, Lily took a nasty fall from her horse," Rand yelled.

Just as the words left his mouth he heard a voice bellow, "What the bloody hell did you do to my daughter?"

"I didn't do a damned thing to her, she fell from her horse. Help me take care of her."

Torrington reached to take Lilliana out of his arms, but Rand refused to relinquish her over to him.

"I'm not handing her over to you, she's fine where she is and I'm taking her upstairs until a physician can look at her."

Rand could hear them discussing the situation as he walked with huge steps toward their bedroom.

"Thor leave the man be, can't you see how distraught he is?" He heard Lilliana's mother say, stopping Viscount Torrington from going after Rand.

"He's manhandling my little girl."

"Sorry Thor, but I have to disagree with you again," Jamieson said.

"On which part, ol' friend, the manhandling or the fact that she's my little girl?" Thor asked.

"Well both actually. What I see is a man looking out for his wife."

"I fail to see your point." Thor's angry voice bellowed through the plantation walls.

"Rand and Lily are married. Sorry, Thor, but I believe that trumps your rights a bit."

"Bloody hell, I need a drink," Thor cursed. "What the hell are you waiting for, my daughter needs a physician. Send for one already."

Even though Rand had fear coursing through his body a small smile formed on his face. He heard Thor storm into the sitting room. At least Jamieson had his back. Maybe he could accept him in his life if the man willingly stood up to an ex-pirate.

CHAPTER 19

*P*ain crashed through her skull as someone poked at her body. Tiny shards of agony filled her head with every touch. A constant thrum of torment beat against the back of her head, and every inch of her body was stiff with soreness. Whoever thought it a good idea to add to the throbbing burrowing its way inside of her would soon find the error of their ways. She didn't do well with any kind of discomfort, and the idiot kept adding to it with each poke and prod he made. If only she could open her eyes to tell him to stop stabbing her with his fingers. Her eyes refused to open, but she could hear everyone around her.

"She's just unconscious," she heard someone say.

"I expect she'll be in a lot of pain once she wakes up. Her body is one huge bruise."

"But she will be okay?" a familiar voice asked.

Rand. He wanted to make sure she would be okay. *Of course I will be,* she wanted to scream the words at him. He shouldn't be made to worry about her.

"She better be all right, boy," another familiar voice roared. "Or I'll make sure you take your last breath."

Her father threatened her husband again. When would he stop tormenting Rand? Her mother had to be nearby; she wouldn't leave knowing Lilliana was hurt. Why hadn't she said something? Lily needed to hear her mother's voice.

"You won't be murdering my son, Thor. Back off."

Ah, yes, Jamieson would be there to help support Rand. Happiness filled her at the sound of Jamieson's voice. Rand had someone in his corner. He needed someone on his side. He often let the weight of the world hold him down. Jamieson would make sure he didn't give into his darker side.

"He's right, Thor. You are only making things worse by threatening him. Be happy that Lily chose him. You know we thought she'd never get married. I'm happy she found someone to give her heart to."

Oh yes Mama, I did. He's wonderful! I can't wait for you to know him as I do. She needed to wake up and tell them everything. The pain in her skull throbbed harder and faster as it tried to beat her from the inside out. *Please stop I can't take the pain anymore.*

"There are too many of you in the room," a man she assumed was the doctor told everyone. "Only two visitors at a time or she'll never get enough rest to heal."

"Fine. Everyone can leave. I want to spend some time alone with my wife."

Good for you Rand. Tell them all to leave. It should just be you and me for a while. My head hurts and I can't think with all of them hovering over me.

She heard some rustling as a door opened and closed. She believed that all of them left the room without arguing with Rand. That made things easier on both of them. The silence was blissful and the pain began to ease a bit as it washed over Lilliana. She could feel a head lay down on her waist and grabbed a hold of her hands. It must be Rand. He wouldn't have left her. He must have found a chair to set by the bed so he could keep vigil. She needed to wake up and help ease his pain.

"I will keep you company," Jamieson said.

So she was wrong. Not everyone left the room. Jamieson stayed behind to be with Rand.

"I'm fine. I don't need you."

"Yes son. I believe you do. You don't have to do everything alone."

"I've done it alone all my life. I don't see why I should change that now," Rand said in a bitter voice.

"Right now I'll remind you that you are not alone. You have me and Eliza if you want us, but more importantly you have a wife," Jamieson said. "I'm so sorry son; I wouldn't have abandoned you if I'd known you lived."

"It couldn't be helped. You didn't know. And you're right. Lily needs me. I can't let this eat up inside of me."

"I would never hurt you intentionally."

"In my head I understand that, but my hearts been bruised beyond recognition. I didn't allow myself to feel anything for anyone until I met Lily," Rand said.

"If you give me a chance, I'd like to get to know you."

"I don't know. Give me some time to let it all sink in."

"I can respect that. I hope you give me a chance. Eliza and I were never blessed with children. Since I missed out on raising you, I'd like to have a chance at being a grandfather."

"I can't make any promises. Right now I'd like to be alone with my wife."

"All right. I will leave you be for now. She will get better Rand."

Lilliana heard the door open and close again. Jamieson had left. The only ones in the room were her and Rand. She needed to open her eyes and let him know she would be okay.

"Lily, love, please wake up," he pleaded.

I'm trying! I would if I could.

"I love you, I should have told you sooner I know. I just couldn't get the words out. Last night I heard everything you said. I wish I could have spoken then. Please hear me now. I need you to know how I feel. I have never had these strong feelings before."

I knew you loved me! I hear you Rand, I hear everything you are saying to me. I just can't seem to open my eyes. It hurts too much. Give me some time. I can do it I know I can.

"You are also right about my father. I do need to

give him a chance. It's just so hard for me to accept anyone in my life. I've been alone for so long. I can't be alone anymore. Wake up Lily. Please don't leave me."

"I love you," Lilliana said with a hoarse whisper.

"Did you say something?" he asked with desperation.

"You heard me," she barely got out the words before he pulled her into his arms with a fierce hug.

"Can you open your eyes, love?"

"Hurts...too...much."

"That's okay, you should rest."

"My parents..."

"I can get them for you, if you want," he said.

"Yes, please. Need to speak to them." Lilliana croaked out, her voice hoarse from being so tight and dry. She struggled to get them out and let her Rand know what she wanted.

"I'll get them now. Just relax as I retrieve them."

Lilliana heard him leave the room in a rush. It seemed like hours before they finally came up the stairs. She must have drifted off again because when she opened her eyes only her mother sat at her side.

"Where's Daddy?" she asked with a hitch in her voice.

"I'm over here, princess."

Lilliana turned her head slightly to see her father standing by the window in her room. The afternoon sun streamed through the glass. Her father had a troubled look on his face.

"So happy to see you both," she said.

"You gave us quite a scare, young lady," her mother said. Her blue eyes held an enormous amount of concern and warmth. Her forehead crinkled up as she spoke. Her pale blonde hair was in disarray, as she must have run her hands through it with worry. "What were you thinking?"

"I wanted to make Rand smile. He looked so sad when he found out Jamieson was his father. Instead I ended up with a cracked head. That'll teach me for galloping at such fast speeds."

"I'm glad you are okay. I've never been so scared in my life." Her mother leaned down to hug her. "That doesn't make what you did right. Don't ever do something so foolish again."

"I know and I'm sorry, forgive me."

"Always, princess, we can never stay mad at you, but did you really have to go and marry Jamieson's only son? Right now I'd really like to murder him for putting you in danger," her father said.

"Be kind Daddy. I love him."

"I'll try. I'm not happy about it."

"I know, I promise you'll get used to the idea in time."

"I will make sure he plays nice," Pia said and kissed Lily on the cheek. "In the meantime you need your rest."

"Rand..."

"Is not so patiently waiting for us to leave." Pia smiled. "There isn't supposed to be more than two of us in the room at a time. Rand said you wanted to see us both which left him standing in the hallway."

"I did. I heard you talking. I had to make it right." She could barely keep her eyes open, and they were tiny slits as she looked at him. She fought the struggle her body demanded of her. She refused to succumb to the sleep her body required to heal. She needed to talk to them and make them understand. If she let herself doze back off she wouldn't be able to take care of her immediate concerns.

"You did, princess." Her father leaned over and kissed her cheek. "Don't worry about us. Just concentrate on getting better."

She watched her parents walk to the door to leave.

"I love you both. Thank you for being such wonderful parents."

"The pleasure, princess, belongs to us, you were

one of our blessings. We couldn't have asked for a better daughter."

Rand entered the room immediately after they left and sat down by her side. He lifted her hand to his mouth and placed a quick kiss in her palm. Her husband had been put through a lot in a very short time, and she didn't have a clue how to help him through it all.

His hazel eyes had held so much pain as he looked at her. She would have done anything in her power to ease it, but he hadn't given her a chance. Rand had done a good job of acting like he would be okay, but she knew him better than that. He may have laughed a little and acted untroubled, but she knew inside it shredded him. If he needed a little bit of time to himself to ease the hurt within, then she would ensure he had it.

"Did you say everything you needed to them?"

"Yes, I believe I did."

"I'm glad."

"What about you?"

"I don't know what you mean," he said.

"Have you talked with your father?"

"I had a small talk with him while you talked with your parents. We have a long way to go, but he knows I'm willing to try and build a relationship with him. I talked with Eliza as well. She cried a little bit and hugged me. It turns out she isn't capable of having children of her own. She wants to consider me her son. It's not a huge step, but it's a start. It's all I can offer them right now."

"Well that's good for you. You now have two wonderful people to call your parents," Lilliana said.

"I know it is, but it's still not going to be easy for me. I don't know what I'm doing here. It's all new territory for me."

Lilliana looked into Rand's eyes and just enjoyed gazing into their depths for a few minutes. He had such a sensitive nature, but didn't know how to express it.

"You will be fine. Besides you will have me every step of the way."

"I know. If I didn't have you by my side I wouldn't be able to do all of this. I wouldn't even be here to know who my father was. I owe everything to you. Thank you for agreeing to be my wife, Lily."

Lilliana needed to lighten the mood a bit. It had taken a turn she didn't want to go down just yet. She didn't need his gratitude, but she'd gladly take any love he'd willingly bestow upon her.

"I had my own selfish reasons for marrying you, you know."

"Oh yeah? What were they?" he asked with a smile.

"I knew you wouldn't be able to keep you hands off of me if I happened to be your wife." A hushed chuckle filled the room.

"I knew you were a wanton from the moment I met you."

"Really, do tell, what gave me away?" she asked with coyness.

"You had a devilish smile and you knew how to lure in your prey."

"So you are now my prey? I didn't know I had such power."

"You hold all the power, Lily. You are my life. I'd be lost without you. Do not ever do anything like you did earlier today. I thought I died a million times seeing you lying on the ground."

She could imagine how that scared him. If it had been in reverse and he lay on the ground hurt, she'd have been frantic. If she had a way of doing it all over again she'd never get on the horse.

"I didn't mean for that to happen, I'd never hurt you."

"You can be a bit reckless at times. Its part of why I love you so much, but it scares me at the same time."

"Is that all you love about me?" she asked.

"No, I love everything about you. I adore how your eyes fill with that devilishness I spoke of earlier, I admire your tenacity to get what you want, cherish the way you fight for those you care about, I worship the ground you walk on, but mostly I just love you with every beat of my heart."

"Oh Rand, I love you too. You have a great capacity for love. I knew it from the moment I looked into your eyes. It's why I knew you were the right man, not only to take me to Charleston, but to welcome into my life forever." Lilliana reached up and caressed his cheek with the palm of her hand. "You are the reason I changed my views on marriage. Because of you I started to believe love existed again." Lilliana paused, and looked down at her lap. A lump of emotion welled up inside of her. Once she regained control she looked up into Rand's eyes. "When I first started to socialize in society the men hadn't inspired me to believe in it. None of the ton marriages had been based on love. They only married for some kind of gain, either financial or power. I never wanted a marriage based on such low expectations. I always knew I wanted more. I thought my parents' marriage was a rarity and love only found the lucky few. I'm glad I'm among those blessed with it."

Rand leaned down and brushed her lips with his. At that moment she wished she hadn't cracked her head so hard on the tree branch and on the ground. She wanted to show him exactly how much she loved him, but her body hurt too much.

"I wish we could make love, but it would be too painful," she said with a bit of whimsy.

"We have the rest of our lives to express our love to each other, it can wait for you to heal. I want to be able to love you over and over. As soon as you are ready we are going to spend a whole day in bed doing just that. In the mean time you will have to settle for a few brief kisses and caresses."

"You're going to torture me, aren't you? That will be your revenge for me scaring you so badly. Admit it."

"You know me so well, love. I have to get my kicks in somewhere." He laughed.

Lilliana stuck her tongue out at him.

"I will get even if you do."

"Promise?"

"Always."

With that, Rand got up and lay down next to her

in the bed. Lilliana curled up next to him and rested her head on his shoulder. A small sigh escaped from her at how good it felt to be in his arms. They had come a long way in a few short weeks. They loved each other and had a long happy life ahead of them. Rand treasured her as much as she did him. Lilliana belonged with Rand, their love made them stronger. They could face anything as long as they did it by each other's side. Lilliana couldn't have asked for a better beginning to their story. More importantly, Lily couldn't wait to have children of her own. It would be her turn to craft a fairytale. She would tell her children a tale of true love, much as her father had with her and Liam. It would start with, *Once upon a time a lady asked a gentleman to help her run away...*

Read on for an excerpt from A Sanguine Gem: A Marsden Romance 3

CHAPTER 20

$\mathcal{L}$iam Marsden had a lot of things on his mind. However, he couldn't dwell on what was beyond his control. He had more pressing issues to deal with, starting with a meeting his father demanded. He had never let him down before, and he had no intention of starting at this juncture of his life.

He walked into his family home and strolled down the hallway towards the study. As he opened the door, he got a brief look at his father engrossed in his own work. The viscount had his dark hair pulled back at the nape of his neck; loose strands fell over his forehead as he tilted his head to read the paper in front of him. Liam had always admired his tenacity and willingness to do anything to accomplish any task. He didn't give up easily and believed the world belonged to him to take what he wanted from it.

"Ah good you're here," He glanced up at Liam and set his work aside. "I have a few things I need to discuss with you."

"I came as soon as I received your missive. What's so urgent?"

"A good number of things that I didn't foresee."

On closer scrutiny, Liam could see stress lines forming on his father's face. His eyes filled with worry as he rubbed his temples. What could have happened to make him appear so concerned? Liam didn't think this meeting would be a jovial one. His father didn't often worry about things. No, Viscount Torrington took action and left the fretting to others.

"This is serious?" Liam asked as he raised an eyebrow.

"I received a letter from your sister. Some of it is good news. Most of it is actually."

"It's the part that isn't good news that concerns you." Liam sat down and leaned forward, giving his father his full attention. "What has happened?"

"First, I should tell you that you are the proud uncle of a strapping baby boy. You sister had her child a month ago. They named him William

Jamieson after his two grandfathers. Poor boy has a lot to live up to with that name." He laughed.

"If I'm an uncle that means you are a grandfather. How does that make you feel old man" Liam grinned. He couldn't resist an opportunity to tease his father.

"Bite your tongue, boy. It'll be a long time before I'm an old man," With a devilish grin on his face, his father sat back in his chair and studied Liam. "This is good for you because I don't think you are quite ready to fill my shoes."

Liam hoped his father lived a very long life. He couldn't imagine a life without the man's robust personality filling a room wherever he went. Like most children, he believed his parents infallible. He knew they were mere human beings, but he liked to believe they would live forever.

"No, I can't say I'm in a hurry to take the reins from you. I pray you're here for many years to come. For more reasons than one," Liam said. "But regardless of how I feel about your possible demise that isn't why you summoned me here. Nor is it the news about my new nephew. Grateful as I am to hear about it, something else weighs on your mind. I think it's time to dispense with the pleasantries."

"That isn't all your sister wrote about," he said

with a heavy sigh. "She has some concerns that she asked me to look into."

"Is it about the merger of Marsden Shipping with RandCo? There isn't an issue with its completion, is there?" He needed to dispense with that bit of concern first because it was at the forefront of his mind. "If so, I'd like to take care of it immediately."

"No, that at least is going well. We should have considered a merger as soon as Lily and Rand married." Viscount Torrington sighed and stood up. He strolled over to a nearby shelf and pulled out a decanter of brandy along with two glasses. "This is something entirely different and I'm not sure how to proceed."

"What's Lily worried about?" Liam's concern rose. What could be so dreadful?

Viscount Torrington handed Liam a brandy filled snifter. He took a sip of his own and set it down. He stared past Liam, his eyes unfocused. "The Earl of Devon was a pretty good friend of mine."

"I remember." Liam nodded.

"At one time I'd hope to have a merger with him," his father paused and stared down at his drink. "It was the reason we attempted to betroth you and Gemma."

Liam would rather forget about that time in his

life. He grimaced and stared up at his father. "Right, that was several years ago." What was his father getting at?

"The business merger and familial one fell through at the same time. We never found a reason to revisit either." He downed the rest of his drink in his glass. "I have to admit a part of me is glad it didn't. As much as I liked the man I abhor the gentleman who inherited his estate."

Liam rubbed his temple; a pain throbbed through his head listening to his father rattle on. "What does Alfie have to do with this?"

"Lady Gemma is my concern."

She wasn't his, so Liam had no clue why he brought her into the conversation. In fact, everything he'd said so far hadn't made any sense to him.

"Father, what exactly is the problem?" Frustration built to the boiling point deep inside him. "I don't understand what Lady Gemma has to do with all of this."

"Lady Gemma keeps in touch with Lily. She wrote your sister about some disturbing news." The viscount sat back and studied Liam. He steepled his hands together as he spoke. "She thinks I might have a solution to the problem. I can think of a couple of ways we could assist her, but you would have to be willing."

"What it is you would like me to do?" Liam replied, a horrible feeling sinking to the bottom of his gut.

Viscount Torrington leaned forward and set his hands on his desk. His eyes bore into Liam's as he appeared to weigh over the issue that troubled him.

"You know I'd never force you to do anything, but I think in this you believe as I do."

"I'm at a loss as you haven't explained anything to me," Liam reminded him. "How am I to know if I agree or not if you don't?" He silently hoped his father wasn't about to ask what he thought he was. After he mentioned the botched attempt to betroth him to Lady Gemma, Liam couldn't help but wonder —he couldn't possibly want him to marry Gemma. *Could he?*

"First, you should be aware of the circumstances regarding Lady Gemma and why Lily is so concerned," his father told him. "Then I will explain my idea and the two possible solutions to it. One is a better option, and the other should only be considered if you are against the first."

"And what is happening with her?" Liam stood up and paced around the room. He stopped a few steps away and pinned his father with a stare. "Quit stalling and tell me what's going on."

"Alfie is—being difficult."

"In what way?"

If his father didn't tell him what was going on soon. Liam wouldn't be held responsible for his actions. Their conversation was driving him mad.

"He has squandered the entire inheritance. If the estate weren't entailed, he'd sell it to pay off his enormous debts. That leaves him in a bit of a bind. He needs money and as fast as possible."

Liam nodded. "I think I see the correlation. Lady Gemma still has an inheritance, and he wants to get his hands on it."

Viscount Torrington stood up and joined him in front of the desk. His eyes had an angry edge to them. Liam knew his father well enough to realize he wanted to do some damage to the new Earl of Devon. Whatever Alfie was doing enraged him. Liam had a bad feeling about what was going on with Lily's friend.

"In a manner of speaking yes and he is willing to use whatever is at his disposal to get it. Lady Gemma is afraid he might force the situation to get his way."

"I see." Liam scowled. "Does she have reason to believe he will act so dishonorably?"

"This is old news." His father frowned and crossed his arms over his chest. "I got the letter today from your sister. It might already be a foregone conclusion. I'm afraid we may be too late with how slow mail travels between England and America. I don't know what we'll find if we go to the Earl of Devon's estate."

Not good news, in fact, they were quite horrid. Liam might have issues with Lady Gemma, but he'd never wanted anyone to hurt her. He'd willingly help her deal with her cousin if he could find a good solution to her problem.

"I hadn't even considered that. We are wasting time. What are your solutions?" Liam asked.

"Lady Gemma needs a husband. She doesn't gain majority and control over her funds for five more years. She only has one solution that will effectively work for her."

With those words, Liam's fears were realized. His heart beat faster in his chest and the pounding in his head intensified.

His father wanted him to marry Lady Gemma.

Liam should be appalled at the suggestion, especially as he'd already tried to betroth them when they were younger. He had never denied that Lady Gemma had beauty in spades. She had luxurious crimson hair and eyes the color of jade. His mouth watered thinking about her beautiful complexion and soft curves. That was until she open her mouth to speak. Listening to her droll on and on for what seemed like forever, he invariably forgot how exquisite her body and face appeared and wanted to put some much needed distance between them.

Why should he sacrifice his life for her?

The brazen redhead had been the bane of his existence for several years now. It took the death of her father for her to back away. Admittedly he admired her tenacity and willingness to make her wishes known, but that didn't mean he ever desired to tie himself to her forever. Perhaps his father's other solution would be easier for him to stomach.

"You are not suggesting what I think you are." Appalled, Liam sat back down in his chair. Shock filled him to the brink. He had to be reading the situation wrong.

"I had hoped that you had some tender feelings for the chit. You are constantly arguing with her." His father sat back down in his chair, a slight knowing smirk resting on his face. "That is a form of passion. Trust me I know a bit about denial in that area."

"Well, you're incorrect in your assumption." Liam

glared. He didn't have any feelings for Gemma. She was a nuisance nothing more. "There aren't any tender feelings on either side. The girl irritates me to no end. I never did understand what Lily saw in her."

"That's too bad. I still have the betrothal contract I signed with Lady Gemma's father. We could have used it to our advantage."

Liam stared at his father with a blank expression. He'd actually signed the contract? How could he have done that? His father had reassured him he'd never force him to marry anyone.

"Excuse me could you repeat that? I don't think I heard you correctly." Liam hoped he'd heard wrong. Sadly he doubted he had. "You informed me the betrothal hadn't been finalized."

"That's correct," His father grinned. "However Devon hoped I'd change my mind and told me to keep the contract. All I have to do to make it legal is sign my name to it."

Liam blanched. His father was losing his mind. There wasn't a chance in hell he'd make him marry Lady Gemma. "But you're not going to, right

"So you are not willing to help?"

"I didn't say that." Liam shook his head. "I'm willing to hear the other plan you have. I'm hoping it is preferable to the latter."

"The other plan involves you basically kidnapping the girl and taking her to your sister in South Carolina."

Relief flooded him at his father's words. Calm now that the storm of anxiety fled his stomach, Liam took a deep breath and considered his father's other idea. He had to agree that the second plan held more appeal. It was preferable, but not that much better in the grand scheme of things. He would still be forced to spend a considerable amount of time in Lady Gemma's company. How would he be able to get through a voyage with her? They would have to take the Sea Rover for the crossing. No other ships were available, and their steamships were only in the planning stages of being built. If he had any luck, it wouldn't take more than three weeks to complete.

The bonus, of course, would be to see his sister and his new nephew. He sincerely wished to see them so that no price was too high for him to be able to spend time in their company. He would even be willing to get to know his brother-in-law as well. Maybe he would find a way to like the rat bastard. His father may have forgiven him for stealing Lily, but Liam didn't feel like he deserved such absolution. The man had a lot of audacity to run away with the daughter of Viscount Torrington—a former pirate. Liam would give him that much.

"That plan is more conceivable to accomplish," Liam said. "But is kidnapping really necessary? Do you believe Lady Gemma will be unwilling to go to live with Lily?"

"I honestly do not know," his father sighed. "I hate to tell you this, but I think you're going to need ammunition to get her out."

"Explain," Liam demanded.

"If you go in prepared Alfie won't have anything to argue about."

"How do you suggest I do that?"

His father grinned. It almost had a wicked tinge to it. "I'm going to sign this betrothal. Go to the bishop and demand a special license. With the right amount of money and the betrothal as evidence, he won't deny you."

"I fail to see why I need to go to such lengths."

"Alfie won't let Gemma go willingly. You're going to have to force his hand." His father paused and looked him in the eye. "I'm not telling you to marry the girl. Just use the tools I'm giving you to save her."

"All right I will go see the bishop now. Afterward, I will retrieve Gemma and bring her back here to plan our next move." Liam said.

"Good. I'd hate to disappoint your sister. I hope we are not too late to help Lady Gemma."

With those words, Liam got up and walked out of the study. He had never been a fan of Lady Gemma Kemsley, but he had never wished her ill will either. If she had more trouble than she could handle, Liam had no choice but to help her. His sister depended on him, and he had never let her down before—he certainly didn't plan on starting with Lady Gemma.

The chit had better be prepared to do everything necessary to leave her home. Liam didn't suffer fools and luckily for him he knew that she didn't either. No matter what he believed, her to be he had always been able to see the keen intelligence in her eyes. Perhaps with age she had also gained some maturity to go along with it.

CHAPTER 21

Gemma Kemsley couldn't believe her rotten luck as she strolled into the sitting room on her father's—her cousin's estate. She still had trouble wrapping her mind around the fact that her father passed away eighteen months ago. Her cousin, Alfie, inherited the title and the entailed estates upon his death. He also became her guardian. A reality that Gemma loathed for many reasons, the biggest being he had lecherous intentions towards her.

He said in no uncertain terms she would be his wife whether she liked it or not. Well, Gemma didn't like it and vowed to find a way to escape his plans for her. She took a page out of her best friend Lily's book and started to scheme her way out of the situation.

The only option for her would be to run away and live in America. Lily would welcome her into her home. She just needed to find a way to leave without Alfie knowing what she had in mind.

"Ah, there you are Gemma, dear. We have some things to discuss."

Disgust filled her at the sight of her cousin invading her space. He smelled just as foul, like a night of overindulging in cheap liquor. Bloody hell, why couldn't he be in London at one of his clubs? They probably wouldn't admit him anymore. No doubt the whole ton had begun to realize the new Earl of Devon was headed to debtors' prison. It couldn't happen soon enough to satisfy her. The horrid man continued to harass her on a daily basis. She didn't know how much longer she could stand to put up with his unwanted advances.

Why did her father have to die and leave her in Alfie's care? She missed him every day. Living without him was hard enough, but to constantly have to defend herself rattled her to her very core.

"As far as I'm concerned we have talked more than I have ever liked. Go away Alfie I am not in the mood to fend off your licentious advances today," Gemma told him.

"I don't care what you want, dear. I came to

inform you that your time is up. At the end of the week, we will wed. Just as soon as I can obtain a special license." His eyes leered over her bosom as he delivered the awful news. "You look especially lovely today. How about we seal the deal with a kiss?"

Lovely? Like that was going to work on her. She'd rather stand outside in a lightning storm and beg to be struck dead than marry her cousin. Kiss him? Not bloody going to happen.

Alfie reached for her. Gemma took a step back to prevent being held in his embrace. She knew it wouldn't stop at a kiss. No, her cousin wanted to do more than press his lips on hers. He wanted to ravish her until she no longer retained any shred of innocence.

Alfie believed she owed him because he allowed her to live with him after he moved in. As her guardian, he got a stipend to provide for her living expenses. He couldn't touch the majority of her inheritance without a valid reason.

Thankfully her mother had left her a large sum of money upon her death. Only marriage or reaching her majority would allow her access to it though.

It took her a while, but she finally understood why her best friend, Lily, had been so against marriage. It was unbelievably ironic that she succumbed to it as soon as she left England, but that didn't make her argument against matrimony any less valid.

"I'd rather kiss a dead fish than allow you anywhere near me." She gave him a scathing look and frowned at him.

Heat filled her cheeks at the idea of him touching her. Not in a good way either. She didn't desire him; rather she wanted never to lay eyes on him ever again. Alfie was the exact opposite of the man she truly wanted—or rather used to long for.

"No reason to be so vicious. You'll like it once I warm you up a bit," he said, an evil grin on his lips.

In her haste to get away from him she tripped and fell backward on the settee. She tried to get up before he could take advantage of the situation, but her efforts were futile. He pounced on her after her misfortunate collapse. His lips pressed hard against hers. When she tried to open her mouth to scream he pushed his tongue inside her mouth and squeezed her breast in the palm of his hand.

Pain shot through her and continued to spread through her nipple. Alfie pulled her onto him and grinded himself against her stomach. She could feel his hardness as he rubbed himself on her. She'd lose the contents of her stomach soon if she couldn't get him to let her go.

What could she do? Not a lot of options were making themselves known to her and she was fast running out of time. An idea came to her as Alfie pushed his tongue into her mouth again. Gemma bit down on his lip and drew blood. She could taste it as a small drop fell on her tongue, it was bitter and disgusting.

"You little bitch," he shouted with rage. "You're going to pay for that."

He yanked Gemma's dress and tore the side of her bodice. He reached forward and pinched her nipple between his forefinger and thumb. She screamed out as his nails dug into the sensitive tip. She had to put some distance between them before something she couldn't escape from happened. It was clear Alfie planned on claiming her against her will.

Gemma grabbed his arm, her nails digging in and leaving half-moon imprints into his flesh. She yanked his arm away from her, ripping his hand off her bruised breast. She fought to get away from him, but it was a struggle she was losing. Her cousin was too strong, and she didn't have the ability to fight him. Tears started to fall from the corner of her eyes. This was wrong, so very wrong, and Gemma couldn't stop it from happening to her.

"Alfie, Ole' Chap, I do hope you are not doing what I think you are."

That voice—Gemma knew that voice. Her heart raced in her chest and tingles of fire danced across her stomach. It haunted her dreams and made her want things she knew she'd never have. Alfie let her go, and she fell back on the settee. She jerked her bodice over her exposed breast, embarrassment settling in the bottom of her stomach like a dead weight.

Gemma looked over and straight into the stormy blue eyes of the only man she had ever wanted—ever allowed herself to love. His pale blond hair hung loosely over his collar making her want to run her fingers through it. She knew that the fine blond strands would be silky if she'd were to touch them.

At one time, she believed he would be her everything, the one person she was meant to spend the rest of her life with.

Too bad he didn't return her feelings.

No man had ever compared to him—no one ever would. This man standing in front of her, glaring at her cousin, filled her with desire and longing. Liam Marsden had ruined her for anyone else.

"I don't know why you feel comfortable waltzing in, but Gemma and I were in the middle of something. You can show yourself out the same way you came in," Alfie said.

Fool. Liam Marsden didn't take orders.

Gemma didn't know why her cousin even thought that nonsense had a possibility of working. She was simultaneously irritated and relieved Liam had showed up. She didn't know why he came out to the country, but he had saved her from ruin. She might be perpetually angry with him—but now, she'd have to set that annoyance aside to thank him. Gemma owed him a debt she didn't think she'd ever be able to repay.

"Well, I came to see my fiancée. I have to say I don't like that I walked into you getting rough with her. Explain yourself, man, before I commit murder."

Fiancée? She stood up her gaze whipping toward Liam's. A blaze of longing rushed through her with that one word. What the bloody hell was Liam talking about? The only place he had ever asked her to marry him had been in her dreams.

Sadly, in reality he ignored her whenever she came near him.

So this little announcement of his baffled her. What was the man up to? Did he know something about her situation and decided to come and save her? It wouldn't work as much as she wanted it to. Claiming to be her fiancé wouldn't make Alfie let go of her. He'd fight Liam every step of the way unless there was proof of his prior claim.

"Gemma is not your fiancée," Alfie said. He sneered, evil apparent in his gaze. "I think I'd know if I had approved of someone for her to marry."

"That's because you didn't approve it." Liam folded his arms across his chest. He oozed smugness as he looked Alfie in the eye.

Gemma hid a smile. That had to goad her cousin a bit.

"Then you can leave. I'm the only one who can approve who Gemma marries." Alfie waved his hand attempting to dismiss Liam.

Liam ignored him and stalked forward. "Her father signed the contract before he died." He turned and gave her a glance that scorched her from the inside out. Gemma only barely restrained from fanning herself. "I have waited patiently for her mourning to end so we can be married. I think it's time that we proceeded with our plans."

"What contract? Why wasn't I made aware of this?" Alfie asked as he glared at Gemma.

Gemma just shrugged her shoulders in his

general direction. She didn't have the answers he sought. She didn't have any idea what Liam was talking about. Surely her father would have told her if he had signed a contract for her to marry someone. This had to be some ruse on Liam's part. Whatever he planned she had every intention of following along with it. Anything to help her get away from her cousin would be very much preferable to submitting to his licentious groping.

"I have it right here," Liam said as he shoved the contract at Alfie. "The old earl's signature is at the bottom giving permission for me to marry his daughter, Lady Gemma Kemsley."

"I don't understand. Why didn't the solicitors tell me about this?" Alfie asked, his face turning three different shades of red.

Liam had the contract in his hands and Alfie attempted to snatch it from him. Liam just shook his head and folded it back up, placing it back in the safety of his inside pocket. Cool, calm, and collected —that was Liam.

"Possibly because they didn't know. This document has been in my father's keeping since I was fourteen years old. They decided to betroth us several years ago." Confidence intertwined with each word he spoke. "Good for business you know. We had no idea Gemma's father would die so tragically before he could tell her about it. It's sad, but well I think it's time we move on."

"I don't care." Alfie stomped his foot like a small child. "I don't approve and Gemma isn't going to marry you."

Gemma had to restrain herself from laughing at the ridiculous situation she found herself in. The only man she had ever loved demanded she marry him and her libertine cousin thought he had a chance of denying it. Not for a minute did she believe the contract had any validity to it. Lily had to have put Liam up to the scheme to help her escape. Gemma knew that Liam didn't want her. She'd learned it the hard way two years ago. It didn't matter though; he was here to save her. She knew Liam would do anything his twin sister asked him. They'd always been close. If she demanded he save her best friend he'd do it without blinking. Liam wouldn't be in her ancestral home stepping in between her and Alfie otherwise.

"Seems like you don't have any say in the matter, Alfie," Gemma said solemnly. "Papa signed the contract. That supersedes your wishes. I have no choice, but to marry Liam Marsden."

This was surely a dream. Marry him? A flutter of

hope started to ignite within her. She squashed it before it could take root. Liam wasn't going to marry her. Gemma refused to give in to something surely destined to destroy her. Hope was an evil four letter word, designed to bring a person to their knees and wrap them up in despair.

"You could refuse him."

"I don't want to." Gemma laughed.

Alfie clenched his fists at his side. His hand flew up and stopped in midair as if he rethought the action he'd been about to take. He glanced over at Liam and Gemma did as well. He was in a position to strike. Alfie would never have gotten the slap across Gemma's cheek.

Gemma grinned with relief. Alfie would have to find some other heiress to get him out of debt. She had no intention of letting him touch her or her money.

"Good. Go pack a small bag, whatever you deem necessary to take today. We can send for your other belongings later," Liam instructed her. "Oh and Gemma, change your gown too. Something pretty, perhaps green to match your eyes."

"I'm to leave today? Isn't that sudden?"

Assuagement filled her at the idea of escaping Alfie.

Her hand flew to her chest as she allowed herself to believe it was going to happen. Liam worked fast, not that she was complaining, but she thought it'd take more time for him to extract her from her cousin's clutches.

"Yes. I have a special license. We're to be married today."

"Give me fifteen minutes. I don't have a lot that needs to be packed immediately. I will instruct the housekeeper to pack the rest of my trunks for delivery to Marsden House."

"I will wait for you here. I need to have a private word with Alfie on how a woman in his care should be treated."

Liam's mouth crunched up into a firm line. Displeasure filled his eyes as he turned to pin Alfie with his gaze. They darkened to a stormy blue, one Gemma had never seen before. She wanted to tell Liam not to hurt her cousin for altruistic reasons, but if she were honest she wanted him beaten.

He would have forced himself on her if Liam hadn't walked in. Her skin still crawled with revulsion from the places he'd put his hands. She shuddered at the memory, disgusted she'd had to endure his groping. Gemma loathed the man as much as she adored Liam. They were two different men and each invoked a different feeling in her. Sadly, she wasn't at all happy with either emotion.

Living with unrequited love was horrible— dealing with Alfie's nasty disposition, however, was a far worse ordeal.

"Liam, don't hurt him—much." Gemma paused and waved her hand dismissively. "I'd hate for this to come back to haunt us."

He looked at her with a devilish smile. That carefree smile so full of sin had always been her undoing. Her heart skipped a beat, and her stomach started to tingle.

"Darling, I promise you he'll be hurting far more than it will show on the outside. He'll feel a pain that will haunt him long after we are gone from his life. Now scoot so I can inflict all those deep seated wounds he fully deserves."

Gemma nodded and ran out of the room. She skipped the steps and walked into her bedroom. She grabbed a valise and put a change of clothes in it. Then she took her jewelry case and a stack of letters. She placed them inside and tied it closed. Gemma didn't need much and everything necessary had been enclosed in the satchel. She found a green gown in her armoire and changed as fast as she could. Thankfully she followed Lily's advice and had had gowns made she could put on herself. She picked up the bag and with much haste went back to the sitting room.

She paused inside the doorway. Her eyes flew to Liam as he lounged on a nearby chair. His legs were crossed in an easy manner as he tapped restlessly on the arm. Alfie sat stiffly on the settee and held his stomach in a tight embrace. Not a mark showed anywhere on him as Liam had promised.

"I'm ready to go."

Liam turned and looked at her. He nodded in her direction and started to walk over to her side.

"You're both going to regret you've crossed me," Alfie spat out.

Liam stopped and turned back to Alfie before they exited the room.

"Alfie, don't do anything stupid." His voice was hard and commanding as he issued the reminder. "As long as you leave us be we will leave you alone. Make one wrong move towards me or Gemma and you will regret it. That isn't a threat. It's a promise. I take care of what's mine."

Gemma snorted. Liam had claimed her. She didn't believe he meant it. Whatever his reasons for helping her, it had nothing to do with wanting her. Still, a part of her couldn't help wishing it were true.

When she'd first heard the words, her whole body lit up with an uncontrollable longing.

Liam turned back to Gemma and placed her hand in the crook of his arm.

"Ready to go, love?" he asked, his tone softening just for her ears.

"Oh yes. Let's go and never look back."

She let him lead her out the door and to his awaiting carriage. Liam helped her as she entered the carriage and followed her inside. He took her bag and placed it under one of the seats and then sat across from her. The carriage started to move, and it jerked her forward causing her to collapse into his arms. She hadn't been prepared for it to depart.

"You always did fall into my arms." Liam laughed as he set her next to him on the seat.

"Don't go ruining a good rescue by turning into an arse," Gemma scolded him. "I know that was a farce. Did Lily put you up to it?"

"Not at all. Well, not entirely. She did ask for my father to help you out of the situation. He placed the particulars in my hands."

"And this is the solution you came up with?" Gemma paused with a sigh. "I'm sorry. I should be thanking you. Instead, I'm harping on how you did it."

She stared at him. "I don't mind really. It worked to get Alfie to let me go without a fight—well not much of one anyway. I truly do appreciate your assistance. I don't want to think about what he'd have done if you hadn't arrived in time." Gemma shuddered at the memory of her cousin's hands on her bosom. "I take it you are going to help me get to America so I can stay with your sister until I reach my majority?"

"No."

"What do you mean no?" she asked. "How am I going to escape from Alfie if I don't leave the country?"

"I thought that had already been settled. You're marrying me. Today. Nothing else is going to deter him."

"I don't want to marry you. I'd much rather go to South Carolina."

"We will do that. It is probably best we leave for a short period anyway. On our wedding trip can go visit Lily," he said.

"Why are you being obstinate? I am not going to marry you."

"Yes, you are." Liam emphasized each word as he looked her directly in the eyes. Gemma's lips pursed, disbelief filling her as he spoke. "Your father gave his permission. You are stuck with me. You just told Alfie you didn't want to refuse me."

Were they actually getting married? The infernal flutter of hope sprung to life. Gemma didn't know if she could eradicate it again. Did her father truly want her to marry Liam? She bit her lip and once again wished he was still around to ask. He'd know what to do. But if the contract Liam had was legit, it was clear her father had wanted her to marry him. She already had her answer.

Warmth pooled in her cheeks. She clenched her fists in her lap.

Gemma wanted to scream with outrage. Damn her rotten luck. She knew Liam didn't love her, and she didn't want to find herself stuck in a loveless marriage. Worse yet he knew she loved him once; maybe he counted on her still having those feelings for him. No matter what she said, she was far from over him. A one-sided love— married to him for the rest of her life—would be hell. She had to make him see that it wouldn't work.

"Can't we just pretend?" Gemma asked. "You don't want to marry me, Liam. Don't make me hate you."

"You are not going to talk me out of this, Gemma.

It's decided. I've accepted it, and now you need to as well."

"Like hell I do,"

Gemma pushed him back and scooted across to the other side of the carriage. She didn't need to sit next to him while he dictated to her.

"No need to make things interesting, love. I'm already willing. Now sit back and relax. The rector is expecting us to arrive shortly."

"What rector?"

"The one in the next town. I've made all the arrangements. I already told you I had a special license, didn't I," he said. "In less than an hour you will be my wife. Don't worry you'll get used to the idea.

If Gemma had something to throw at him, it would have already bounced off his head. Liam Marsden had to be the most stubborn male in existence.

"Bloody hell, you are irritating."

"Welcome to my world," he said with a droll smile. "It's all part of the plan, love. Makes life more... intriguing."

Gemma sat back in her seat and fumed. Winning an argument with Liam was akin to dreams becoming reality. No way would he allow her to get ahead. Just like the real world never compared to the bliss of dreams.

Neither one had a chance of happening for her right now. She gave up on her fantasies a long time ago; just as she now gave up on convincing Liam to forego marrying her. It would amount to wasted energy and useless hope.

Gemma knew when to sit back and lick her wounds to fight another day. If she had to be Liam's wife, she'd need a new plan of attack. She had learned from the best and Lily had taught her well. Her fiancé didn't know what he had in store for him.

Gemma didn't give up anything that belonged to her.

Liam would love her or at the very least desire her as much as she did him. With a plan forming in her head, she relaxed, and her lips lifted into a half smile.

Thank you so much for taking the time to read my book.

Your opinion matters!

Please take a moment to review this book on your favorite review site and share your opinion with fellow readers.

www.authordawnbrower.com

Broken Pearl

Deadly Benevolence

A Wallflower's Christmas Kiss

A Gypsy's Christmas Kiss

Snowflake Kisses

Begin Again

There You'll Be

Better as a Memory

Won't Let Go

Enduring Legacy

The Legacy's Origin

Charming Her Rogue

Scandal Meets Love

Love Only Me (Amanda Mariel)

Find Me Love (Dawn Brower)

If It's Love (Amanda Mariel)

Odds of Love (Dawn Brower)

Bluestockings Defying Rogues

When An Earl Turns Wicked

A Lady Hoyden's Secret

One Wicked Kiss

Earl In Trouble

All the Ladies Love Coventry

Marsden Descendants

Rebellious Angel

Tempting An American Princess

Marsden Romances

A Flawed Jewel

A Crystal Angel

A Treasured Lily

A Sanguine Gem

A Hidden Ruby

A Discarded Pearl

Novak Springs

Cowgirl Fever

Dirty Proof

Unbridled Pursuit

Sensual Games

Christmas Temptation

Linked Across Time

Saved by My Blackguard

Searching for My Rogue

Seduction of My Rake

Surrendering to My Spy

Spellbound by My Charmer

Stolen by My Knave

Separated from My Love

Scheming with My Duke

Secluded with My Hellion

Heart's Intent

One Heart to Give

Unveiled Hearts

Heart of the Moment

Kiss My Heart Goodbye

Heart in Waiting

ABOUT THE AUTHOR

USA TODAY Bestselling author, DAWN BROWER writes both historical and contemporary romance. There are always stories inside her head; she just never thought she could make them come to life. That creativity has finally found an outlet.

Growing up she was the only girl out of six children. She is a single mother of two teenage boys; there is never a dull moment in her life. Reading books is her favorite hobby and she loves all genres.

bookbub.com/authors/dawn-brower

facebook.com/AuthorDawnBrower

twitter.com/1DawnBrower

instagram.com/1DawnBrower

EXCERPT: ALL THE LADIES LOVE COVENTRY

BLUESTOCKINGS DEFYING ROGUES

Dawn Brower

All the Ladies Love Coventry

April 1794

Charles Lindsay, the Earl of Coventry surveyed the building he was hoping to purchase. The structure was sound and would work splendidly for what he had in mind for it. The street it was located on was also ideal. A secret gentleman's club would be well hidden in the neighborhood, and its residents wouldn't question the constant comings and goings that would be involved. He had a lot of plans and this townhouse was only the beginning.

"The owner is willing to part with it?" He turned toward the solicitor in charge of the sale. Charles didn't want to seem too eager. It might give the solicitor a reason to raise the price. He wouldn't pay a penny more than it was worth.

"He is, my lord," he answered. His salt and pepper hair was sprinkled around his ears and the back of his head, but the top was completely bald. The solicitor had beady eyes that made him appear untrustworthy. Not a good look on someone that should invoke that particular feeling. "Would you like to make an offer?"

"No," he answered. "It needs major renovations and I'm not sure it'll work for what I have in mind." That was a lie, but he didn't want to make the man aware of his complete interest. "The entire bottom floor would need to be stripped and the walls rebuilt. Your employer is asking too much."

"I see..." The solicitor swallowed hard. Charles wished he could recall his name, but as it hadn't been important to him he'd dismissed it upon hearing it. He fumbled with some parchments and then glanced up. "Is there anything that will convince you to purchase it."

Charles held back a grin. It wouldn't work in his favor and he did want the property. He tapped his chin and tried to act as if he was considering his options. The truth was he knew exactly what his next move would be. That was the benefit of being several steps ahead of his opponent. He had a gift of seeing the larger picture and how all the pieces around him could fit together. This project of his was going to be big and he had to do everything right for it to work. "I might consider it if the owner will take off a thousand pounds from the selling price. I won't pay a shilling more than that."

He shuffled his feet and then met Charles gaze. "That sounds reasonable, my lord. I'll inform the owner that you're willing to purchase it."

Charles lifted a brow. "Is that all?" He shrugged and headed to the exit. As far as he was concerned their business had been concluded. If the owner took the offer the solicitor could send him a missive about it. He had a good feeling though. Soon he'd have the building necessary to start his club.

He hadn't reached the exit before the solicitor called out to him. "Lord Coventry."

He turned toward him and said, "Yes?"

"I have the authority to approve the sale within a certain amount. If you want the property it's yours."

This time he did allow the smile to form on his face. The Coventry Club was now one step closer to becoming a reality. He couldn't wait to tell his good friend the George, the Earl of Harrington about it.

They could plan the development and reconstruction of the townhouse together.

"Wonderful," he told the solicitor. "I'll let my solicitor know and you two can handle the details." Charles nodded at him. "Thank you for your assistance." With those words he did exit the building and headed home. He had an appointment later with George and they could make their final plans then.

CHARLES TAPPED HIS FINGER ON HIS DESK impatiently. Where the bloody hell was George? He was supposed to arrive several hours ago. He sighed and poured a glass of brandy from the decanter on his desk. They would have to discuss his plans for Coventry Club later. He sipped on his brandy and wondered what could have held his friend up. For the life of him he couldn't discern a reason for George to stay away. His friend never missed an appointment. He was the most reliable man of Charles acquaintance.

He set his glass down and peered at the deed to his new property. He'd already sent out missives to start the repairs and renovations. In a matter of months, no more than a year, his dream would be a reality. A safe haven for men who had no place else, a den of iniquity for those that needed it, but mostly a place where loyalty would prevail more than anything else.

The door to his study flew open and George stepped inside. His face lit up with a huge grin as he exclaimed, "I'm a father Charles."

He'd forgotten George's wife was enceinte. That was a damn good reason for his friend to be late. Now that he realized why he felt like a right arse. Charles reached for a glass and poured two fingers of brandy into it, then handed it to his friend. He lifted his own glass and toasted, "To fatherhood." He sipped his brandy, and then asked. "I must ask—an heir or a daughter?"

"It's a boy," George answered. "The most perfect little bundle of joy I've ever held. We named him Jonas after my maternal great grandfather. It'll make my mum happy."

Charles knew he should look for a wife and carry on his line, but the idea of tying himself to one woman for the rest of his life didn't appeal to him. He hadn't met a woman that inspired that kind of commitment. George had married his wife because of his father's demands. The Duke of Southington was a difficult man to say no to. Charles didn't envy his friend's situation in that regard. "I'm sure she'll be ecstatic to just have a grandchild to dote on. I hear women like that sort of thing."

"You're probably correct in that assumption. Either way I'm grateful it's a boy. The birth was hard on Sarah. I don't think she could handle another pregnancy." He sighed. "Jonas is a blessing for us both. My father will finally leave us alone about carrying on the family line."

"Your father is brutal." He was an overbearing arse who browbeat George whenever he could. Charles wished he could find a way to remove the Duke of Southington from his friend's life. Unfortunately, it wasn't up to him to extricate George from the control of his father. His friend had to find the bollocks to do it himself. It was the only way he would ever know what it felt like to be free to make his own decisions.

"I have news," Charles began. "I've purchased the building I need for Coventry Club."

"You did?" His face lit up with happiness. "That's wonderful. Now you can achieve your goals and we'll all have a place to escape the realities of life."

"I'll have to discern the rules of the club before

we invite new members. I'd like you to be the first head of the club if you're willing." He wanted George to have the responsibility so he felt included, and it would give him something else to focus on other than the terror his father was.

"Me?" George asked surprised. "You don't want to run your own club?"

"I'd much rather enjoy it at first. One day I'll take over the duties, but I'd like the time to experience it first. You're much more level headed than I am and will be able to enforce whatever rules we put in place. I think the first one will be—the leader of the club is the only one that can be married. I don't want a bunch of cheating husbands to take their mistresses to the club."

"So once they marry they have to hand in their key?" George asked. "That's not a bad idea. So you're not going to take over until you find a bride? That's going to be a long ways off isn't it?"

Charles smiled. "I know one day I'll have to marry someone, but you're correct, I don't plan on finding a lady to wed for some years to come. I'm going to depend upon you to keep things running smoothly until then. But there isn't a requirement to wed to hold the position. If you find it is too difficult I can take over. If I marry before that...I'll have to take over is all."

"Yes," George agreed. "That makes sense." He nodded at Charles. "All right I'll run your club." His lips tilted upward into another grin. "I can't wait to get started."

Charles picked up his glass and tipped it at his friend. "I already have my friend. Now let's drink to that new son of yours."

"That is a fabulous idea," George replied. He picked up his glass and clinked it with Charles's. "And to your future club. It'll be as successful as you imagined it would be."

They both drank the contents of their glasses, and then Charles filled them again with brandy. They drank several glasses before George left. They had all the rules of the club in place by then and the future of his Coventry Club would be a reality before long. Charles loved when a good plan came to fruition.